P9-DTI-309

THE STRAW MAN
is a
MASTERPIECE!

THE STRAW MAN
is
DAZZLING!

"*A beautifully written and entertaining novel . . .* an amazingly accurate portrayal of both sides of the art world." —Roy Lichtenstein

"*Knowing, understanding . . .* a witty oasis among recent fictions—*if* it is fiction."
—Truman Capote

"*Remarkably entertaining . . .* thoroughly wicked!"
—*New York Magazine*

"*Smashing . . .* absolutely fascinating!"
—L. Rust Hills

THE STRAW MAN
is
SENSATIONAL!

THE
STRAW MAN

Barbara Goldsmith

BALLANTINE BOOKS • NEW YORK

FOR FRANK

Copyright © 1975 by Barbara Goldsmith

All rights reserved. Published in the United States by Ballantine Books, a division of Random House, Inc., New York, and simultaneously in Canada by Ballantine Books of Canada, Ltd., Toronto, Canada.

Library of Congress Catalog Card Number: 74-34398

ISBN 0-345-24953-4-175

This edition published by arrangement with Farrar, Straus and Giroux, New York

Manufactured in the United States of America

First Ballantine Books Edition: April, 1976

1
___

*At the start of that nineteenth summer, I drew up a list
of my friends and a list of people who came to use
the tennis court. The tennis court list had twenty names
on it. There were two people on the friend list. I wasn't
positive about one of them.*

*It's not easy to be the son of a very rich man. It
abstracts you from life. Don't think that I regard myself
as a poor little rich boy or anything like that, and I'm
not the first person whose parents ever got a divorce.
Maybe the way it happened was rough, but we did
have those seven summers, from the time I began
remembering until the time it was over at eleven.
On my dice that's a winning roll.*

*It is my observation, however, that as a group the
sons of extremely wealthy men suffer damage. A few
escape. In England they say the neglected, penniless,
fourth son of the duke usually turns out fine. But the
first-born, trapped beneath the shadow of power, never
sees his own sun. Others overcompensate. My father's
that kind. Smarter in business, more perceptive in art,
he became richer and more powerful than his father.
Driven, goal-oriented, he surpassed the goals set for
him, neglecting only certain things: neglecting only
warmth and humanity.*

*I could never surpass my father the way he
surpassed his. I am not equipped. To me the only
course is not to compete. I have arrived at this
conclusion in a logical manner, over a number of years.
If you know you are going to fail, it's better not to try.*

*There are two kinds of rich men's sons, the over-
compensators who have some chance of becoming*

1

*men, and those who don't enter the competition and
remain forever boys. I'm one of the latter. . . .*

Excerpt from *Nineteenth Summer,* an unpublished
manuscript by Bertram Ogden Royceman, 1962

───

I have always enjoyed constructing model ships. I was
working on a model that night when Missy, my mother,
came into my room. The sticky, sweet smell was all
around her, and she was crying. "Birdie," she asked, "if
four people were drowning and you could save three or
let all four drown, you'd save the three, wouldn't you?"
I didn't know what she meant. Then. Now I know who
the fourth person was. Me.

That was years ago, but I still build model ships. I
had just finished gluing the thirtieth oar on an Egyptian
barge when the telephone rang. I had seen this particular
model in a toy shop on King's Road the day before. The
label on the box proclaimed *Cleopatra's Barge—Queen
of the Nile.* It was prepainted black and gold, the balsa
wood thin as onion skin, not at all like my other models.
It was too easy. I didn't mind being interrupted.

My sister Ellen's cotton-candy voice chirped, "Birdie,
thank God I got you. I wanted to know if you wanted
me to pick you up at the airport tonight or tomorrow?"

"What the fuck are you talking about?"

There was a pause, and then Ellen said, her voice very
small, "Birdie, I thought you knew. Daddy Bert died
early this morning. I spoke to Jack Weisman; he told me
he'd sent you a cable. The funeral is tomorrow, at the
house. Weisman said he'd made all the arrangements,
but then I thought, well maybe I could meet you. I
mean, it never occurred to me that you didn't know.
Anyway, it's tomorrow . . . Birdie?"

"If he sent a cable he dropped it in an elephant's ass.
I just got off the fucking plane. Oh Christ, I was just
there three days ago." Then I stopped yelling at Ellen
and said, "Look, I'll get back as quickly as I can. Absolutely. Without fail." As soon as I said that, I began to

smile: that was the exact phrasing my father had used the day Aunt Adeline died.

We'd been at Saratoga when he received the call telling him of his sister's death. We finished lunch and waited two hours until it was time for the fifth race. His horse Fly-by-Night (my other so-called sister, Tammy, had thought up that name) was in that race. The royalblue and navy Royceman colors flashed past us like a smear of fingerpaint. The horse placed. Then we drove to the airport where our plane waited. "We must compose ourselves, Birdie," my father said as he leaned forward to fasten my seat belt. I felt no sorrow about Aunt Adeline, only a giddy warmth, because my father and I had become conspirators. By the time we reached New York we were in a properly somber mood.

"Birdie, are you still there?"

"Yeah."

"I'm sorry."

"Sure. Don't try to meet me. I don't know what flight I can make. Call the Chelsea for me, will you? I'll need a couple of rooms."

"Right away."

"Good. See you." I put the phone down.

I sat quite still on a bridge chair next to the table where I'd been working, and then very carefully rolled a joint. I lit it with a match that I struck on the fireplace.

I looked around the room of my London townhouse —the parquet floor gleaming in the amber afternoon light, the whitewashed walls, the double-story cathedral windows with leaded panes—all that spoke of an ordered life. In a room like this everything had to be all right, to be safe.

I'd bought the house because of that feeling of solidity and serenity. When I met the agent, the first thing he said was, "Is the client meeting us later?" One day I might get around to furnishing the place, but a bridge table and chairs, a bed, a chest or two do fine for me. I don't like my life cluttered. Furniture isn't what it's about.

I took a long drag on the joint. The phone rang again. It kept ringing. I picked it up. "Yeah?"

"Mr. Bertram Ogden Royceman, please."

"Who is it?"

"Mr. Jacob Weisman calling. Is Mr. Bertram Ogden Royceman in?" That whole formal name, the one I never use. They call me Bertie, or sometimes by that baby name, Birdie. My name, in fact, is the same as my father's except for the Ogden in the middle. That was my mother's maiden name; but therein lies the difference. As different as black and white. Correction: Jew and Gentile.

Jack Weisman, Jack-off Weisman, was calling: keeper of the keys, lawyer extraordinaire, pimp particular, controller, user, friend to Presidents and to Bertram (no middle name) Royceman.

"Put him on," I said.

"Is this Mr. Bertram . . ."

"Oh for Christ's sake, cut the shit and put him on."

"Hello, Bertie. This is Jack Weisman. Ellen Billings just called to tell me that you never received my cable."

"That's because you never sent it."

"I did."

"Like hell you did."

"I can send you a confirmation copy if you'd like, but you'd better get moving, because your father's funeral is tomorrow at three."

"No, it's not," I said. "The last time I saw him he said he wanted *me* to arrange things. So it can't be tomorrow. I may not be able to get there until tomorrow."

"I've arranged everything already. Don't worry, Bertie, just be there."

"I'll be there, but you can't have it tomorrow."

"I'm not going to waste time arguing with you. I've got to hang up. Your mother's on the other line."

"Hey, wait. Hey, you bastard, wait." He didn't.

Missy would be speaking to Weisman from her villa on Cap Ferrat, where she was presently in residence with this year's lover. I could imagine her drenched in sunlight, wearing a flowing yellow caftan, her canary-diamond ring (which covered her index finger from base to center knuckle) flashing as she lifted her hand to stroke her pale hair. In certain moods I thought of Missy in these tones of bright youth and yellow. Then it was the romantic, the beautiful, the unreal storybook Missy that I conjured up, although the last time I'd seen her she'd looked shriveled, crowlike, face tanned leather, legs reed-thin, distended stomach. The years of alcohol and boredom and loss finally erupting through the glossy surface to reveal to the world what had been well concealed.

My earliest memory: Missy dressing me in "The Fifer" costume. She'd called out each part of the costume by name in a childlike voice that Ellen had inherited. "Here are the bright red trousers. Here's the jacket with its beautiful brass buttons. Here's the shiny fife case." Missy's macaw, Harry, circled her head, his stubby yellow and blue wings flapping like nervous hands. He settled on Missy's shoulder. "Remember to hold the fife to your lips," she instructed. Then we walked down the long corridor to the Impressionist Room. My father sat behind the immense desk under the rock-crystal chandelier. There were wax flowers in a silver bowl on the corner of the desk: great magenta wax peonies, yellow wax tulips: I kept looking at them as Missy pushed me forward. "Here's your fifer," she said, laughing. My father smiled. "He's my living Manet and you are my living Renoir, or with that exotic bird on your shoulder, perhaps I should say Gauguin." Then my father lifted me up into his lap and hugged me. This is not one of my romantic fantasies. It really did happen.

I started packing my blue and white plastic BOAC flight bag. In went the shaving kit, shirt, socks, underwear. I'd carry a blue suit over my arm, a concession to Jack the Jackal. I wanted to take some grass but figured I wouldn't risk it. The last thing I put in the bag was the eye drops. The damned iritis had started three days ago, right after I'd left my father at Mount Sinai. It was my third bout. Iritis, the doctor had explained, is a rather rare eye ailment. I think he said it makes the iris adhere to the cornea, but I know for sure that it makes your eyes red and runny and sensitive as hell to light. I'd had it once at ten, once at twenty, and this was my thirty-year-old bout coming a year early. The doctor says I've got the most interesting scar tissue he's ever seen. The treatment is atropine and cortisone drops, and after a while it just goes away. There are three possible causes—tuberculosis, an allergy, or undetermined. I'm undetermined.

I stuck on my shades. The car and chauffeur would be waiting outside. There were three drivers. They worked eight-hour shifts, waiting outside the house in my gray Rolls (the model was called Silver Shadow, which reminded me of a spy story). The drivers weren't allowed in the house. I wondered where they went to relieve themselves. They cost me damn near half my income, but it was worth it to me to stay mobile.

I guess I have transportation hang-ups. At seventeen, I drove a car for the first time alone. I pulled into a service station and asked for gas. "Where's the gas tank?" asked the attendant. I didn't know. I just didn't know. I drove home, but never drove again.

Not driving is damned inconvenient. Once I was asked to a party on Eighth Street and I only had a fifty-dollar bill in my pocket. I couldn't get into a cab with that and I couldn't stop in a strange place to change the bill, so I walked. I had no alternative.

I jumped into the front seat of the car. I've never been comfortable Little Lord Fauntleroying it in the back. We made Heathrow in twenty-two minutes—flat. Then I waited. The field was fogged in. If I couldn't get there, would they postpone my father's funeral? Not a chance. That bothered me, but I felt no sense of loss about his death. For me, a sense of loss was standing by the elevator when my mother and Tammy and Ellen stepped inside, when the doors snapped shut, when I thought I'd never see them again. Now I only felt unhooked at the back of my brain. After a four-hour delay, the fog lifted and we took off.

A half hour into the flight I was reading *The Guard-*

ian when the columns began running together and my eyes started feeling gravelly. I switched off the reading light, pressed the seat button, leaned back, and stretched my legs. There was a lot of leg room. I fly Tourist. It saves a lot of money when you travel as much as I do. This time, Tourist was full-up, so I bought a First Class ticket and requested seat 1C. My father called it a Bertram Royceman theorem: "Never fly commercial unless absolutely necessary, but if you do, request row one; you'll have room for your legs and you won't have to look at the other marsupials." This is typical of my father's useful advice. Correction: was typical.

I put some drops in my eyes. Then I fell asleep. I remember my dream. There was to be a theatrical performance for a very important audience. Everybody was required to perform. Missy sat in front of a dressing-room mirror, with tiny light bulbs all around. She dipped a long thin brush into a glass of clear liquid. Then she applied the tip of the brush to her lips and began stroking, around and around, circling her mouth. She inserted the brush back in the liquid and repeated the gesture over and over again.

I wandered into the wings and looked at the stage. Ellen and Tammy were performing. Mimicking the gaits of their horses, they trotted around in tight circles. My father marched on stage, wearing a tuxedo, and set up the jumps. The girls ran and hurtled over them. My father pinned a blue ribbon on Tammy's jacket. He patted Ellen on the top of her head.

I realized that it was time for me to get started. I knew I couldn't perform unless I could find a suitable costume. In front of me stretched a vast corridor of rooms which ran on as far as I could see and disappeared over the horizon. I began opening doors, one after another, looking for a costume. Every room was empty. I felt terribly afraid. Finally, I saw my father walking down the hall toward me. When he reached me he said, "Don't worry, you can wear mine," and he held his hands out to me. They were empty. I didn't see anything in those outstretched hands. I said very politely,

"No, thank you. It would never fit. It just isn't right for me."

I was first off the plane, carrying my suit and flight bag. I headed straight for Ellen's apartment on East Sixty-eighth Street. She lived on the sixth floor but I could hear the dogs barking the minute I got on the elevator. Ellen was like Missy in her love of animals, but a lot less imaginative.

Ellen had dogs and cats, and I remember one visit when she harbored a deodorized skunk. But our childhood had been the whole box of Animal Crackers come alive. Apparently, Missy had started out mildly enough, with six dogs, four cats, two canaries, and a parrot. By the time I came along, she was on intimate terms with a macaw, a chimp, and eight gogos. He summer zoo featured fawns, bears, raccoons, opossums, skunks, owls, hawks, and an ocelot.

Right before she checked out, her outré palate required a declawed leopard and a python who spent his time curled up like a black medicine ball under her gold, swan-shaped bathtub spigot. It didn't matter much. I suppose Missy used the stall shower, and the year before my father had moved down the hall into a small converted maid's room which he announced was strictly off limits.

Ellen opened the door wearing a brown flannel robe and carrying a snifter of brandy. Two papillon puppies, a whippet, and a terrier eddied and flowed around her feet. Ellen was puffy and frowsy but her upturned nose and china-blue eyes gave her the look of a perpetual child.

"You made it," she said, giving me a half hug. "I'd about given up on tonight. Are you hungry? Want a snack?"

"Like yours?" I asked, looking at the brandy.

"It's not exactly your typical two o'clock in the morning," she replied amiably.

"It's breakfast time by my stomach."

"Then I'll make breakfast. Come on into the library.

I made the kids go to bed. They're going to school to-morrow and coming home early to change for the funeral. I thought it would be good if they had something to keep them busy."

Ellen gestured at the coffee table on which reposed *The New York Times*. "It's Daddy Bert's obituary. I bought it a while ago when I was out walking the dogs. Maybe you'd like to read it while I make something."

When Ellen left the room, I looked at the chaos that surrounded me. The bookshelves contained a mixture of leather-bound volumes, paperbacks, and jacketless books squeezed into random fellowship. Silver trophies, with black tarnished patches blighting their surfaces, stood on the shelves along with what once must have been blue and red ribbons, now faded to purple and amber. Magazines littered the floor, and on a bridge table in front of the window was a half-completed jig-saw puzzle. I was uneasy with that mess and I wondered how Ellen could function without orderly perimeters to her life.

I sat down, picked up the paper, and turned to the beginning of the second section, where you find the obituaries. It was there all right, five full columns, but the top line read, "Continued From Page 1, Col. 8." I carefully closed the paper and turned back to the front page. In the lower right-hand corner was a photograph of my father looking stern, white-haired, and impeccably tailored. The photo credit read Yousuf Karsh.

2

BERTRAM ROYCEMAN,
ART COLLECTOR AND BANKER, DIES

Bertram Royceman, the eminent banker whose private art collection is valued at over 100 million dollars, died yesterday in Mount Sinai Hospital after a prolonged illness. He was 71 years old.

Mr. Royceman was senior partner of Royceman Brothers, the distinguished investment banking firm. During his lifetime he succeeded both in multiplying his own fortune and in placing the firm in the top echelon of prestige on Wall Street.

Scion of a wealthy and famous family, Bertram Royceman numbered among his close friends and confidants many of the most important men in government, philanthrophy, corporate finance, and the arts. He was recognized as one of the foremost art collectors in the world. His taste was princely, combining an exquisite aesthetic sensibility with an immense checkbook.

The Royceman Collection is without a doubt the finest private art collection in this country. Liberally represented are the Old Masters: El Greco, Goya, Velázquez, Botticelli, and the Impressionists: Renoir, Manet, Monet, Cézanne, Pisarro, Degas, and Sisley. The collection also contains 200 thirteenth to fifteenth century Italian Primitive paintings. . . .

Consisting not merely of paintings and sculpture, the collection is encyclopedic in scope, encompassing over four thousand items including drawings, tapestries, illuminated manuscripts, jewelry, Fabergé objects, majolica, Venetian glass, and religious artifacts.

10

Mr. Royceman served as vice president of the board of trustees of New York's Urban Museum of Art from 1950 to 1958. During this period, he lent almost all of his treasures for exhibition at the museum.

For undisclosed reasons, in 1958 he transferred the collection to the East Side mansion constructed by his father, Paul Royceman, in 1909 and used as his home until his death. Here Bertram Royceman created a private museum accessible only to art collectors and art students. In the same year he selected a thousand objects and paintings from his collection, forming an exhibition called "A Private View." These works of art toured the United States and received the highest critical praise. . . .

In 1968, Mr. Royceman donated a million dollars to Princeton University to endow a chair in the history of art. In 1969, he was made chairman of the board of trustees of New York's Urban Museum of Art, a new position created for him by Douglas Watson and Bartholomew Spencer Hayes, president and director respectively of this institution. In a joint statement issued yesterday said: "Mr. Royceman was a great leader in the art world and one of the finest trustees in the long and distinguished history of this institution. He exemplified all that was sensitive and aesthetic . . ."

Excerpts from the obituary of Bertram Royceman, *The New York Times,* September 2, 1972

———

Pretentious shit. Jesus, what crap. And I hadn't even gotten off the front page. Bartholomew Spencer Hayes. *B. S.* Hayes, that supercilious snake, had his tongue so far up my father's ass he was seeing daylight.

I could see Hayes standing in that hospital room wearing a black velvet cape at eleven o'clock in the morning, no less, making you-and-me-in-it-together small talk with the old man. "We received a rather sizable donation last night for the refurbishing of the Great Entrance Gallery. Two million five to be exact."

"So you softened up Adele Laskoff? I knew you'd do it," said my father, a thin grin spreading across his parchment face.

"No, *you* softened her up. That idea of telling her we'd install two islands of shrubbery and trees in the Gallery was genius. The architects' rendering looked like horticulture heaven. We presented it to her at a tiny private dinner upstairs in the European Paintings Gallery. As Willie Sutton used to say, 'There's nothing quite as impressive as the inside of a bank vault at night.' "

The old man smiled again. "You should be in politics, Bart," he said.

"I am," replied Hayes. Then he turned to me. "You might be interested in seeing our newest exhibition, which opens tonight. It's called 'Gateway to America' and it's absolutely fascinating. A multimedia presentation tracing the history of the immigrant groups of New York: the Irish, Jews, Italians, blacks, and Puerto Ricans. It's my most forward-looking show and should create quite a stir. I expect attendance will soar. I'll leave your name at the door."

"O.K."

"Well, back to the slave galley. I'll return soon again though, since I count on this diversion to get me through a day."

"I look forward to it too," said my father.

I was fascinated by the stiff phraseology of their conversation. This ritualistic non-communication. "I look forward"—idiomatic phrase of an extinct culture—connoting what? I wondered.

After Hayes had left, my father asked, "Will you go to the exhibition tonight?"

"Hell no, it just seemed simpler not to argue."

"Hayes is rather full of himself. I'd call him a dedicated egomaniac."

"There's something off about him."

My father leaned forward. "Plump up that pillow for me, will you, Birdie?" I removed the pillow, shook it vigorously, and replaced it. He settled back. "I think your instinct is right. There *is* something off about Hayes and the way he goes about things. He sees himself as the hero of the Great Unwashed. But, personally, I think he has no more conception of who these people are than I do.

"What he's doing is trying to get the masses to come to the Urban by merchandising the museum as if it were a supermarket. Hayes presents a dazzle of film, slides, tapes, and guides which explain but fail to illuminate. He promises people something valuable, and then you know what he gives them? Do you, Birdie?"

"What?"

"Nothing."

"Nothing?"

"That's right, because in reality art exists only if you explore and discover it in your own private way. No one can give it to you. It's a ridiculous assumption. Art is an acquired taste that requires knowledge. It is a one-to-one experience, a contemplative pastime. It's not at all the easily acquired treasure Hayes has made it out to be."

"But Hayes says thousands of new people are flooding to the Urban. He must be doing something right."

"Increased attendance, community involvement, relevant exhibitions—I've heard it all, son. In the long run it will only cause resentment. Just imagine how you'd feel if you'd waited in line five hours for a three-minute view of a multimillion-dollar painting or object. You'd feel cheated, that's how you'd feel, and you'd be right. After all, what have you really seen? A painting or a pot or a statue. That's what. And that's all! No, people should not be talked into coming."

"Then how will you get them there? I don't think a museum should just be a private club for the wealthy and elite."

"It may surprise you to know, Birdie, that I agree with you. But I am a very old member of the club and so is Hayes. Historically, few aristocracies have transformed themselves. Revolution comes from the outside. In the meantime, Hayes is simply playing at being democratic. He is Czar Nicholas with his token reforms, and the very masses he wishes to cultivate will eventually turn on him. People should not be sold the ephemeral."

"But you were thinking of leaving your collection to the Urban?"

"Not thinking of it, Birdie, I've finalized on it. I believe people will, in time, come to appreciate art, not in Hayes's way, but in their own way. They will make their own discovery. When they do, I want my collection to be there for them. Besides, it's the only game in town."

I remember this conversation very well, because it was the only time my father explained something to me without condescension on his part or resentment on mine. That day, when I left the hospital, I walked down Fifth Avenue, aware of the slate-blue New York light, and stopped in front of the Guggenheim. There was a sculpture outside of a gleaming gold man, soft and featureless, with wheels for arms and legs. I thought it very powerful. I went inside the museum and spent an hour walking up and down the curving ramp looking at the paintings. I really tried to understand what it was about these inanimate objects that obsessed my father.

As I was growing up, again and again my father would show guests through our apartment as if conducting an extended series of student tours. He was an articulate guide. He would pause in the living room, where the paintings hung in tiers three deep, and gesture toward the walls and say, "These are my children." That always drew indulgent smiles. I'd really spent a lot of time hating the Royceman Collection.

3

. . . Bertram Royceman succeeded his father as head of the firm. His position on Wall Street was such that he could raise millions of dollars with little more than a phone call. He was not easily impressed by news of a financial coup. Once a partner bounded into his office to tell him that he'd pulled off a transaction yielding a million-dollar profit to the firm. Royceman replied softly, "That's good, just keep on making those little deals and the big ones will come."

In 1937 Bertram Royceman liquidated a holding company, Phoenix Securities, which controlled Pepsi-Cola, Bendix Washing Machine, Loft Candy Company, and several other smaller companies. He set these companies up as separate entities, retaining stock in each, thereby making millions of dollars for himself and for his firm.

He proved the adage "You can do well while doing good." In 1946, Royceman owned sixteen acres of New York real estate bordered on the north by Forty-eighth Street, on the south by Forty-second Street, on the west by First Avenue, and on the east by the East River.

He was rumored to be influential in the transaction by which John D. Rockefeller, Jr., donated $8,500,000 to the United Nations to enable this organization to purchase Royceman's site for their General Assembly Building. Through this purchase, the United Nations came to be located in New York City. After the construction of this building, the land Royceman owned adjacent to the United Nations property skyrocketed in value. . . .

Excerpt from the obituary of Bertram Royceman,
The New York Times, September 2, 1972

———

Ellen came into the room, carrying a tray which held a
coffee pot, two mugs, and a Sara Lee coffee cake still in
its tin-foil container. She sat on the couch opposite my
chair. The papillons leaped into her lap, a mingling of
black, white, and tan fur. "I made Sanka, no caffeine."

"Thanks."

I removed my dark glasses, put the paper down, and
pressed my thumb and index finger into the corners of
my eyes. I put my head back, and applied the drops.

"You must be wiped out."

"My eyes really hurt. Would you mind reading this to
me?" I extended the newspaper.

"Sure." She took the paper. Her eyes skidded down
the columns. "You're mentioned twice, once by name.
And I'm in it too."

"Congratulations."

"Listen to this: 'His office was only nine feet wide and
twelve feet long, an unprepossessing rectangle. On his
desk were eight family pictures including one of a
laughing young boy emptying a watering can over his
head.' That's you, right? And here's the other time.
Right at the end. 'Mr. Royceman married twice. His
first marriage to Mrs. Melissa Ogden Crowley ended in
divorce. In 1954 he married Miss Gina Mazzo. Besides
his widow, he is survived by a son of his first marriage,
Bertram Ogden Royceman, and two former stepdaughters, Ellen Crowley Billings of New York City and
Tamara Crowley Held of Greenwich, Connecticut. The
funeral will be held at Royceman House. Attendance is
by invitation.' That makes two for you, one for me."

"For Christ's sake, will you just read."

"O.K." She bit the tip of her finger. "There's a lot of
human-interest stuff here. It tells about the thirty brood
mares at Bird Hollow Farm in Virginia and how Flight
Plan earned over half a million dollars. There's a whole
thing about how soft-spoken Daddy Bert was."

Ellen's skipping around was getting to me. "Just give the fucking thing back," I demanded.

"As you like," she said in her polite, little-girl voice. "I was only trying not to make it read like what it is—his epitaph. You want to be by yourself?"

"I'm glad I'm here, but I think so."

"Your room's ready. See you tomorrow. Try to get some sleep."

"Not tonight."

"I understand." Ellen stood up. The dogs spilled like rubber balls to the floor and bounced after her as she left the room.

That Ellen and I have remained in touch seems pretty odd under the circumstances. I call Ellen my sister, but she's my half-sister to be exact—Missy being the dam that had us both. My sire was Betram Royceman, Ellen and Tammy's was Missy's first husband, Mr. Crowley. His first name escapes me. My father wanted to adopt the girls, but Crowley said he wasn't going to let any kike adopt his kids.

There's a five-year difference between Ellen and me, and Tammy is three years older than Ellen. In fact, I can only remember about seven years of our being together. I remember summers best. After Missy and the girls left, Ellen and I would see each other weekends. If I went to her apartment, I did so in secret, because Missy had no visiting rights. Soon we were both away at school. At school they called me B.O., naturally, and I was pretty much of a loner.

I started to read again but found my concentration wasn't much better than Ellen's. The next three columns were about what a business genius he'd been. It was full of names like Bankers Trust, Chase Manhattan, Syntex, IBM, Christiana Securities.

They mentioned my cousin Robert Royceman, the "esteemed ambassador," four times. They traced the family from its "humble beginnings" as fur trappers in Mississippi, through the cotton brokerage business, to the Chicago commodities exchange, and then to the investment-banking business.

I knew all this of course, and seeing it written out made it appear simple enough. I wondered why it had seemed so mysterious and threatening. Over the years, those papers had come to me with penciled notes attached: *Sign twice. Sign on page 1 and on page 7. Sign in place indicated by penciled X and paper clip. Use complete signature*. I signed whatever it was, next to the paper clip, next to the X, my complete signature, over and over. Always, I'd felt powerless, manipulated. He said it was because I didn't care: not about business or about art or about anything. But I did care.

The Impressionist Room was my father's study. He spent a great deal of time there. On the wood-paneled walls were thirty-two Impressionist and Neo-Impressionist canvases: Cézanne, Degas, Renoir, Manet, Monet, Seurat, Sisley, Vuillard, Bonnard, lots of other names. I was about seven when Ellen and I had the spitting contest. It was my idea. Our aim was directed at a pail carried by one of the girls in Renoir's "Children at a Beach Picnic." The pail was bright red. I hit it four times, but Ellen kept missing.

Later on, when the apartment was empty, I used to whack off in this room. It seemed the perfect place for it. I'd lock the door, spread a Turkish towel on the damask sofa, and devote my full attention to a nubile Degas ballerina, her opaque, crisp white tutu pinwheeling about her waist as she grasped her glowing white satin ballet slipper.

In the evening, cocktails were often served in the Impressionist Room, and as a small child, I was required to attend. Sitting on the edge of a plush wing chair in the gray-flannel shorts and dark-blue blazer which were my school uniform, I felt stupid and uncomfortable ...

"Marshall, the E.R.P., ridiculous! That's 5.3 billion of our money this year to start the blasted thing. I say, let Europe go to hell."

"The Olympics were divine and it was great to be back in Switzerland, if only you could stand to hear them shout *achtung* every second of the day. I gained ten pounds at tea in Hanzelmanns. Cottage cheese is all I eat from here on out."

"Now's the time for Giacometti. He's solid but he hasn't peaked yet."

"It's called *Other Voices, Other Rooms* and he's only twenty-three."

"A real renaissance in church art—Matisse, Moore, Léger, Miró, Chagall—they're all into it. It'll be next."

"Bertie, do you know all the words to 'I'm My Own Grandpa'?"

It followed that the Impressionist Room was the appropriate setting for the (I suppose) obligatory father-son talk, which took place two days before my nineteenth birthday. My father requested the meeting at 8:30 a.m. promptly, which was late for him. His masseur arrived every morning at six-thirty. You could hear him thumping away as my father spoke on the telephone. My father's business partners didn't need an alarm clock. He called them every weekday morning between six-thirty and eight. I carefully selected my oldest Levi's for the occasion and sat in front of the vast Regency desk, he on the other side, and between us the Harvard Catalogue. I called it that because it was a catalogue of the Royceman Collection he'd started during his senior year at Harvard. The catalogue was three feet long and eighteen inches wide. It, and my father's concern, seemed to weigh about a million pounds.

"You see that I have the catalogue here," he began in that tentative, barely audible voice of his. He stroked the pigskin cover.

"I nearly missed it."

He looked at me then with those strange green, amber-flecked eyes. "Turtle eyes," Missy called them. "Not now, Birdie," he cautioned.

"O.K. No laughs."

He opened the book to the first page. Liver-colored

spots were sprinkled over an inscription which read "The Royceman Collection, New York," and underneath, in letters about a block high, TEXT BY BERTRAM ROYCEMAN.

"I worked twenty months on this catalogue," my father said, looking down at that page with intense concentration. "I think I can say without pretension that in that time I discovered myself. I went to live at Bernard Berenson's I Tatti. I stayed four months, and then Berenson came home with me and lived at my father's, your grandfather's, house for six months more, helping me complete the text and the authentication of the paintings. Incidentally, I am still considered an expert in paintings of the Italian School. After I completed this catalogue I was so devoted to art that I went to work for Lord Duveen. I thought at the time that I would never enter Royceman Brothers, although my father pressured me incessantly to do so. At thirty I gave in. If I consider Royceman Brothers my vocation, I do not consider art an avocation but a parallel vocation. Therefore, I feel twice enriched."

My father cleared his throat and continued. "It is important to me that you also find yourself and I hope it will be along similar lines. In the past, it has distressed me that you have shown no interest either in our collection or in the workings of Royceman Brothers. You may not have been aware of it but last summer when you worked at the firm I observed you quite carefully. It is my opinion that you not only made no effort to learn the business but went out of your way to seem as inept as possible. Correct me if I am wrong."

I said nothing. What was there to say?

"I'd like to discuss your plans for this summer, Birdie. This summer it would gratify me if you would make an effort to interest yourself in either of the two great heritages that we possess."

"I want to write a book."

"Will it be a book about art?" he inquired. His hand began stroking the cover in small quick circles.

"Perhaps," I answered. "Maybe it will include art. I don't know yet."

"Well, that's a start," he said, and slapped the palm of his hand down on the catalogue. I thought the sound was that of a judge's gavel. "Let me know if I can help you in any way."

4

December 17, 1966

Dear Bertie,

This is to inform you that your father has established a Trust Fund effective as of December 15, 1966. He intends that this Trust will generously provide for all your necessary expenses. A copy of this Trust Agreement is enclosed herewith.

As you will note, the sum of one million dollars has been invested largely in municipal bonds and stocks, which should yield approximately forty to fifty thousand dollars per annum before taxes. As a convenience to you we will set aside whatever taxes may become due.

These figures, which are for your information, are rough at best, and in no way should they be considered binding.

You will note that I am the sole Trustee of this Fund. If at any time you wish me to invade the capital of this Trust, your father has instructed me to inform you that you may contact me, and only me, in writing or in person.

You will also note that it is my discretionary right to give you such funds from capital as I deem in your best interest, without considering your other resources.

In conclusion, I would like to add that I am executing a waiver of my commissions for serving as Trustee except to the extent that any surcharge is ever asserted against me.

Sincerely,
Jacob Weisman

Even now I'm not sure what caused the rift that only his final illness could begin to repair. It took years to happen. The worst four started with the novel and ended with the stock.

That novel was the first piece of work I ever really cared about. I wrote every day, digging deep into myself, getting rid of a lot of feeling. There was a great pleasure in the discipline. My father and Gina were at Birdwood, our summer place, but I remained in that still, shrouded, dark apartment, where white sheets engulfed the furniture. There were several telephone calls asking me to come up to the Adirondacks and be outside and not neglect my body. "The trout are biting," or "Walmsey is due for a visit and she's dying to see you," my father would say to tempt me. I didn't go.

I finished the book in August. I never thought about whether it was good or bad. I knew there was a lot of pain in it: my pain and that of my father. I sent it to a publisher whose name had been suggested by my adviser at school. I wasn't surprised to receive a rejection letter. (The only surprise was that up to that time I'd really believed they sent you a pink rejection slip.)

In September my father returned, and soon after Weisman came for dinner and my father mentioned the book and Weisman urged me to send a copy to a literary agent who was a friend of his. I sent him the manuscript and subsequently received a call inviting me to see him. He said he wanted to buy the novel outright for twenty thousand dollars. Since I was nineteen, my father co-signed the contract. When the check arrived I deposited it in a savings account that I opened myself.

I called the agent six weeks later, but he was out of town. Eight weeks later he was still gone. Two months after that he told me he didn't think he could interest a publisher in the book.

In subsequent phone calls I asked him to return the manuscript. I said I'd give the money back. I said I'd take it around myself. He replied I couldn't do that because legally it was no longer mine. It took me a long time and maybe five or six more phone calls to understand what was happening. My father denied the accusation that he and Weisman had decided to suppress my novel. He also said, "I've signed my name to a contract. Unfortunately, there is nothing to be done." Those were his exact words. It's important to me to recount this accurately and without undue emotion. When I do that, sometimes I can switch off the feeling.

I don't think I ever won a single round with my father. In November 1966, when I was living at the Chelsea, a messenger arrived at my door with a form to purchase ten thousand shares of the Standard Oil Corporation of California for my account. The form was accompanied by the usual small white slip of paper with a note asking for my signature. A penciled X indicated where to sign.

I have always thought of myself as apolitical but the spring before, I'd read an article in *The New York Times* stating that Standard Oil of California had leased a plant to the United Technological Center for the manufacture of 100 million pounds of the newest type of napalm. The enormity of that figure got to me.

I turned the paper over and wrote, "Napalm Burns— no thanks. B.O.R." I put it back in the envelope with the form and gave it to the messenger.

It must have been no more than an hour later when my father called. "Birdie," he said, "Standard Oil is a very secure stock. I'm purchasing some for myself and for Gina, and I want you to have it."

"Standard Oil is involved in the making of napalm. I don't want it."

"The company happens to be the special interest of my friend David Rockefeller. Rockefeller is an old business associate of mine, a fine man, and a patriot. He's also chairman of the board of trustees of the Museum of Modern Art. I should not be required to explain these things to you. You should not question my judgment. Now, Birdie," he continued, "I'm sending those papers up again and you sign them. Is that clear?"

"Not me," I said and hung up.

I spent about three weeks thinking I'd won, until a

confirmation order arrived in the mail. His office never sent me confirmation orders, so I knew this was some sort of message from my father. I called him and said, "How could you buy me that stock? You forged my signature."

"That is not the case," replied my father in an exasperated whisper. "We have on file several power-of-attorney forms which you signed for us. Furthermore, your unreasonable conduct upsets me a great deal."

Two weeks later I received a letter from Jack Weisman and, in the same envelope, a copy of my trust agreement. I took it to mean that the ragged connection between my father and me had been severed.

They wanted me out of the way. I just wanted out. I tried Paris first, then London. For more than four years my only contact with the family was through Ellen's letters. I didn't come home, not even when she wrote that her husband, Ben, had died and she wanted very much to see me.

I heard from Weisman though, in regular monthly installments. If I was the prisoner in the tower, then he was my keeper, pushing sustenance under the door via those checks. I loathed Jack Weisman and he returned the compliment.

Weisman's been a part of my life for as long as I can remember. Years ago, he and my father owned a fishing camp in Canada. At night he'd sit in front of the rough stone fireplace, his hands crossed across his protruding stomach, relating tales of his Brooklyn boyhood. Way back then, I must admit, I couldn't get enough of those stories. "Every morning at six I'd be out there selling pretzels, the cold coming up through the newspaper that covered the holes in the soles of my shoes. I did that for about a year until I saved enough to buy her a phonograph. She loved music so—my mother. I gave it to her on her birthday, with ten records. That night my father came home for the first time that week. Drunk as usual. They say just goys are drunks. Believe me, it's not exclusive. First he smashed the phonograph and then he began beating me with his belt, yelling about how we didn't have bread and I was buying music. Hey, Bertie, what's that, tears? Cut it out. I'm not crying and it happened to me."

Weisman did make me cry. Once. Later I realized his stories fell into two categories and I could pretty well anticipate the punch. First there were the ones that I categorized as price-tag stories. Stories about walking across the Brooklyn Bridge to save a nickel. How he'd wait in the rain with two cents for a boy with three cents so they could go to a movie at two-for-five-cents. How in those days a hot dog cost three cents and a lemonade one cent. How his weekly music lesson cost thirty-five cents.

The other category of stories stressed discipline and drive. How he'd gone to night school for eight years, first to become an accountant and then a lawyer. How he'd slept on the subway between school and his job as a bellboy at the Hotel Astor. He was disciplined all right. He still walked every weekday from his Fifth Avenue apartment on Seventy-first Street to his office on Wall Street, stopping en route at the Whelan drugstore opposite Grand Central Station, where the counterman plunked down scrambled eggs, a toasted English, and coffee. Weisman left two dollars. They rarely spoke.

I figured Weisman could afford all those humble-pie stories because he was one of the best-known lawyers in America and certainly one of the most powerful. He was so close to two Presidents that his apartment had been nicknamed the New York White House. He did for both Presidents what he did for my father—*everything:* from exporting Nathan's hot dogs to Washington to preparing messages to Congress.

One of the reasons I hated Weisman was that, when my father gave up on me and created that trust fund, he placed Weisman smack between us. I didn't appreciate Weisman and his legal documents because they prevented my father from dealing with me direct. Sometimes, though, I ask myself, Why is my anger directed at Weisman when the whole thing was my father's idea?

Also, I hated Weisman because I had to go begging to him for what I considered to be my own money. If I wanted any of the principal of my trust, I was required to request it from the sole trustee, Jack Weisman. I did request extra money twice. One time, I wanted to invest two hundred thousand dollars to bring *Hair* to Broadway, but try to explain that to him. Request refused. The other time, I wanted to buy the London townhouse and the car. Request granted.

5

December 10, 1971

Dear Mr. Royceman,

I know it is not my place to write this letter, but I wanted you to know that two days ago your father was taken to Mt. Sinai Hospital with what all the physicians consulted seem to feel is, in plain words, terminal cancer. They have not told him this, but I am sure he knows.

I know that your relationship with your father has been strained. At first I thought you would probably hear of this from other sources. Then I thought, what if no one tells you? Therefore, I am taking the liberty of doing so, realizing full well that it is a liberty.

Sincerely,
Mary Constanziakias
Assistant Curator
The Royceman Collection

We hadn't seen each other in nearly five years, but when I walked into that canary-yellow hospital room he just looked up and said, "Hello, Birdie. It's good to see you, son." After that I flew in from London about once every ten days, usually staying at Ellen's or the Chelsea. It would have cost a lot less to live in New York, but I couldn't. Not yet. I never thought it would take nine months.

When I saw that there was nothing they could do for him, I wanted them to let him go home. The doctors wouldn't, I couldn't persuade them. It was as if they'd been entrusted with a priceless piece of merchandise. They wanted it to be where they could keep an eye on

28

it. "We can do more for him here," they'd say. "What can you do if he's going to die anyway?" I'd ask. "He'll be better off here . . . He'll be more comfortable here . . . We won't be responsible," they'd reply. So he stayed—nine long months.

It was during this period that I began to feel some self-confidence and ease in his presence. My first visits had been perfunctory, and I'd fooled myself that they'd been duty calls. After a time, I began to acknowledge the fact that I enjoyed them. As his life ebbed, I began to open to him as I had never done before. Perhaps it was because he was dying, growing weaker, less of an adversary.

One afternoon in late January I arrived from London exhausted, trailing airplane odors, to find him sitting in a chair by the window. He was laughing, a great open laugh I had never heard before. Sitting opposite him was a slim woman, about forty, extremely tall, aquiline nose, chalk-white skin, hair drawn back in a tight bun. Beautiful, mature, a face from an ancient Greek frieze. She had a stenographer's pad in her hand. She was laughing too. I knew instinctively, even before he said, "Birdie, this is my assistant curator, Mary Constanzi-akias," that she was the person who had written me of his illness.

My father gestured to the one remaining chair. "At long last we're compiling a master catalogue of the collection and I'm trying to write a proper introduction. It's rough going. I get so high-flown and opaque. I was about to analyze our religious works, but Mary just said I'm not fit to do that, being such a pagan."

"I wouldn't call you a pagan," I said. "They spend their time having fun."

"You're right, I don't. I just work and slave and get ulcers."

"I'd hardly go that far," interjected Mary.

"Actually, I don't get ulcers. I give ulcers; to my partners, my friends, my wife. Maybe even to you, Birdie."

"Not me."

"That's good. I know sometimes I push hard, but people are supposed to push back. Standing up for your rights is an acquired taste. First you have to find something worth fighting for, then after a while it becomes a modus operandi. I was a late bloomer, Birdie. I suspect you are too. I was even older than you are now when my father dragged me down to Wall Street, a most reluctant bride. But I ended up loving that firm. I'm quite good at it."

Mary Constanziakias stood. "I'll be down the hall in the lounge if you need me."

"No, don't go," my father said. "Birdie can stay while we work. I call it *work:* I dictate, Mary types it up, then I read it when I can't get to sleep. I find art writing is more effective than Seconal. Can't write. Can't spell either. Birdie, do you know the word that means to understand things without specific knowledge?"

"Intuitive?"

"Yes, intuitive. I knew that."

At first, a good hospital day for my father began with several messengers delivering envelopes marked CONFIDENTIAL, the contents of which he'd arrange in neat stacks on his white formica bed table. Weisman would arrive promptly at eleven, carrying his black attaché case. He'd stamp the snow and slush from his boots, remove his gloves, hang his coat in the metal closet, and begin talking. What they talked about was the disposition of my father's worldly goods, but always in abstract terms, as if the discussion concerned the estate of a client they did not know. In fact, on my father's best days, they'd argue fiercely and constantly, Weisman shouting while my father's voice became less and less audible. The only one who was made uncomfortable by these discussions was me.

"I want that building completed and the collection installed and open to the public eighteen months after my death. Eighteen months is enough time. That's it," my father said, banging his hand down on the formica table.

Weisman sighed. "That's crazy, Bert, it takes at least eighteen months just to build a building."

"Very well, Jack, twenty months. The National Gallery says they'll ante up to build me a wing and maintain it in perpetuity. If the Urban wants the collection and a bequest for a special wing, they'd better not drag their heels."

"There are legitimate reasons for delays that we can't control—pestilence, war, and famine." Weisman was beginning to shout. "What if there's a national building strike? What then?"

"You can put in your Latin provisions about all that, and we'll discuss what protection we need for the collection, because I'll not have it sold. Look, Jack, as executor you'll be in charge. You'll be my lawyer, architect, protector, my everything—but they get twenty months. What's more, I want them to know that this stipulation comes directly from me."

"It's a pigheaded thing to do, Bert," Weisman said, his knuckles white on the black attaché case.

"Pigheaded or not," my father whispered, "just do it. I know how to deal with those milk-train aesthetes."

In April, I began to notice the deterioration. When you're away ten days or so, it's harder to deny the change. My father was propped up in bed, cranked up, I should say, because that's what they do. There's a lever you turn that puts any section of the bed up or down. When I entered the room he was studying the catalogue of "A Private View," the exhibition of one thousand works from his collection that had toured the country several years before. He held the blue leather cover broadside so I could read the title. "I can't see them any more, so this is the next best thing," he said.

"Maybe I could arrange to have some of your paintings brought here."

"That would be nice, but I don't think the hospital would permit it."

"I could see."

"Yes," he said, "you and Jack might look into it."
Then he added, "You look well, Bertie, you know."

"Thank you, sir."

His eyebrows compressed over his turtle eyes. "Sir?
That's a rather new mode of expression for you, isn't
it?"

"I wasn't aware of it."

My father reached out and adjusted the white sheet
in front of his body. He looked down at it as if concentrating on its border. "A strange thing just happened. A
while ago a man came in, sat right down, called me Bert,
and talked and talked. Wore me out. Wanted us to do
an underwriting for him. I have no idea who he was.
Everybody in this town knows me, but that doesn't mean
I know everybody. I did tell you the collection's going
to the Urban?"

"Yes, you mentioned it."

"I'd like them to build a duplicate of Royceman
House and keep everything exactly as it is now, but
that might be impossible. I've heard a million reasons
why it's impractical and I suppose a townhouse would
be out of keeping with the rest of the museum. Anyway,
I wanted you to know I am planning to withhold a
small part of the collection. I've recently decided to keep
two paintings for you. The Degas 'Girl Combing Her
Hair,' because I think you admire it, and the Ingres
of 'Countess Di Cavour,' because it was the first painting that I personally acquired for the collection. I want
those for you and for your children, should you have
any."

I didn't know how to reply to my father, so I blurted
out, "Let's not talk about that. Let's talk about something else."

"No," he replied, "let's not talk any more at all today. I'm feeling quite exhausted. Put the bed down a
bit, will you, Birdie?"

As I walked to the end of the bed, I saw him stare
fixedly at the wall behind me. I noticed his eyes were
misted over with the glaze of narcotics. "And, Birdie,
don't forget," he murmured.

"What?"

"About the crabs. When you get home do tell Mrs. Dowdy to order the soft-shelled crabs. The season is about to begin and you know how we both love them. They'd be excellent with a '59 Montrachet."

"All right."

"The food here is terrible. Sometimes I think they're trying to poison me."

As summer neared I knew that it would be soon, not from the crutches that stayed always within his reach, nor from the increasing insubstantiality of his body, but from the air of gaiety pervading that room. It was as if his imminent death made only the frothiest of conversations permissible. Weisman spoke not of business but of his golf game. "I lost two balls and a caddy on the water hole." Tammy and Ellen came and left, chattering of children and inconsequentialities. Gina, who is technically my stepmother, would arrive dressed for a ladies' lunch, dark curly hair perfectly in place, her large-breasted figure encased in clinging jersey, bracelets clanging. She bore glazed strawberries, sweet biscuits, champagne, which she distributed with gracious smiles. My father accepted these offerings with a formal "Thank you, my dear." He put them aside—always. It did not discourage her.

One morning I arrived to find his room empty. I walked to the front desk. "Don't worry. He's just down having some tests," the supervisor informed me. Walking back toward his room I saw Gina running down the corridor. I reached out and caught her arm. "Jesus, where is he?" she gasped.

"Getting some tests."

"Oh Jesus, I thought . . ."

We sat in his room, waiting. Gina opened her purse, produced two gray capsules, and swallowed them. No water. Nothing. "Want one? calm you down."

"No."

She reached forward and grabbed my hand. "It's a

bitch. Monday's the pituitary operation. I ask you, why do they put him through this when it won't help?"

"They say it will buy him time."

"Buy it with his pain. Not their pain. Why do they go on? Why don't they just let it happen?"

"I don't know."

"They should just let it happen."

The door opened and my father appeared, a slight pretty black nurse pushing his wheelchair. "Welcome back," said Gina, strident-voiced. "You're just in time to hear the story of the week: Rosalind de Fels has left Pierre for his seventeen-year-old son."

You never know when the last time will be. I sat on the radiator in that hospital room and looked out at Central Park. I could see a sparse smattering of children, lilliputians in the playground below. Most were shirt-less, some wore bathing suits. Heat waves rose from the playground pavement. It was as if I were peering through a curtain of undulating water. My eyes hurt.

I turned away from the window toward my father and noticed a photograph in a red leather frame on his bedside table. It was of Missy and me on the beach at Birdwood. I wore bathing trunks and carried a pail, and Missy wore a white one-piece bathing suit. It had not been there before.

My father was prone. He was so emaciated that I could see the sharp outline of his bones through the sheet. When he spoke his body did not move. "Tammy was here about an hour ago, but they wouldn't let her stay very long. They said I shouldn't talk too much."

"You shouldn't. I'll just sit here and you don't have to talk at all."

A glimpse of a smile crossed my father's fragile face. "It doesn't matter, it's quite silly of them really, and I want to talk. Birdie," he began. Then he paused and began again. "*After*, if you want to publish the book, I'd have no objection."

"I can't, I burned it," I lied. I no longer wanted it published.

"Well, no matter then," he replied. I couldn't tell if he said it with relief or regret. "Your book was one of the things I thought about, lying here last night. I also thought that when it happens, Birdie, I want *you* to take charge. Let's make it private and small. You know what I mean."

"I know what you mean, but let's have none of that talk. You're looking good, you shouldn't . . ." I didn't finish the sentence because at that moment a nurse barged into the room. She wore a wrinkled white uniform, and wisps of gray hair escaped from her hair net. I hated her for being there.

"We were talking," I said.

She answered in a voice of such insensitive cheeriness that I felt like striking her. "That's just what you shouldn't be doing, he needs to rest now." She turned to my father. "Time for our private little things, Mr. Royceman."

I looked over at my father's sharp profile; he did not move or respond. "Well, so long for now," I said. "I'll fly in again next week. I'll see you then. Next Saturday afternoon at two," I added. I'd said it brusquely and I'd fixed upon an exact day and hour. The saying of it, the securing of a place in time, would make it true. I could not, would not, consider the alternative.

"You bet, son." His voice floated up to me with renewed vigor. Then he turned his head and looked me full in the face and winked, in mute acknowledgment of our pedestrian charade.

6

*Art is the purest form of communication. It can lift a
person out of himself and open him up. It teaches you
to understand other human beings and yourself. When
you comprehend an artist's view, you have extended
your own aesthetic horizons both on a conscious and
on an intuitive level. . . .*

Excerpt from the introduction to the catalogue,
The Royceman Collection, 1972, by Bertram Royceman

The funeral was called for three. I left Ellen's at noon,
thinking that if I arrived early I would have some
private time to be with him. I walked down Lexington
Avenue. As I paused for a light on the corner of Sixty-
second Street, a red Volkswagen halted about a foot
from where I was standing and a laughing, bloated, redheaded woman leaned out of the window and dumped
a paper bag full of garbage at my feet. Out rolled soft-
drink cans, pieces of sandwiches, and other indistinguishable debris. I quickened my pace. Then, there it
was, the house on Fifty-second Street.

I'd always thought of it that way, not as my grandfather's house, or as a museum called Royceman House,
but as the house on Fifty-second Street. As a child I
had been awed by it: the somber, forbidding interior,
the engulfing velvet draperies, the silence. It was an
appropriate place for a funeral.

I climbed the gray marble front steps. Dirt-em-
bedded cracks ran the length of those steps. The pearl-
gray silk curtains behind the heavy iron-grilled doors
were shredded, light peeking through. I rang the bell.

One of the doors was opened by a man in a black suit, and when I gave my name, he let me in. My father's body would be in the upstairs living room, where they had held the funerals of my Aunt Adeline, my grandfather, and my grandmother. (I hadn't gone to my grandmother's funeral, I was only a baby then, but I felt as if I'd been there. When people talk about an event that happened when you were very little, it seems like a memory, although you know it couldn't be.)

I walked up the staircase and entered the upstairs living room. It was full of tiny gilt chairs, the kind you use at a dinner party. They had delicate caned seats covered with dark crimson velvet cushions, which were tied to the frames with lengths of gold cord ending in thick tassels. No coffin was in evidence. Only row on row of those gilt chairs lined up as if for a theatrical performance but facing nothing but the blank wall. I was puzzled.

I walked downstairs to the second living room, the one directly underneath that one, and there it was, the gleaming ebony casket resting on a platform at the end of the room. The casket was closed. It was covered with a blanket of white flowers. In front of the platform were more of those gilt party chairs in endless rows.

When I looked up at the walls, I saw the loudspeakers. Black wooden boxes with rough brown material, glistening with gold-lamé streaks, stretched across their faces. Then I spotted a microphone standing on the platform behind the coffin. I began to understand why I had not received the cable. Only four days ago my father had said, "I want *you* to take charge. Let's make it private and small." He *had* said that.

I looked at the chairs. There were hundreds of them in this room alone, and it was the wrong room. It wasn't even the room we used for funerals. Oh God, Oh God, I thought, they're not going to do this. They're not going to do this to me, to us. He's dead and he's a private person. He's dead and he's my father. Those bastards, they knew it would be too late for me to do anything about it.

I could feel heat surge through my body and white lights burst in my head. No, fuck it, it's not too late. I stood on one of the chairs, reached up, and wrenched a loudspeaker from the wall. I climbed down, carrying the speaker, and moved to the nearest double window, grasped the black iron handle, and pushed. The window gaped wide. Several panes of glass shattered as I heaved the speaker through the opening. You could hear a crack like lightning and then a tinkle as the glass fragments settled. A dark-suited guard appeared in the room, his face a rosy mask of incredulity. I ignored him as I tore another loudspeaker free and threw it out.

Then the chairs—I had to get rid of them—those velvet-cushioned, blood-colored, fucking party chairs. "It's no party, it's no party," I screamed as I hurled the chairs through the window. Those death-textured, gore-colored, intrusive chairs. I had to get them out. Then it would be pure again, and his again, and mine, and no party, but death as it was.

I must have gotten rid of at least twenty before the guards closed in on me. It wasn't much of a fight. I'm only five feet six and pretty puny. They grabbed my arms and pushed me into the library next door. They shoved me into an armchair and left. I knew it wouldn't be long before Jack Weisman arrived.

I sat in that chair, trying to catch hold of myself by concentrating on the Gospel according to Paul. My grandfather, Paul Royceman, had believed in bringing children up in the country, so he constructed a place in Morristown, New Jersey, that included two dozen bedrooms, thirty-four servants' rooms, a stable for my father, twenty greenhouses, four grass tennis courts, and other such necessities of life.

In 1908, Grandpa Paul had his first stroke, which left him with a slight limp and somehow convinced him that he should move to the city and summer abroad. Thus, the Royceman townhouse. The day the townhouse was completed, my grandfather ordered the

Morristown house demolished. He said he didn't want anyone else to live in his home.

For his townhouse, my grandfather wanted architect Charles Haight, who had designed the Havemeyer house at 1 East Sixty-sixth Street. My grandmother visited there, however, and said it looked like a cliff dwelling. She wanted something "less exotic." All her friends lived in traditional houses decorated with Louis XVI furniture and my grandmother was no groundbreaker.

Grandpa Paul built her an altogether traditional house, but indulged his penchant for "the exotic" by commissioning the Tiffany Studios to design the upstairs living-room fireplace, the staircase, and the ceiling of the library in which I sat. Right up over my head was a spiraled brown and tan cornucopia pouring out fruit. There's your average everyday fruit—green and red apples, and oranges—but there are also pomegranates, persimmons, mangoes, and figs. (The figs are ugly, really bruised.) There's a lot of fruit I've never seen anywhere else: violet pears, ruby-colored grapes, and a yellow melon resembling a large summer squash.

This house was completed in 1910. That's when Grandpa Paul decided that he needed some paintings to hang on the walls. Durand-Ruel supplied a Courbet and Lord Duveen provided a Corot and a Duccio crucifixion. These were my grandfather's first three paintings. He often talked of how the Duccio obliterated the other paintings. It depicted a rather languid Christ suspended on an ebony cross. The background of the painting was gold leaf. At the base of the cross the Virgin Mary stood, leaning her head on the shoulder of Mary Magdalene. My grandfather frequently said it was the "fragile power" of this painting that attracted him. I've always thought he was attracted to the "fragile power" of all that gold leaf. I also think that Duccio was the beginning of his finding a legitimate way to fill the house with Christ and Mary and angels and Peter and Paul and Mark and Matthew and Judas: a legitimate way for a Jew to surround himself with the trappings of Christianity.

In the next two years Grandpa Paul managed to acquire about two hundred thirteenth- to sixteenth-century religious works. Chronologically, the last one was a Tintoretto, "Saint Theresa and the Angel," painted in 1590. Then he bought his first El Greco and then two Goyas.

Early on, I memorized a lot of proper names. I knew that Duccio was Duccio di Buoninsegna and that Goya was Francisco de Goya y Lucientes and that El Greco was really Domenicos Theotocopoulos. I remembered that by the eo-to-co-po combination. I never let on that I knew.

From the time I was five until I was ten, every Sunday that we were in New York we went to the house on Fifty-second Street for lunch. The pervasive mood was always the same—dark, forbidding. It has never changed. Even the fireplaces (which were lit every afternoon from October to June regardless of the weather) have always emitted a cold red flame. The menu too was unvarying: consommé, roast beef, creamed spinach, roast potatoes, a salad with cut-up hard-boiled egg in it, and for dessert, chocolate soufflé, then fruit if you had a niche uncrammed. Never once do I remember a different vegetable or a different dessert. My seat, which never varied either, faced a tapestry of Judith and Holofernes, and every Sunday I was confronted with the dismembered head of Holofernes dripping Aubusson blood down the length of the tapestry into a pool around Judith's feet. That tapestry reappeared frequently in my childhood nightmares.

When there were guests for lunch, the talk usually revolved around art; when there were no guests, the topic was finance. Everything was discussed in single digits. "Jack says our commission will be two but I say three is the very least we'll accept," my father would say. Or my grandfather's knife would flash into the taut skin of a persimmon as he remarked, "Participation will be six or seven, I'm not sure which yet."

The people around the table were the same too. My grandfather, my father, Missy, Tammy, Ellen, me, and always Aunt Adeline, my father's sister. Aunt Adeline had gray lacquered hair that never moved and a prominent bump in the middle of her small nose. My father called Aunt Adeline "Little Miss Do-Good-Drop." He said if a charity ball was being given anywhere in the world, you could count on her being the chairman. He also said his sister had headed a committee that raised half a million dollars for research into a disease which affected only the residents of one town in Poland (with a population of 873). I couldn't look at Aunt Adeline without remembering a story Missy had told me. It seems Aunt Adeline was giving a dinner party the night her daughter, my cousin Penelope, went into labor. Aunt Adeline insisted that Penelope sit through dinner so that the seating at her party would not be ruined. After dessert, Penelope was rushed to the hospital, but her baby was born dead. I don't know why Missy told me this.

After lunch at the house on Fifty-second Street, invariably we walked up Fifth Avenue to an art gallery, invariably Knoedler's. In the company of a man dressed in a morning coat we'd take the small elevator to an upstairs floor where we'd sit on a gray velvet couch in a dark paneled room in a hush stiller than stillness, while discreet white-gloved hands would place paintings like sacrificial offerings on a wooden easel standing in a pool of light on an elevated gray-carpeted platform. My father and grandfather would murmur quietly while I would glance longingly at the high narrow window divided by mullions into small squares of glass and wonder how other boys would be spending that particular Sunday. I could imagine them, in the bright sunlight, each throwing a ball to a laughing man who was not stiff as a new linen handkerchief. Each ball would soar high, and a man and boy would race after it and dive for it and wrestle and laugh in the warming sunlight.

During these Sunday outings, while concentrating on

the window mullions, I observed that they formed a series of crosses, twenty-four in all, if I remember correctly; cross after cross after cross. I thought about these crosses, then about Christ, then about us. That's when I began my personal analysis of what was wrong. When I thought about it, and I did, I came to the conclusion that my father's biggest problem was simply a three-letter word spelled J E W. Of course it took me years to think of it in these simple terms. It's a confusing thing, this self-hatred, and my father never licked it. Aunt Adeline was a victim too. Her husband changed his name from Gutfreund to Gallin, and once I heard her boast, "Our family hasn't been Jewish for generations."

It was important to my father that Missy was descended from John Adams and therefore I was too. He was really proud that I was only half Jewish. Case in point: When Tammy was thirteen, Missy took her to the Foxcroft School in Virginia for an interview. The colonel in charge of admissions (the ladies subscribed to the military system) told Missy in the course of conversation, "If Tammy is Mr. Royceman's daughter, she can't come to Foxcroft. You must know we don't take Jews here." Missy simply stood up and without a word walked out of the office and drove back to New York. That night at the dinner table she re-created the scene for us, her face flushed with remembered indignation. My father listened, carefully spooning his vichyssoise in a rhythmic motion from the orange and blue flowered bowl in front of him. When he had finished his soup, he dabbed at his lips with a napkin and said, "But, my dear, Tammy is *not* my daughter and I want her to go to Foxcroft."

Stepdaughters who attended the right schools and hot-walked your horses, a wife and son who were descended from John Adams, being a trustee of the Urban Museum of Art suited my father fine. It all suited him fine, but then it backfired. In 1957, he was slated to be the next president of the board of trustees of the Urban, but the trustees wouldn't elect him, and you know why. When he knew why, he sent a fleet of trucks to the museum, picked up the Royceman Collection, then valued at seventy-five million dollars, and created his own museum in my grandfather's house.

It was over a decade later that Bartholomew Spencer Hayes became director of the Urban Museum and after he'd been there for a while he found a way to get my father back and still soothe everybody who thought that a Jew shouldn't rule Wasp heaven. Hayes created a brand-new honorary position, chairman of the board of trustees, and awarded it to my father, who by that time was too ill to do very much anyhow.

The whole thing is very complicated really, because my father wasn't just a Jew, he was a sort of a Prince of the Jews. For a long time he even served as president of the Federation of Jewish Philanthropies, and once he took me to a dinner given in his honor by that organization at the Waldorf Astoria. He introduced me like this: "This is my son, Birdie." (As if I had no last name. He didn't even call me Bertie, but used that puerile name, Birdie.) There must have been seven hundred people there and all of them paid homage to my father. One woman in a white satin dress, her neckline plunging between pendulous breasts, actually squeezed my arm and said something about how "blessed" I was to have him for a father. But personally I knew he wanted out of this world within a world. He wanted to belong to Wasp America, to be one with all those people who thought of him as a money merchant. That's the irony; with all his art and horses and clubs he thought of himself as an American, but they still thought of him as a Jew.

Weisman was in the room. He was wearing a blue-black suit and a black tie. Sigmund Rudd stood by his side. Tweedledum and Tweedledee. Rudd had been my grandfather's secretary. My grandfather had sent him to law school and now he was a partner of Stern and Stern, the other law firm along with Weisman's firm, Stuyvesant and Chisholm, that handled all the legal business. Although Weisman handled a lot more than strictly legal matters.

Weisman stood directly over me and, looking down, began: "That's quite a mess in the street out there, but I understand your grief. We are all quite shaken by this."

"My grief!" I exploded. "Listen, you bastard, microphones and loudspeakers, for God's sake! What is this—Madison Square Garden? He told me he wanted it private."

Weisman's enormous round face remained calm. His tone was one you'd use on a not-too-bright child. "It *is* private. Your father was a great and distinguished man. He had many friends in the Wall Street community and the art world who wish to say farewell."

"Fuck that," I said. "Friends. You mean the partners of Royceman Brothers and all those other suck-ups who lapped up the golden stream when he pissed on them?"

"Your language has always left something to be desired, but I do respect your grief. It's too late to do anything about it now."

"That's why you did it behind my back. You knew I'd object. That's why you never sent me a cable."

"Let's not go over that ground again," said Weisman in a weary voice. "I did send you a cable. I can have Western Union send you a confirmation copy. No matter what you want, young man, I owe it to your father to see that his funeral is treated with proper respect."

"Please, Jack," I was begging, "please get rid of all that stuff and let's do it the way he wanted it."

"It *is* the way he wanted it. He spent half a century with his business partners and as a mover in the art world. It's my responsibility to see that nothing interferes with a proper tribute to him."

I looked at him and at Rudd, who had not uttered a word. I knew I'd lost. "You've even got the wrong fucking room," I said.

"What?" asked Weisman.

"We use the upstairs living room for our funerals."

"We're using that room too. It's wired for the overflow. Anyway, it doesn't matter."

"It does to me."

Weisman simply turned and walked to the door. His back was to me as he said, "Rudd will stay with you till it's time." As the door swung open I noticed three guards stationed outside.

Rudd sat next to me but we did not speak. I could hear the hushed voices and the footfalls, smell the intermingling of heavy perfume and flowers: people were arriving for the funeral. After what seemed like a long time, Rudd stood up and, holding my arm as if I were some sort of a cripple, he guided me into the living room. The room was a tableau of mannequins frozen on those gilt chairs. I could feel their eyes on me as I walked to the front of the room. In passing, I recognized several of them: three partners of Royceman Brothers, the public-relations man with the walrus mustache to whom my father had presented the standing Giacometti that we kids had dubbed "Mr. Nourishment," Gina, the bereaved widow, wearing a skin-tight black dress and a grotesque black net veil with round spots of velvet the size of nickels creating scattered blemishes on her face. Rudd led me to an empty seat next to Tammy and her husband Ned Held. Further down the row I saw Ellen sitting between her dark-haired daughter Sally and her young son Ben.

I don't remember what the speeches were about, only that they took a long time. I looked at the gleaming dark box that contained my father and wondered if he would have liked this funeral. I guessed that he would not. I could hear him saying, "Went to that funeral today, it was a bore. Took two hours of my valuable time. They made Royceman out to be a saint, when he was really just a shrewd old duck."

My mind drifted in and out of the speeches. Sometimes I listened and sometimes I did not. There was a lot of that exaggerated and unrelated praise they give to dead men. At one point my cousin Bob (the "esteemed ambassador," that is) mentioned that my father was a great "communicator." He said my father once told him, "I read faces, not balance sheets." That was absurd: my father did just the opposite.

The eulogies floated past my ears. My attention shifted to a price tag safety-pinned about one inch under the armhole of Tammy's black crepe dress. I concentrated on that tag a lot of the time.

Suddenly there was a burst of organ music—I have no idea where it came from—and people stood up and began to leave the room. I followed. On the sidewalk a woman approached—Mary Constanziakias. She reached out and drew me to her, arms encircling my shoulders in an awkward embrace, her chin resting on the top of my head. After a time, she released me and was gone.

Then I was in a car with Tammy and Ned and Ellen, and we were on our way to the cemetery. We made small talk as if driving to the country for a weekend. We never mentioned *him*. I like Ellen's face, it's real, but Ned and Tammy both have the kind of face you see in *Town and Country*. They're the people sitting on that plump Billy Baldwin couch in front of a blazing fire, with cocker spaniels curled up at their feet on the needlepoint rug. Tammy has unusually unattractive hands, with broad fingers and large knuckles, which she accentuates by wearing scarlet polish and a ring on almost every finger. Ned's tailoring is English Impeccable. He looks like a male model. He would be well groomed if he didn't overdo it so. You yearn for a scuffed shoe or a hair out of place. Only one thing spoils the image: Edward (called Ned) Held picks his nose. At frequent intervals his index finger disappears up that nasal cavern. It doesn't bother me, but Gina has refused to have him at the apartment for dinner.

I hardly remember what happened at the cemetery except for the sharp stab in my chest when the first clod of earth smacked the surface of the coffin. I saw stringy roots and pebbles mixed with that hard brown dirt.

That part didn't take long. Less than two hours later we were standing on the sidewalk in front of Ellen's apartment. That was when Ned Held said, "I imagine you'll be needing somebody to represent you, dear boy, and I'd like it to be me."

For a minute I didn't know what he meant, but then I got it. I stared down at his mirrored shoes and said, "When do they read the will?"

Ned laughed, but shifted his weight uneasily from one foot to the other. "They only do that in Victorian novels. I'll call Weisman in the morning and get a copy of the will. I represent Ellen, and Tamara too, of course, so we'll have all our begs in one askit."

"Yeah," I said. "Call Ellen after you've read the will. She always knows where to get in touch with me."

"Good. And don't give out any autographs until you check with me."

I would have chosen Held to be my lawyer, even if he hadn't chosen me. Ned was a member of the family, so to speak, and that made me feel safe—well, safer. He'd been president of the *Harvard Law Review,* and after he married Tammy, my father got him a job at Weisman's firm. Just last year, he'd formed his own firm and had taken several big accounts with him. He was no friend to Weisman.

I was surprised at how quickly Held called. The phone rang at 11:00 a.m. three days after the funeral. The next day I was in his office. A rosewood door bore his name in gold letters. Everything in Held's office looked as though it had been made tomorrow. There was a Spanish tile floor and a ceiling to match. A desk of some sort of new wood carefully stressed to look ancient rested on a wrought-iron pedestal. Held sat behind the desk in a soft English worsted suit, a yellow striped shirt, and a matching tie. On his desk there was nothing but a stack of thick white documents, a yellow pad, and a stainless-steel pen holder. It was like a carefully arranged still life—de Chirico vacant.

As I walked into the room, Held stood up, leaned across the desk, and handed me a white document, on the cover of which was printed:

LAST WILL AND TESTAMENT
OF
BERTRAM ROYCEMAN

Will Dated: May 22, 1972
Date of Death: September 1, 1972

Stern and Stern
Attorneys for Executors
120 Broadway
New York, New York 10005

It was the size of a small book.

"Here it is," said Held. "Sit down and we'll talk."

I sat in front of the fake-wormy desk: there must have been a million holes in its surface. I put the will on my lap. Held said, "I'll try to give it to you without the usual legal jargon. I think you'll want to know right off that you are the recipient of two million dollars outright."

He picked up the yellow pad from his desk, studied it for a moment, and put it down. "You also get Birdwood, but that place is a white elephant. I figure in about two months you'll begin paying all the maintenance—grounds crew, taxes, electricity—everything. I guess you'd better sell the place. Well, that's it."

"What do you mean—that's it?" I picked up the will. "Look at this thing. How can that be it?"

Held looked at me; his finger approached his nose, then paused. He brushed at his nose as if removing a speck of dust. "That's it for you," he answered.

"Where did all the money go?"

"Your father left almost everything to the Urban, his collection and eighteen million to build and maintain a wing."

"And no one else gets anything?"

"I didn't say that. There are some other smaller bequests. I was shocked to discover that Tammy and Ellen get only two hundred thousand dollars outright and the lifetime income from some oil stocks yielding approximately twenty thousand dollars a year. Pretty outrageous when you consider that my wife and Ellen were the only friends the old man ever had. My children, that is mine and Tammy's, and Ellen's children receive the paltry income from those oil stocks *per stirpes* after we're dead. Which I hope will be a long time off."

"*Per stirpes?*"

An equal share for each living child. If that child dies, then his children divide up his share. Held picked up the yellow pad again. He looked down at the pad, then over at me. It was the eye and head movement you use when watching a tennis match. "The largest other bequest goes to Gina, who gets the apartment, most of the furniture, and five million. She can't claim more because she and your father had an ante-nuptial agreement." (Look down . . . Look over.) "Two Royceman partners, Hector Stone and Joseph Wormsley, get the paintings hanging in their offices at Royceman Brothers." (Look down . . . Look over.) "There are some rather small bequests to a cook, a chauffeur, and a secretary averaging about fifteen thousand dollars each." (Look down . . . Look over.) "There are some small charitable bequests, but they don't amount to much."

Held put the pad down. "That's really all, except for a bequest of ninety thousand to Jack Weisman. Incidentally, Bertie, the will was not prepared by Weisman's firm, Stuyvesant and Chisholm, but by Sigmund Rudd's firm, Stern and Stern. We both know that Weisman masterminded this will and Rudd merely executed it at his instruction. I presume that the reason Weisman didn't officially draw up the will is that he is the beneficiary of a legacy. He would have had to file an affidavit with the court to show that there was no improper conduct. Under these circumstances, it is simply easier to have another firm draw up the will.

"I must say the bequest by your father to Weisman puzzles me. Although ninety thousand dollars is a considerable amount by some standards, it's not much to

Weisman. Perhaps it was some sort of honorarium. I don't know, but it does interest me . . . Anyway, that's about all I can tell you. Any questions?"

"It's a lot to digest," I answered. "I'd have to think about what questions to ask. How about the paintings he willed to me?"

"I saw no such provision."

"An Ingres and a Degas, he said they'd be mine."

"Well, dear boy, they're not. I wouldn't have missed that. You get cash, some cash, that is. And that's it. As I said, the Urban gets eighteen million and the collection, with the discretionary details in the hands of the executors of the estate, that's Weisman and his pawns, Rudd and Wormsley."

"My father wanted me to have those paintings. I'd better tell that to Weisman."

"Tell him. It won't do you any good. Take my word for it."

"I'm not sure of that, Ned. You know how I feel about Weisman, but this is a point of honor. He might respond to that."

"Look"—Held tapped the white documents in front of him—"all I can deal with is what's written here. What's written here says to me that we've been screwed."

"I don't feel that way. I just want my two paintings."

"You can't get them unless he chooses to give them to you. And he won't."

"I'll see Weisman." I lifted my copy of the will from my lap and put it on the corner of the desk. "Those paintings are mine."

"In that case, go try it. I wish you good luck," said Held.

"Fuck luck," I replied.

7

*. . . The undersigned, Gina Mazzo, hereby waives and
releases all rights to contest any disposition made to
charity by Bertram Royceman in his Last Will and
Testament or any Codicil thereto, now or hereafter
executed; without restricting the generality of the
foregoing, said waiver shall apply with respect to such
rights as the undersigned may have under Section 17
of the Decedent Estate Law of the State of New York,
or any successor thereto (or under any similar provision
of any other jurisdiction whatsoever). The undersigned
further waives all rights to participate and all rights to
share in any funds which may become available as a
result of such a disposition being contested by or on
behalf of any other person. . . .*

Excerpt from ante-nuptial agreement,
Bertram Royceman/Gina Mazzo, December 3, 1954

I telephoned Weisman for an appointment. As soon as
I'd hung up, Gina called. Her voice kept faltering, and
she began sobbing when she asked me to meet her. Gina
sobbing—that wasn't the way I thought of her.

A few months after Missy left, a long brown and
white striped rectangular box arrived at our apartment
containing seven seemingly identical fur coats. The fur
was dark and bushy. Over the next year, one by one, the
coats disappeared from the closet in the entrance gallery. I never saw any of the women my father brought
home during that period but sometimes I could hear
them laughing and talking late at night in his bedroom.
They were always gone the next day.

I did see Gina though. I was eleven then, and we'd been studying Greek myths. I loved all that heavy stuff about fathers sacrificing their daughters for a fair wind. That night I read till around eleven-thirty, when I decided to go to the kitchen and poke around in the refrigerator. Just as I was about to walk across the entrance gallery, I saw them silhouetted in the light from the gallery vitrine, which held the Fabergé icons, boxes, cases, and commemorative eggs.

Once my father opened one of the eggs for me. Inside was what he called "the surprise," a tiny fairy coach made of gold with red-lacquer upholstery, no bigger than four inches around. He let me spin the wheels with my finger.

I stopped and watched as my father opened the door of the lighted cabinet. He removed a cigarette case and in that almost whisper of a voice started to explain the history of the case. While he was talking, the curly-haired young woman who stood by his side shifted her weight from one foot to the other, and then putting her arms behind her, at a 45-degree angle, let her gray cloth coat slide to the marble gallery floor. Next my father removed an egg, explaining how Czar Nicholas had commissioned Fabergé to create this rock-crystal egg for the Empress Alexandra. He opened the egg and withdrew a tiny gold and jeweled tree. He held the tree in one hand and with the other handed the translucent, diamond-encrusted egg to the woman.

She took it, held it for a brief period, and then very deliberately snapped the egg shut, raised her arm above her head, and opened her fingers. The egg shattered.

Everything seemed to decelerate, as if I were watching a slow-motion film. My father turned and placed his left hand on the woman's shoulder. With his right hand he struck her full in the face. "Cunt. Stupid whore," he hissed. She put her hand to her face where he had struck her and then began to laugh. Laughter filled the gallery as she sank to her knees, kneeling on the gray coat, and moved toward my father's trousers. She opened his fly, reached inside, and guided his penis into her open mouth. She moved with piston precision, forward and back, forward and back, sliding her mouth and fingers down the length of his now-erect penis.

My father reached down and pushed her shoulders so that she collapsed back on the rumpled coat. I'd never watched anybody fuck before; as a matter of fact I've never watched anybody since, but I watched them right there on the gallery floor, and all the time he was spitting out words like bitch, cunt, filthy whore, over and over. That was the first time I ever saw Gina.

By the time I was sixteen (during my infrequent visits home from school) I'd completely mastered the art of holing-up. In the afternoon, I'd lay in a supply of food, and when the first guest rang the bell, I'd lock my door. One evening as usual I was on my bed reading, vaguely aware of the tinkle of glasses and the hum of voices, when I heard a knock on my door. I opened it and there stood Gina in a black turtleneck dress, wearing a necklace of diamonds and emeralds and a matching bracelet. She had a highball glass in her hand. "Can I use your can?" she asked.

"Be my guest."

Gina walked in and flopped down in a chair. "I came here because they're all over my room like locusts, ogling the paintings and looking in drawers to find the secret of my success. I've just got to take off my girdle before I die." Gina gestured with her glass. "Want to share?"

"No thanks. I've had my fix for the day."

"All those people might stay out of my underwear if they had something more exciting to do than look at the fabulous Royceman Collection. I wanted to hire a trio. Nothing spectacular, just a piano player and two other guys, but your dear father said no soap. With all the dough he spends on art and horses and jewelry, I just don't get it. You'd think he was too tight or something. Do you know what he said? 'What would we have to-morrow to show for it?' "

"You, on the other hand, will have one hell of a hangover to show for it," I said.

"Snotty kid," she replied with a laugh. "You know what all those people want to find out? They want to know how I landed Bertram Royceman, Mr. Eligible. Well, I landed him by giving him what he wants. Do you know how we got married?"

"For Christ's sake, Gina, I'm trying to read. Let's not have the saga of your life tonight."

"You *are* a snotty kid. You really are. After your father and I had known each other for about six months, I got kind of bored with the whole number, although there were certain advantages. One night he was working late, so I left him a note and went to a party at the loft of an artist friend of mine and everyone got pretty drunk and there was this big bed behind a screen right in the middle of the room. We moved the screen, and this spade boxer and another girl and I took off our clothes and started to perform while the other guests stood around the bed cheering and clapping and splashing drinks on us. You'd be surprised how well you perform when you've got an audience. I mean, it really makes you want to give your best." She smiled. "Somewhere along the line I turned over onto my stomach and looked up and there he was. Your father, I mean. He was standing right there at the foot of the bed. That night he took me home and two days later we were married."

Gina got up and walked to the dresser. She looked in the mirror and patted her hair; then she turned, surveyed my room, and said, "I like this room. Nice and plain. No paintings or crap on the walls. Your old man just gave me hell out there."

She took a long swallow from her glass. "It seems the lamb at dinner was raw and the embroidered shadow-work tablecloth was on upside down. It's supposed to go bright side down. What the hell does it matter? I ask you. You know what I told the bastard? I said, 'I'm your wife, not your cook. And don't blame me. Blame your secretary, she invites everybody. I don't even know who's going to be here.' "

Gina sat on the bed next to where I was lying. I could feel her body pressing against my hip. "Listen, Bertie, don't you ever want to get out of this mausoleum? Maybe one night you and I could go over to my mother's and she'd make us a great pasta dinner. One night when he's buying the moon or the Mona Lisa or something." Gina brought her face level with mine and for a moment I thought of Missy, it was her smell. Then she leaned down and kissed me on the lips. I couldn't think of anything very clever to say, so I said, "No thanks, Gina."

She stood up abruptly and rolled her eyes toward the ceiling. "I only came to use the can anyway."

I spotted Gina a block away. She was standing under the gray awning of our building wearing a sable coat and tan slacks; a tiny green chiffon scarf anchored her hair in place. She waved when she saw me. "Let's walk," she said, brushing my cheek with her lips. We crossed Fifth Avenue, walking parallel to the black-stained stone wall bordering Central Park. "I couldn't meet you upstairs, they listen to everything."

"They?"

"That's one reason I wanted to see you, they've got Pinkerton guards all over the place. It seems that Bert left some of the furniture and paintings to the Urban and they say they're there to guard them. Weisman won't talk to me. I got that from Sigmund Rudd, who also said if it makes me nervous I should just take a suite at the Plaza until it's settled. Those bastards, they're not going to drive me out. This is my place. My home. They're not shoving me out into the street."

Gina clutched my arm. "I'm enough of a mess, Bertie, without being watched twenty-four hours a day. I take Valium all day long and two Seconals every night, but I can't sleep knowing there's that sweaty man in the kitchen.

"I wanted to bring you his cuff links and his watch

today. Rudd warned me that every single item has been inventoried and I couldn't touch a thing, but I never thought . . ." Gina stopped talking and pulled her coat around her. Then she said, "Jesus, Bertie, it scares me. I got to the door with the box and this big lunk of a guy took it right out of my hand. Then he reached out and cupped his hand around my breast and squeezed it. He kept his hand there and said, 'We have a saying where both of us come from—old chickens make the best stew.' I was scared to death. I just ran into the elevator hall. Honest to God, Bertie, I can't believe this is happening. It's times like this when I really miss him. I'd forgotten how rough it is out there."

I touched her arm, but said nothing.

"Bertie, you're the head of the family now, I want you to get them out of there. Your father made me feel safe, you know. I hadn't felt like that since I was a little girl and I used to sit in my father's bakery smelling the bread baking. My father would get up at five every morning and sometimes I'd go with him and help get the ovens ready and, oh Jesus, why am I carrying on about that, it's now that counts. Now they're closing in on me again, and without Bert I can't even remember who I am. Or was. I'm invisible to myself. I don't know how I got so empty. I need something, someone. I can't take it. Help me, Bertie."

I could see the sweat on her face and she was trembling. "I'll try."

We turned into the park. I looked at the spare September trees and then down at the gray sidewalk. Gina as victim, that was a new one.

I dug my hands deep into the pockets of my jacket until I felt tiny hard balls of lint and grit and the tight stitches at the bottom. I looked on the lobby board of 200 Broadway for the offices of Stuyvesant and Chisholm. Although I'd been there before, I couldn't remember the floor. White metal numerals on the black felt board specified 29. In the reception room were copies of *The Wall Street Journal, Time,* and *Newsweek,* and a desk with a grandmotherly secretary wearing a tweed suit and gray pearl-button earrings. She buzzed for an acned young man, who conducted me to Weisman's office. The office was seedily impressive, the kind of place designed to instill confidence with its carefully studied look of stability and lack of pretension. It was paneled in dark walnut. On two sides were floor-to-ceiling windows, which overlooked nothing at all, by that I mean, just other buildings. The other two walls were covered with bookshelves containing massive gold-embossed loose-leaf leather binders. There were cabinets underneath the bookshelves, topped by a wooden ledge on which rested several heavy-silver framed photographs. One was of my father, the same Karsh photograph that had appeared with his obituary. It had an inscription across the front. There was a photograph of Weisman with President Johnson and one with President Nixon. Another showed Weisman in mortarboard and gown, smiling into the camera, his jowls accentuated by dark shadows. To his right stood Clare Boothe Luce and to his left a black man who resembled Sammy Davis, Jr.

I saw all this in the time it took to walk toward the desk. I wanted to stop and study the photographs, especially to read the inscription my father had written, but I didn't. I sat down in a barrel-shaped, green leather chair in front of Weisman's desk. The chair had the distinct disadvantage of being somewhat lower than the desk, and lower than Weisman's own chair. I shrugged off my jacket, and as I did Weisman said, "There's a closet just behind you."

"No thanks, it's O.K. here."

"As you like," he said, tipping back in his chair and crossing his hands over a stomach that looked like a swollen balloon. "I could see you better without those dark glasses," he commented.

"Do they disturb you?"

"I like to look a man straight in the eye when we're talking. It makes things seem less devious, which is what we're all trying for. At least, that's my philosophy."

"Sorry, I like my shades. They make things seem more devious, which is what we're all trying for. At least, that's my philosophy."

Weisman's tongue made a full circle of his lips and disappeared back into his mouth. "Where's your mother?" he asked abruptly.

"How should I know? Why?" I hadn't thought about Missy. Not even at the funeral.

"It's just a formality. The court will require that she be cited, so we need her to sign a consent to probate the will. It's common enough in cases of Mexican divorce. You've received your consent to probate from Held, haven't you?"

"Yes," I lied.

"Good. What's on your mind?"

"First of all, I just spoke to Gina. How long are those Pinkertons going to stay there?"

"Oh, indefinitely, I suppose; at least until we can arrange to ship the large parlor furniture and paintings to the Urban."

"You can't expect her to live like that. My father would never have allowed it. There were no guards when he was alive and the stuff was just as valuable then."

"When your father was alive he had the best insurance agents in the world, the United States and the New York State governments. If anything happened to an object, he could take a deduction up to the percentage allowed by law. In your father's case, in general terms, he could deduct in a given year from 80 to 90 percent of an object's value. We are now faced with quite a different set of circumstances and in my fiduciary capacity it is my duty to see that these valuable objects are protected until they are disposed of in the way he directed."

I knew Weisman and all that long-winded legal gobbledygook he could throw around. This time I was determined to stay clear and in control. "You can insure them, can't you?"

"I can but I won't. Pinkertons are just as effective,

and in a cost study we made, we ascertained that we can employ three private men twenty-four hours a day at a fraction the cost of insurance. Contrary to what you think, these things are not done arbitrarily. It might interest you to know that certain small items have disappeared from the collection. Small in size, not in value."

"Like what?"

"A priceless Fabergé Imperial Easter Egg is missing. It infuriates me to think that anyone could have dropped it in his pocket and simply walked out the door."

Lost—round one. I began to feel my foot prickling and my back getting wet, because I knew I'd have to get to the real reason I'd come. "About the will," I began. I paused and started again. "My lawyer informs me that you, Rudd, and Wormsley, as executors, must give me permission to have certain objects. I'd like to request certain personal items."

Weisman said nothing but looked at me with a curious intensity.

"Specifically, I'd like my father's cuff links and his wristwatch. And I'd like two paintings which my father told me would be mine." Weisman still said nothing. "Well?" I asked.

"What paintings?"

"The Ingres portrait of 'Countess Di Cavour' and Degas's 'Girl Combing Her Hair.' "

"And Goya's portrait 'Carmelia'? The most expensive painting in the collection valued at over two and a half million dollars. You'll be wanting that, too, I suppose."

"No, I don't want that." I wasn't sure what he was driving at. "I don't particularly like Goya."

Weisman ran his fingers through his gray hair. "Your father's will was well thought out. If he had wanted to give you paintings or personal effects, he would have so designated. I am merely an executor of this will. I can't give you valuable property that has already been relegated elsewhere."

"I'd be willing to buy the paintings from the estate.

My father said they'd be mine, so if you can't give them to me, then you can let me buy them at a fair price."

"Buy them? No, that's impossible. If I let anyone, for any reason, invade the estate, then I leave us open to criticism by the Urban Museum and investigation by the attorney general. The paintings which your father left the Urban Museum are a charitable gift, tax free. If he'd willed the paintings of which you speak to you, they would have been subject to estate tax. I'm sure your father had this in mind when he designated that they go elsewhere, and I would have advised him of the wisdom of this course of action."

"And his personal effects?"

"I have no authority in this matter," said Weisman, exasperation pulling at the copious folds of his mouth. "Perhaps it never occurred to your father that you'd want these things. Knowing you as I do, it certainly would never have occurred to me.

"Bertie," he said, "believe me, if I invade the estate for a toothpick or for a ton of gold, the principle is the same. I cannot and will not take the risk, and you must understand that."

"No, I don't. I don't understand it and I'm going to get what's mine."

"Not this time, Bertie," replied Weisman, his voice very loud. "You are very clever coming here with requests for cuff links and watches and offers to buy to soften me up for the big ones—the Ingres and the Degas."

Weisman leaned forward, picked up a freshly sharpened yellow pencil, and bore down on the tip with his thumb. He removed his thumb and replaced it again in a rhythmic motion, as if trying to release emotion in small gasps through his fingertip. After perhaps a thirty-second repetition of this gesture, he began speaking in a more modulated voice. "Your erratic nature is no secret, and I think you will find that we shielded your father from it in death as in life, an act of which we are justly proud. Your lawyer, and I know Edward Held is astute, will certainly inform you that we expected trouble from you. We have therefore taken pains to produce a document that is Bertram-Ogden-Royceman—proof. Is that quite clear?"

"Don't pull this crap on me, you cocksucker. Just don't try to do this to me."

"You've always wanted it your way," replied Weisman. "You were a spoiled and petulant child, and I'm afraid you're a spoiled and petulant adult. The fact that you have no gift for finance is at best regrettable, but that you go out of your way to be pugnacious and foulmouthed is unforgivable. I repeat, you came here to take what is not yours and I for one am glad that I am able to prevent it."

I stood up then, grabbed my jacket, and headed for the door. I knew if I stayed another minute I'd lean across that desk and hit Weisman in the center of that moon face. I started moving fast. I kept going until I was in front of the bank of elevators and there was nothing to do but stand watching the red electric arrow that indicated down. I walked about three blocks while the hatred crystallized in me. I saw a phone booth, went in, found a dime, and dialed Ned Held.

"How did you make out?" he asked.

"Make out! I struck out."

"Cheer up, dear boy," Held laughed. "Just remember, where there's a will there's a way."

"Cut the comedy," I replied. "What's that supposed to mean?"

"If you come to my office tomorrow at eleven, I'll explain exactly what that's supposed to mean."

Held was sitting at his desk drinking espresso from a white china demitasse with a pattern of gold ferns around the edge. He looked up and said, " 'Into the valley of death, into the mouth of Hell . . .' Want some coffee?"

"No. Why the quote?"

"You know. You've seen Weisman. We've all been *had,* you more than any of us. You went to him to plead for two lousy paintings. If it wasn't for Weisman, that entire collection would be yours. When your grandfather died, did he leave his collection to a public institution? Not on your life. He left it to your father. It was *meant* to be passed down from father to son. Your father knew that; that's why his first impulse was to leave the collection to you. I know, because I was working for Weisman in 1965, when a will to that effect was drawn up. Even then Weisman kept badgering him about the exorbitant taxes it would entail. He's the one who talked your father into this new will. He's the one who cheated you.

"Not that your old man was altogether blameless. He remembered to leave his partners the paintings that hang in their offices, but he forgot about you. You, dear boy, simply slipped his mind."

It was true.

"The trouble with you, Bertie, is that you just sit there and take it. They've conditioned you to knuckle under, to beg."

I must have sounded very bitter when I replied, "There isn't a great deal I can do about that."

"You're wrong—you can get those paintings and whatever else you want—you can sue. Don't sit there looking so bewildered, for God's sake. How much do you think the Royceman Collection is worth?"

"I don't know exactly. A lot. What has that got to do with it."

"That collection is worth approximately 100 million. Your father willed the collection and eighteen million cash to the Urban. The total of all your father's other bequests is perhaps twenty-two million dollars, and I'm being generous in that estimate. Bertie, there happens to be a New York State law that says a will which leaves more than half the estate to charity may be challenged."

"Let me get this straight, Ned. You can't leave more than half your estate to charity?"

"Not in New York. You can leave it to your dog or your mistress but not to charity."

"Why not?"

"There's the question. I guess if you had to find a culprit you'd pin it on Henry VIII."

"Henry VIII, terrific! That makes a lot of sense."

"Actually it does. Almost all our laws are based on English jurisprudence. Henry, as you may remember, wanted to marry a little trick named Anne Boleyn. For this he needed sanction to divorce from the Catholic Church. When he didn't get it, he broke with the Church and decided to try to vitiate its power. Henry limited the amount one could leave to the Church and also ruled out deathbed bequests. You know, those last-minute attempts to buy your way into heaven.

"Now, four hundred years later, most of our states are still bound by some form of these percentage or time requirements. California, for example, is a time state. In California, until recently, if you died within six months of making a bequest to charity, the bequest was automatically void. New York is a percentage state."

"And you can't get around that restriction?"

Held clasped his hands behind his neck and focused his eyes on the ceiling. "Getting around things is what we lawyers are all about. For every law there is a concomitant abuse of the law. If you lived in California, for example, and wanted to leave your collection to the Los Angeles County Museum, you might do so and add the provision, "If I die within six months of this bequest, I direct that my collection go to the then director of the Los Angeles County Museum.' That would get around it for you, providing the 'then director' turned over the merchandise." Held chuckled to himself at this, his chair emitting a series of squeaks as he rocked back and forth, still staring at the ceiling.

I could feel my eyes begin to sting. "Let's get on with it, Ned."

"In your father's case, the device for getting around the law is in the form of a Straw Man. Your father provided that, if for any reason his collection did not go to the Urban Museum, it would then be given to your cousin, Ambassador Robert Royceman."

"Bob? Why would my father do a thing like that? He didn't even like Bob."

"He didn't have to like him. Robert Royceman is the Straw Man. Let's say you decide to object on the grounds that your father clearly violated the statute prohibiting him from leaving more than half his estate to charity. But this statute is not automatically enforced. It applies only when and if it is challenged. According to law, the only persons who can challenge are parents and issue, descendants like children and grandchildren who stand to reap direct benefit from such an objection. But the Straw Man device disqualifies you from challenging by preventing this direct benefit. The will states that the collection goes to the Urban or, failing that, to the Straw Man, Robert Royceman. There is simply no way for you to benefit."

"If I understand you correctly, it's really Catch-22. If I challenge and win because my father left more than half his estate to charity, I still can't benefit directly because the collection then goes to my cousin Bob. But since there's no way I can benefit directly, I'm not allowed to object in the first place."

"You get it. It's Catch-22, all right. What's more, the Straw Man is just that. He can't get anything either, because now no one can challenge the will."

"Jesus, why are you giving me all this sophistry if I've had it? You said I could sue."

"You can. I think we have a shot at proving the Straw Man device invalid and winning the right to challenge the excess charitable disposition."

"That's beginning to make sense. The Straw Man device is outrageous. Anyway, I've got nothing to lose."

Held took a sip of his coffee, then put the cup down. "I wouldn't exactly say that. If we press suit we've got to be able to go into a lot of areas. We need to have a clear road to pursue whatever course we feel is right. Weisman has put an obstacle in our way. He expected trouble from you so he inserted an *in terrorem* provision in the will directed against you."

"What's that?"

"In terrorem. It's what it sounds like—in terror. You'll find the provision on page 23. It states that if you contest your father's will you'll lose whatever you've been given. It would be as if you had predeceased your father. Your share would then go into the residuary estate, that portion of the estate still remaining after every other obligation is fulfilled. Incidentally, Bertie, you, Tammy, and Ellen are the heirs to the residuary estate."

"In other words, by the simple act of suing I lose everything I've been left in the will and Tammy and Ellen split what I lose, two million dollars plus whatever money is in the residuary estate. And you're asking me to sue? I may be crazy but I'm not stupid."

"In terror," intoned Held. "You see, it's doing what it's supposed to do."

"So what. Why doesn't your dear wife, Tammy, sue?"

"Tammy's in no position to derive benefit from a suit. She's no blood kin of your father. He was in no way legally obligated to leave her anything. It's you or forget it."

Held paused, then asked, "Wouldn't it be great if there were no *in terrorem* provision?"

"But there is."

"That's right. Therefore, I suggest you look at your father's will and then at the agreement I drew up last night. As a matter of fact, I stayed up most of the night working on it."

Held smiled as he handed me the documents. "I want you to see for yourself how they tried to block you. Then read my agreement, which is self-explanatory. I don't want you to think I'm pressuring you."

"How could I think that, just because you happened to forget to ask me to sign my consent to probate the will?"

Held remained calm. "I didn't want you to sign anything until you understood the situation."

"If I don't sign, won't Weisman know what's coming?"

"We're lucky. They'll have to postpone the date of return because no one can find Missy."

"Do you know where she is?"

"Well, almost. She sent Tammy a cable from Switzerland. It said, ALIVE AND WELL AND DRY AS THE SAHARA."

8

... D. The provisions of subdivision A of Article
SEVENTH *and paragraph (5) of Section D of Article*
FIFTH *and Section II of Article* NINTH *of this Will for
my son,* BERTRAM OGDEN ROYCEMAN, *or his descendants, as the case may be, shall be in lieu of any and
all claims which he or they may have as heirs, distributees, devisees, or legatees of this Will. If any
claim inconsistent with the provisions of this Section D
shall be made by or on behalf of* BERTRAM OGDEN
ROYCEMAN *or his descendants, as the case may be,
his personal representatives, distributees, heirs, legatees,
assignees, or appointees, then any rights which he or
they may have under subdivision A of Article* SEVENTH,
and paragraph (5) of Section D of Article FIFTH *and
Section II of Article* NINTH *of this Will shall cease
and terminate and my estate shall be disposed of as
though* BERTRAM OGDEN ROYCEMAN *and his descendants had predeceased me. . . .*

In Terrorem clause—page 23,
the Last Will and Testament of Bertram Royceman

That's the way it's always been. That's how many
clauses within clauses I am. I'm so many sections and
articles and letters that I'm not really there any more.
Not as a person, that is. You're powerless when you're
a subclause in a subsection in an article in an extrap-
olated equation that you cannot begin to comprehend.

The Straw Man device was there too. I found it by
locating my cousin Bob's name and working backward
up the page.

When I finally got to Held's document, it was as he'd said, self-explanatory. It stated that if I sued and lost, Tamara and Ellen, who would receive my share of the estate, would give it back to me. In return, if I won, we'd split, one third for each of us, whatever was over and above my present share of the estate. That's what it said, although the language was legalese dense.

When I thought I had it all sorted out, I went back to see Held. "This agreement gets around the *in terrorem* provision all right, but is it legal?"

"Quite."

"And I get everything back even if I lose my suit?"

"Everything except what the girls would have to pay as a gift tax. It's considerable but well worth it, I believe."

"Why are you doing this? What's in it for you?"

"The difference between the allowable charitable gift of half your father's estate and what he's actually given away is in excess of forty-seven million dollars. If we win, there are two possibilities. The first is that all the excess in money and art will revert to the residuary estate. The second is that the court will insist on reverting to a previous will, if one exists. One does. The one in which you get the collection. If you sign this agreement and we succeed, you get a third of the residuary estate or you give Tammy and Ellen each a third of the collection. Either way we'll all be very rich."

"I understand. The answer's no. We can't do that. The collection is supposed to go to the Urban. If that's the plan, then count me out."

"You're just going to let them shit on you? You're not going to fight back?"

"No, I only want a couple of paintings. I don't want to destroy the collection."

Held's index finger burrowed into his nose. We sat staring at each other for a long time. Then he said, "Look, I can't do anything without you. You're in charge. I'm only your lawyer. We'll do what you want to do. We're in good shape even without the collection. What would you say if I told you that two weeks after

we press suit Weisman will settle for your paintings, a
written apology, and nine million dollars?"

"Where'll he get the nine?"

"From the Urban bequest of eighteen."

"But that's for the building."

"They don't need that much. Your father only did
that so there'd be very little money left in the residuary
estate. He even stipulated that the Urban couldn't use
more than half the bequest for construction. The rest of
the money just sits there in a great big pile and the net
income goes to maintaining the collection, which is absolutely ridiculous, since the city contributes millions
every year to the Urban for that very purpose. Nine
million is plenty for them. More than enough. We
should get something for our trouble. How about it?
Nine million for us, your paintings, and a written
apology."

"A written apology. You could get that? You're
sure?"

"Within two weeks."

"And you can't do anything else unless I agree to
it?"

"How can I? You're the one who has to sign everything."

"O.K., we'll fight."

"Good. Just relax and I'll have the girls in tomorrow
to sign the agreement."

But as it turned out, it wasn't that easy, because
Ellen wouldn't sign.

"It's the way Daddy Bert wanted it and I don't think
we should try to change it," Ellen said. A tiny fox
terrier puppy nestled in her lap. She was feeding him
with an eye dropper, her hands in constant motion as
she dipped the dropper into a bowl of milk and brought
it to the animal's mouth again and again.

"I want what he told me would be mine. You believe he told me about the paintings, don't you?"

"Yes, I believe that."

"Ned says I'm the only one who can sue. But I can't even do that if you don't sign."

Ellen's hands began stroking the puppy. "Ned Held is a bad man and a drunk."

"Come on, Ellen."

"Really, really he is. He beats Tammy up. He kicked her in the stomach when she was pregnant with Addie and she nearly lost her. He's ugly, I don't trust him."

"We don't have to trust him. We only have to use him to get what's fair."

"Fair! You say you want two paintings but Ned Held says we'll be nine million richer. I'm not a complete Neanderthal. I do understand what's going on."

"The nine million makes it worth his while. That's why he's out there working for me. Believe me, Ellen, taking that money won't hurt anyone or anything. It's just extra money."

"It's Daddy Bert's money, not yours."

"It's maintenance money. They don't need it."

"First you wanted two paintings. Now you want two paintings plus nine million. What's next? It's going to go on and on."

"That's not true. Held says that two weeks after we sue it'll all be settled."

"No, it won't. I don't believe it. What'll stop you from grabbing off all you can get? If I let you sue, maybe there won't be a Royceman Collection. You don't care about it, you never have."

"But I told Held that the collection is going to the Urban and he's promised . . ."

"He promised, but so what? He's a damn liar. Who'll protect Daddy Bert if I don't? You know, Birdie, I always thought of myself as the one who really loved Daddy Bert best, right from the very beginning when he first started seeing Missy. We lived in a run-down house in the Village. I was quite little but I remember him driving up in a big black car with a curved back seat. He told me the name, it was fancy and foreign, and after that I called the car his Hispano Squeezer. The presents he brought us: matching brown velvet dresses with crimson streamers down the front, a toy barn with a tack room and china horses, a model of the frigate *Constitution*. I always remember those good things. You know, Birdie, memory is all we have left of him now."

It's all we ever had, I thought. Nothing exists until it becomes memory. We are our memories. They shape us. Ellen and I, crippled by our memories, sought constantly to re-examine the genesis of our deformity. And why not? Even now she was saying, ". . . Missy wore caftans and walked barefoot. It wasn't even fashionable way back then. We had all those animals in the house. Daddy Bert nicknamed Missy 'Rima' after Rima the bird-girl in *Green Mansions*. 'Rima,' he'd say, 'your chair is full of cat hair. Will you get the girls to brush it off so I can sit down in your jungle?' It was all fun then. We went to a crummy progressive school where we danced naked but never learned how to read or write or anything.

"When we moved in with Daddy Bert it got real formal. Our own nurse in a pink nursery with flowers painted on the walls, but Missy insisted on bringing the animals. The first week we were there, I looked up at a painting of the Virgin Mary and thought she'd grown a beard, but it was Missy's gogo, her South African bush-baby, who'd crawled up the wall and perched right on Mary's chin. Things like that were always happening. But Daddy Bert didn't seem to mind at first. It was years later that he began calling her a slovenly bitch and saying how he couldn't live in all that filth, but that was after you were born, so you probably remember that."

"No, I don't remember," I said. But I did. My memories: Missy disappearing into her room for days at a time. Waking in the night, the scent of her all around my head as she kissed my eyes. Missy going out only to return with a grotesque new animal, an armadillo, an indigo snake, an alligator whose repulsiveness was designed to pay my father back. My father's voice hissing at her in the darkness outside my door, "I'll throw you back in the gutter where you came from." And then the memory that for me has always meant loss, irrevocable loss, and pain: The girls and Missy are in the elevator. The doors close. That's it. "I don't remember," I repeated. "Let's get back to business."

"All right. What's your plan?" asked Ellen, picking up my tone.

"We're going to try to knock out the device that prevents our challenging the charitable bequest. Then we'll contest on the ground that Father left more than half his estate to charity, which is illegal in New York."

"That's funny. When Ned called he kept giving me the third degree about how dotty Daddy Bert was toward the end. I was sure he wanted to use senility as a reason to sue."

"He never mentioned it."

"Well, I'd bet you that he's going to use it. That's why I didn't tell him anything, although, God knows, Daddy Bert was unclear a lot of the time. The last time I brought Ben Junior to see him he kept calling him Birdie. He thought Ben was you. The poor kid kept looking at me because he didn't know how to handle it. Daddy Bert had no idea who I was, so he simply ignored me. He asked Ben if he still had 'The Fifer' costume Missy had given him. It was really sad. The next time I saw him, he was all right though, perfectly clear."

Ellen removed the puppy from her lap. There was a ragged wet spot on her skirt where the animal had been. She placed the puppy in a basket on the floor. "Birdie, I like money too. I'm as greedy as the next one. Once we get started we'll take the money and the collection and everything for ourselves. We won't be able to resist. I know that, so I won't sign."

"Look, Ellen I just want to show Weisman that he can't put me down as if I were a piece of crap. All my life they've treated me like a cipher. This time I have a chance to be in charge. My first chance. This is something I want to handle myself. Please let me."

That seemed to get to Ellen, because I saw her

wince and tears were near the surface. "Exactly what is it you want, Birdie."

"I want to win."

"Win what?"

"I don't know. Just win."

"And I want to leave the dead alone. I don't want to talk about it any more."

9

October 6, 1972

Dear Bertie,

In the past you have mentioned that I did not keep you informed of events relating to your father's estate. Therefore, I enclose the press release which will mark the gift of the Royceman Collection to the Urban Museum of Art, October 13, 1972.

The collection will be presented to the museum at the annual Benefactors' Dinner.

Thank you for your kind attention.

> *Sincerely,*
> *Jacob Weisman*

―――

For Release 10:00 p.m. Friday, October 13, 1972

BERTRAM ROYCEMAN COLLECTION
DONATED TO THE URBAN MUSEUM OF ART

Mr. Jacob Weisman, on behalf of the executors of the Royceman estate, announced at the Benefactors' Dinner this evening the gift of the Royceman Collection to the Urban Museum of Art. The collection is described as one of the most important private collections ever amassed.

Formed over a period of more than seven decades by Paul Royceman and his son Bertram, both in their times senior partners of Royceman Brothers, it is comparable to the great American collections of Morgan, Mellon, and Freer.

. . . In accepting the gift, Bartholomew S. Hayes, director of the Urban Museum of Art, termed this announcement "my greatest achievement as director of

74

this institution and the greatest achievement in the history of a museum which has dedicated itself to acquisitions of the highest quality."

. . . Douglas Watson, president of the Urban's board of trustees, noted that "the collection will immensely enrich the institution which Bertram Royceman served so long and with such consummate skill." Watson then thanked Weisman for "this generous contribution to the culture of New York City and, indeed, to the nation."

. . . Mrs. Adele Laskoff, speaking on behalf of the trustees, said she regretted that "Mr. Royceman could not attend this gathering, as he would have adored to see this moment." She noted that her favorite paintings from the collection were the beautifully selected Italian Primitives, including many of the Sienese School of the fourteenth and fifteenth centuries. . . .

Excerpts from the publicity release
concerning the donation of the Royceman Collection
to the Urban Museum of Art

I put down the release. Jesus, what a trip. This wasn't going to happen until tomorrow and yet it was written as if it had already happened. Four mimeographed pages telling what each person said, what each person replied, only they hadn't. Imagine that cocksucker Weisman writing "Dear Bertie" as if nothing had happened. He'd accused me of always wanting it my way, when it was always his way. I couldn't fix the past but I could still alter tomorrow, or at least try. I dialed Weisman.

"Hello, Bertie. I was about to call you."

"About what?"

"Your mother. We still can't find her. Our letter was returned. The next step is to advertise in the newspaper. Most undignified. You're sure you don't know?"

"I don't know. This is Thursday, right?"

"What's the matter with you, are you stoned?"

"Why, Mr. Weisman, I had no idea you were au

courant with the patois of our drug culture. No, I am not stoned—I just received your letter."

"I mailed it last Friday. If you had a better sense of time, you might pick up your mail more promptly."

"My sense of time is fine. I know precisely when my father died. Tomorrow is six weeks to the day."

"Yes?"

"It's too soon."

"We have considered that fact and decided that for optimum coverage the Benefactors' Dinner provides the perfect spotlight in which to make our presentation. It's ideal timing."

"It's Friday the thirteenth. What's so ideal about that?"

"Don't give me any trouble, Bertie. I was not required to tell you that we were making this gift. We were trying to keep you informed."

"Who's we?"

"The executors of the estate. I'm making the presentation on behalf of the estate."

"No, you're not. If it's going to be done at all, I'll do it."

"You?"

"Yes. I'll make the presentation. I'm his son. His only son. I should do it."

Weisman was silent. Then he said, "As long as it's done. Six-thirty for cocktails, dinner at eight. Promptly," he added.

"I'll bring Ellen," I replied.

I'd take Ellen with me to the presentation to prove to her that I wasn't going to be greedy. Also I wanted very much to have Ellen there when the Royceman Collection left the Royceman family.

Ellen opened the door, looked at me, and said, "Oh no."

"Leprosy?"

"A blue suit and a blue turtleneck. Oh Birdie, you know it's black tie. I went four years ago with Daddy

Bert. Everybody is 108 and dripping ermine that smells like mothballs, and it's definitely black tie."

"So what."

"Let's have a drink and think about it."

"There's no time."

"I know! Ben's tuxedo. It's still in the closet. I could never bear to give his clothes away."

"Ben was twice my size. Forget it, will you, Ellen. I'm giving them over a hundred million. They won't care how I'm dressed. At least one of us is together," I added. Ellen was wearing a pale-green chiffon dress with a tiny jacket. She did look great, except her lipstick seemed too bright on her mouth.

"I had my hair done," she said. *"And* a manicure." Ellen extended her hands toward me like a child seeking approval. "I'm so proud of you for doing this."

"I'm not giving them everything. I've thought about it; I've got to get those paintings and his watch and cuff links. Even if you don't help me, it's what I have to do."

"You'd risk it all for that?"

"I have to do it."

"For two paintings? For his watch and cuff links? I don't even remember what they looked like."

"Neither do I."

"Then why? You're putting too much pressure on me. It's not fair. You must be very angry at me."

"I'm not. You have a point, it is a temptation to take it all. After I give it away, maybe you'll feel you can sign the agreement. Besides, the Straw Man device is wrong, and that should count for something."

"I'm scared what Ned will do, although I suppose there isn't much he *can* do once you give the collection to the museum."

"Then we'd better get going."

The south entrance of the Urban was draped with a long gold canopy; a gold carpet unfurled on the pavement, extending into the parking lot. As we started down the carpet flashbulbs began to pop. Ellen clutched at my arm. I reached in my pocket, grabbed my shades, and put them on. We walked fast, not running, but fast. I was glad to get past all that.

Inside there were perhaps two hundred people drinking and talking. Waiters in short red jackets with black satin lapels passed trays of hors d'oeuvres. The men looked like Xerox copies of one another: black tuxedos, white shirts, gray hair, pale skin. But the women were a Jim Dine palette, dabs of pure color moving about the Great Entrance Gallery.

I spotted a bar to the right. "I could use that drink now," I said.

"Me too; bourbon, if they have it."

"Wait here. I'll be right back."

As I moved toward the long table that served as a bar, I caught fragments of conversation . . .

"I know Manet and Monet are not the same. It's that they *seem* the same."

"I told them, we need *youth* in the Century Club."

"It's true the committee did have a deficit of thirty-five thousand dollars, but then Uncle Harold . . ."

"I'm sure both his ex-wives are trustees of the Met."

"There simply aren't any elegant people any more," said a blue-haired dowager in a russet jersey dress. *"Their* idea of something smashing is a square dance with a live donkey making ca ca on the white shag rug."

"They say he was worth well over 200 million," said a clear female voice behind me. "Their tribe was always very good at that," answered a male voice.

Weisman was moving toward me, his bulk strait-jacketed into a tuxedo. I saw him and felt him simultaneously. What I felt was a combination of frustration and suppressed anger. It was not new. Even in childhood, I'd felt this way when my nurse, Walmsey, commanded, "Clean your plate. You are not permitted to leave the table until that food is gone." Weisman stopped beside me, looked at the drinks, and said, "I need one too. It's been hell. We were given only fifty seats and everyone has been fighting over them as if they were tickets to the Inaugural. I'm afraid I've offended some pretty important people." His eyes traveled down my body. "Is that what you're wearing?"

"So it seems."

"It's not appropriate, it's lacking in respect."

Weisman made a sharp gesture with his wrist; his sleeve shot up as if attached to an elastic band. He looked at his watch. "There's no time to change before we go upstairs. I should have sent someone to dress you."

"Preferably blond, naked, and *Law Review*."

"There's nothing I can do about it now," he said, shaking his head. "I'll see you upstairs."

I returned to Ellen and handed her a drink. She was talking to a tiny matchstick of a man. His lank black hair fell in a straight Dutch-boy bob about his pale face. "Mr. Royceman," he said, extending a moist hand, "I'm Harold Linsky, curator of contemporary art. I was told to keep an eye out for you and Mrs. Billings." Linsky puffed on his cigarette and the unmistakable smell of grass surrounded us. "It's a pleasure to see a contemporary here. The benefactors are annual contributors of twenty thousand dollars or more. You can imagine how that eliminates painters, sculptors, intellectuals, critics, in fact anybody with an even moderately serious interest in art."

"I'd like one of your cigarettes."

"American or Mexican?"

"Mexican."

"With great pleasure."

The whiskey and grass helped. I was feeling a little more relaxed when we went upstairs to the European Paintings Gallery. Linsky guided me to a long table on a slightly raised platform. It faced about twenty round tables. "I'll be with Mrs. Billings," he whispered and departed. Then I was bracketed by Adele Laskoff and Weisman.

At my place was a fruit cup. Maraschino-cherry stain bloodied the colorless membranes of the grapefruit. The shank of my vermeil spoon was decorated with an eagle; a banner at his feet was engraved with the initials

U.M.O.A. I picked up the spoon but did not eat. I couldn't. I felt the pressure of Adele Laskoff's elbow as she nudged my right arm. She handed me a small piece of white memo paper folded in half. I opened it and read, "Speeches follow seating order. You are after Laskoff, before Weisman." Three initials were scrawled at the bottom of the note, not Hayes's. They were unrecognizable.

I crumpled the note. Next I remember being served lamb, mashed potatoes, and limp yellow canned asparagus. I drew my fork over the potatoes, making ski-trail impressions on that lumpy white mound. The speeches began while they were still serving the Baked Alaska. I realized that soon it would be time for me to get started. That I would be required to perform for this very important audience. I felt I had experienced this before, somewhere. The speeches reinforced the feeling. They were, word-for-word, that press release.

I became aware of a repeated sound, a tap-tap-tap-tap-tap. I looked down and saw that my own foot was beating a tattoo on the raw planks of the dais.

To my right, Adele Laskoff stood and began her speech. It too was exactly as I'd read; only when she said how my father would have "adored to see this moment," she began to cry and, removing a white handkerchief from the cuff of her dress, dabbed dramatically at her eyes and nose. This surprised me, because the release hadn't included stage directions.

It was my turn. I stood. The tapping stopped; in its place small electric shocks caused tremors in my legs. "Ladies and gentlemen," I began. That's how all speeches begin. "There's been a lot to think about since my father died. Especially for me, since I'd lost the habit.

"The reason I came here tonight is to give you my father's collection. It's not really my father's but our family's, since my grandfather started the whole thing. But that makes no difference to you."

For the first time I looked out at the audience. I spotted Ellen sitting next to Harold Linsky. Her fingers bent, then straightened, forming a tiny wave, and she nodded in agreement. I focused on her as I spoke.

"Anyway, I'm here to give away the Royceman Collection. I'm doing this because it's a great temptation to keep it for myself and I don't want to give in to that."

I heard soft laughter, but I didn't see what was funny. I waited for it to die down. "You can have the collection, four thousand items or thereabouts, but I'm keeping two things for myself. I haven't completely made up my mind, but I'll probably keep half the money too. Let's face it, you don't need all that money, and for nine million you could build the pyramids."

It started again, the laughter. This time it was louder. Weisman leaned toward me. "Stop this disgraceful display. I warn you." His words were covered by the sound.

At least Ellen wasn't laughing. She placed her mouth to Linsky's ear. He picked up a knife and began tapping his water glass. The laughter subsided.

"I guess it's pretty obvious that I'm not a speechmaker, but I do feel obligated to be here tonight. I'm also not an executor of my father's estate, or anything for that matter, so I don't even know if technically I can give you this collection. But if I can, I do. My father wanted it here. He said this place was the only game in town."

A thunderclap of laughter. Laughter everywhere. Loud, seething, mindless laughter. I held up my hand, palm flat, fingers spread wide to push it back. It continued. Weisman rose to his feet. His right arm encircled my back and I felt his hand on my shoulder. He was smiling a benevolent smile. I felt his fingers tighten. The immense force of his weight was in those fingers, holding me fast, pushing me down into my chair, and all the time he was smiling. At the instant I felt my knees giving out, Weisman said, "I know we all want to thank Mr. Bertram Ogden Royceman for his witty and most original speech. On behalf of the executors of the Royceman estate I wish to present . . ."

As I listened to Weisman's presentation, Hayes's acceptance, and all the other speeches, I began to realize that it hadn't mattered what I'd said. No one paid any attention. It had all been prerecorded.

10

August 26, 1937

My dear Father,

I am appealing to you to lend me the sum of $750,000 for a period of approximately one year in order that I might purchase the magnificent Saroque Collection of Fabergé commemorative eggs and boxes. If I had the actual cash at this time I am sure you would encourage the purchase of this collection, which is unique in all the world.

In the past when I have purchased paintings and objects for our collection, it has always been with your generosity, encouragement, and approval. I know that you have expressed a certain lack of interest in the work of Peter Carl Fabergé, but I hope you will approve of this new direction that I wish to take. The study of Fabergé objects has provided me with great recreation and knowledge. I feel these items, while costly, will prove a significant addition to our collection.

I hasten to point out that the money invested will neither be lost nor squandered. The value is there at present and, while not income-producing, I have every reason to believe that, under ordinary circumstances, in the future these objects will appreciate considerably.

I look to you to correct me if you feel it is unwise for me to gratify my intense desire for this collection, which will be a source of constant joy to me. However, I feel that so quiet and unobtrusive a passion must certainly be agreeable to you.

Your devoted son,
Bertram

I can't put a name to it, but I began to feel it right after I read the newspaper accounts. I'd woken up fine, gone out, bought two newspapers, and taken them back to the Chelsea. Neither account mentioned my speech or even the fact that I'd been there. If I couldn't alter that tiny fragment of reality, if I were truly that insignificant, if I were invisible, it would all begin again—everything I had tried to escape—the use, the helplessness. I felt it and I wanted not to feel it.

I lay on the bed. A great lethargy began to infuse my body. I had no conception of time. After a while I realized that I could trace the pattern of cracks on the ceiling above the bed with my eyes closed. I made many trips to the bathroom. I drank a lot of water.

I became aware of peaks and lows in my moods. I woke and was shocked to see cold sunlight coming full in the window. Once I heard wrenching sobs. They surprised me with their intensity. Some time later I woke again, filled with such a sense of well-being that I wanted to float on that feeling forever. I slept, woke, drifted, and slept again. If I was looking for a revelation, there was none in that room.

My timelessness was filled with apparitions. I knew I had dreamed but on waking could not remember the content. I could not remember if that recurring vision came as one of those lost dreams: a flash of cadmium yellow and brilliant blue, a beating sound and a bird calling, "Where's Missy? Where's Missy?" I follow the bright bird into the dim tangle of woods.

I knew I would go. As I began to dress I was momentarily startled by a haggard, unshaven face in the mirror, a ferret face. I went outside and began stopping taxicabs. The fourth driver agreed to do it for $250. One way. Cash in advance.

My little trip down memory lane took nearly eight hours, what with stopping to take leaks, eat, and get gas. Twenty minutes beyond the town of Lake Placid, we were there. The cab dropped me at the entrance gate. I watched him turn around and disappear down the road.

About three feet from the ground a heavy chain stretched across the two stone entrance posts. I climbed over it and stared up the long road that led to the houses of Birdwood.

The main house was called the Lodge. There were two children's houses. My house was Bird's Nest, and Ellen and Tammy's was Tam O'Shanter. Then there was the barn, the stable, the boathouse, the servants' house, the animal house, the garages, and a party house called the Folly, down by the lake. You could call the place rustic manqué: twelve thousand acres of studied simplicity. This was where I'd spent my summers when we were a family.

In those days we'd arrive in two Grumman amphibians, one for us—Ellen, Tammy, me, and the two nurses, Miss Jones for them and Walmsey for me—and one for the supplies and animals. My father, Missy, my grandfather, and his companion always came a day or two later.

When the plane lands on the lake you feel as if you're diving underwater. Water comes right up over the windows and you look out and you're deep in the heart of the lake. Then it levels off, and you pop up into the air and taxi to the dock and get out on the rough wood planks. You feel the sun on your back. There's an open pickup truck by the dock and the men unload the animals, the entire city menagerie, and take them to the animal house, where they join the wilder creatures that stay here all year round. Only Harry the macaw is permitted to remain with Missy. Once the caretaker tried to cage him and the bird pronounced the word "no," reached out, and pecked a hole in his cheek. There was a look of surprise on the caretaker's face as the dark well filled with blood.

The camp lay empty but not deserted. You could hear the animals in the underbrush and the birds. The trees were beginning to color, and there was a sharp smell to the air.

It took me about half an hour to walk to the Lodge. The wide veranda encircled the house like the deck of a deserted ship. On that veranda my grandfather used to sit in his wheelchair, dressed in a light-beige suit, wearing a straw hat, waving indiscriminately, smiling mindlessly, at any passing person or animal. My vegetable grandfather, being propelled around that broad expanse, spoken to as if he understood by his tall, gentle, beefy-handed companion. "We'll go for our nice bath now, Mr. Royceman."

My grandfather was the smell of incontinence. I could never quite reconcile this grotesque, uncomprehending doll with the powerful, focused man of those Sunday lunches. When I was ten, Grandpa Paul had a second stroke, a massive one. Until he died some five years later, he was locked inside himself. My father arranged for his care, insisting that his companion dress him in a suit every day and feed him at a table set with silver, crystal, and china. In the summer his vacant husk of a body was transported to Birdwood.

The front door of the Lodge was locked behind the screen door. I entered easily through a downstairs window, my feet hitting the deep-red Oriental carpet of the living room. It was dark now. I touched the light switch and the cavernous room went bright. The antlers of deer and elk cast dark attenuated shadows high on the walls. A fieldstone fireplace dominated the end of this vast room; a fireplace so large that every member of my family can stand up straight in the middle of it, even my father, who is three inches taller than I am.

Then I remembered that this was my fireplace now; my antlers, my stairs, my floors, my walls, my ceilings. "This belongs to me," I said aloud. I couldn't believe it.

In this place were memories to be sorted out, sifted through. Valuable clues to what had been and therefore *is*. I was compelled to search.

The bookshelves contained several photograph albums. I lifted them down and stacked them on the rug, then sat and opened the top album. The photographs were held in position by tiny black paper corners. Many had come unglued. As I turned the pages, snapshots tumbled onto the rug. The background of all these photographs was clearly Birdwood, but only a few of the faces were familiar. My father on horseback, and Missy too. Did she ride? A smiling group in front of the Folly, the woman in the foreground wearing a patch-work shirt and a diamond necklace. Who was she? Then one I recognized: Ellen holding a blue ribbon. There were braces on her teeth. More unfamiliar faces, a man and woman canoeing on the lake, a young boy holding a tennis racket, a laughing woman pointing at the camera. The next was me, dressed in a gypsy costume with shiny black boots, a gold earring, and a scarf knotted around my neck. I studied the photograph, unable to remember that day, that costume, that child. I tore the picture out of the book, removed my dark glasses, and brought it close to my eyes. The image became clearer but not the memory. I wasn't there. That made me very angry. I ripped the photograph in half and slammed the book shut. No answers here.

I began moving around the room, opening every drawer, box, cabinet—probing. The desk contained a veterinarian's bill, an old party menu (not Missy's writing), and a note in a neat, round, childish hand:

To My Mother

> Flowers are something you smell
> Trees are something you climb
> Birds are something that fly
> They are beautiful
> You are beautiful
> I know

Your Birdie

I moved then to a side table which yielded an age-yellowed envelope on which was scrawled "Check Sent—Good Boy." Inside the envelope was a letter from my father asking my grandfather for money. It was dated August 26, 1937. That was six years before I was born. It told me something. Not much.

I felt hollow. How long had it been since I'd had
anything to eat? In the kitchen cabinets I found some
food, not what we'd eaten, but what we'd called help's
food: corned-beef hash, spaghetti in tomato sauce, ravi-
oli, creamed corn, chipped beef, and soup—lots of soup.
I opened a can of tomato soup, found a spoon, and sat
down at the worn white-marble baker's table. The surface bore a familiar black tracery of lines which always
reminded me of a spider's web. With Walmsey at my
side, I'd watch Mrs. Dowdy fling the dough on that
floured marble surface, knead it and shape it, shape and
reshape it.

Mrs. Dowdy to Walmsey: "Twelve o'clock and she
hasn't even rung down yet. *He* was up at six. I wonder
what the good Lord thinks of such hours. Yesterday I
sent her up some fresh-baked bread with her breakfast,
but Della brought the tray back just as it had gone up.
She'll waste away to nothing, that one. She doesn't eat
enough to keep a fly alive, and him barring spirits from
the house as if that'll change it."

Walmsey: "Well, you have plenty of customers for
your bread sitting right here."

Mrs. Dowdy: "Maybe next time I'll put a bit of the
juniper in it and then she'll eat it right enough."

Walmsey: "Not in front of the lad, Mrs. Dowdy."

I spooned the cold soup directly into my mouth and,
when I'd finished, opened another can and repeated the
process. Then I returned to the living room, intending to
start a fire in the fireplace, but there was no wood, and
by then it was too dark to gather any.

I climbed the wide red-carpeted stairs and walked
down the corridor to the last room on the left, my
father's bedroom. Not the bedroom he'd shared with
Missy and later Gina, but the one he'd kept for himself. His own room. I'd never been permitted in that
room. Now it was mine. I mean, I owned it. Mine in
that sense.

I opened the door and felt for the light switch. Three
floor lamps and a tubular wall fixture came on at once.
Sparta revisited: one oak dresser, one straight-backed

oak chair, one small slant-top desk, one narrow bed
with bare mattress, wood floor, no rug. The room was
spacious, accentuating the sparseness of the furnishings.

I moved about the room cautiously and opened a
closet door. Inside were bookshelves packed tight: mostly art books, some history and finance. I closed the
door. On top of the oak dresser were four wood-backed
military hairbrushes in a straight row. On the desk was
a silver plaque which read:

BERTRAM ROYCEMAN
Through his devoted and selfless service
he fulfills the biblical injunction
"to do justly, and to love mercy,
and to walk humbly with thy God."
With grateful appreciation,
The Federation of Jewish Philanthropies

Next to the plaque were three pens and a small silver
letter knife. There were no other objects visible in the
room. I picked up the letter knife and sat down on the
black and gray striped mattress. This room was him:
ordered, disciplined. Part of him.

The other part was down the hall in that majestic
shared bedroom with linen sheets in the royal-blue and
navy colors of the Roycemans. With the lighted cabinet
full of majolica. With the smell of potpourri. With the
heavy silver frames. With the gold hairbrushes. Objects. With the blond descendant of John Adams. Copu-
lating in that bed to produce an heir worthy of his
dynasty. Impeccably spawned in that luxurious bed.
Objects. All objects.

Was this sparse room an escape for him where he
could be pure and solitary, to read, to retreat, to display
an object of Jewish approbation? Or was this room a
penance for indulgence, for the vanity of pleasure, for
his hated heritage?

My father was a man whose life was two rooms. One
of sensuality and wealth, and one of abstinence. They
existed side by side just down the hall. Why? I would

never know. Death leaves no chance to ask. I knew only that the restless unbelonging was us both. That encapsulated, we had not touched and now could never touch. Death permits no repair. There existed only this visible evidence that he had been unreconciled. And I his son. Unreconciled.

I cried. I held his silver letter knife in my hand and drove the point into my palm, seeking pain, perhaps the pain he sought in this room. Again and again I bore down, and when I felt the warm flood and saw the bright blood stream forth, I opened my hand and let the object fall, and slept. In his bed.

The water in the enormous white tile shower ran brown for a while; then it cleared and hot water came gushing out. He'd taken care of that. Although we were rarely there except in the summer, he'd keep it all going, in perfect year-round condition. Everything, just there. Soon it would be my responsibility; two months, Ned Held had said. Soon I'd have to decide.

I stood in that steamy, glassed-in enclosure until the skin of my fingers began to crease and shrivel. I dried myself. There was a razor in the medicine cabinet but no shaving cream. I rubbed my good hand over the cake of soap on the sink and applied the thin lather to my face. The shave took a long time and was difficult. I liked that. I dressed and went outside.

The air was clear and cold enough for me to see the vapor of my breath. I gathered some branches and piled them up. I found an ax and a hatchet by the side of the house. Because of my hand, I chose the hatchet, and began to chop the branches. It was awkward. Pretty soon my arm ached and the cold came through my denim shirt. "Out of condition," my father would have said. "Why don't you play tennis, you're out of condition. If you don't exercise more you'll never be in condition." Like that. He always kept "in condition." He rode and played tennis with a sense of furious concentration that demonstrated this was maintenance rather than amusement.

I stacked the wood by the gray front steps, turned, and began the ten-minute walk to the stable. The stable is down in a gully, and as you approach you can see only the black peaked roof, but as you climb the hill, the building seems to ascend, revealing red walls and, to the left, a riding ring circled by a birch fence. Several stall doors gaped open, swinging on their massive iron hinges in the October breeze. I could hear my father saying in that proud voice, "Tammy and Ellen sleep at Tam O'Shanter but they *live* at the stable."

Inside the stable, in that cool dimness, implements hung on hooks on the rough pine wall. Brushes of all description, combs, crops, picks, bits, bridles, water buckets, black-velvet hard hats. Ellen and Tammy would work face to face, the dark bay and the chestnut crosstied with perhaps ten inches between their muzzles. "Stupid idiot!" Tammy's voice pierced the still air. "You should use the currycomb before you start with the dandy brush."

Ellen was the better rider and Tammy paid her back by being an unmerciful boss. "He's not stained up, he doesn't need it," replied Ellen, rhythmically brushing her horse.

"You know," said Tammy, patting her blond hair, "in last week's show you would have been pinned in Equitation except for your lousy posture. Your spine looks like an S-curve."

Ellen paused, her brush in mid-air, "In case you forgot, I won four blues." She bent the fingers of her right hand as she enumerated her victories. "Two over fences, one under saddle, and one in the cross-country event. Daddy Bert and Missy said I was super."

"They were judging Royal Wings, not you. He's so pushbutton."

"You only won a yellow last week."

"Well, last year I was Pleasure Champion with Spring Dancer."

Ellen disappeared around the rump of the horse and began to currycomb his tail. "That was last year."

I loved to watch Tammy and Ellen in the stable, but

I was afraid of the horses. The summer I was four, my father bought me a small white pony, and Ellen, with Job's patience, led him around day after day, as I sat frozen in the saddle. Add the horse department to the ways in which I disappointed my father.

Everywhere I could see evidence of that disappointment. I knew my next stop must be down the long oak-shaded path that led to the swimming pool, a large rectangular affair with blue mosaic-tiled steps across the entire shallow end. The pool gaped empty except for a sparse sprinkling of leaves, and a long jagged crack like a lightning bolt splitting its concrete bottom.

Missy sat on the pale-green terry-cloth chaise, her one-piece white bathing suit shining in the sun. I sat in a wooden sandbox with a striped awning, shoveling sand into my silver pail with my tin shovel. Missy came toward me and sat on the platform at the side of the box. "Time for a swim, little bird," she said, gently touching my cheek. I kept shoveling. "Come on, Birdie." She extended her hand. I kept shoveling, denying her existence. Everybody had tried coaxing me into the water that summer. Walmsey had bought me a bright-orange jacket. She said it was guaranteed to hold me up. I knew better.

Missy picked me up, carrying me in her tanned arms toward the pool steps. "Birdie, my little Birdie, it's all right, you're safe, it's all right, Missy's here." We were on the third step when I began to scream.

Quite suddenly there was Walmsey, running across the lawn and splashing down the steps. Then I was in her arms as she carried me back up those steps and placed me on the grass. Missy stood at the shallow end of the pool, the water around her waist like a skirt. She looked bewildered. Walmsey's white uniform was drenched and it clung to her pink body. The laces of her white shoes dripped water onto the lawn. She turned and faced Missy; her voice was quavering. "Mr. Royce-man has instructed me that you are *never, never, never* to touch this child." Then she picked me up again and clasped me tight against her breast. I felt the small contractions of her sobs as she carried me home to Bird's Nest. Did I know even then?

I turned and walked into the woods, guided by an internal compass, following a course set two decades ago. The tangle of trees was a blaze of orange and scarlet. After a time I came upon a small clearing with a granite boulder at one side and memory focused. The boy perched on the gray rock. He was wearing blue shorts and a white T-shirt with Donald Duck's humanoid face emblazoned on the front. The beak, rimmed by smears of crimson, gaped toothless, vacant. He carefully removed his shoe, inspected his toes, rubbed them, and replaced the shoe. Then he lay back on the boulder, face upturned.

The call came from the far distance. "Where's Missy? Where's Missy?" Missy had trained the bird to say that, rewarding him with grapes plucked from her lips by his short arched bill. "How clever," they'd say. "Where's Missy?" The boy stood as the macaw, in a flash of yellow and blue, flew into the clearing.

The bird circled slowly and began moving on, the boy following after, jogging through the woods. The trail became wider, soft pine needles crunching underfoot, leading to a stone paved path and then a tiny cottage: a cottage from the fairy tales Walmsey read each evening. He felt the elation of discovery. He had found what no one knew.

The bird perches on the roof next to the stone chimney. The boy hesitates at the end of the path and then moves slowly to the leaded-glass window and looks in. And sees. She lies on her back on the bed. Her chin is thrust up, hair tumbling toward the floor, mouth agape. Between her legs is a tangle of rough, ringleted hair. Further up, two round mounds of flesh are brown-circled, and centered in each circle is a hard, flushed knob. One arm is tossed above her head, the other extended straight out, and in the hand, a bottle, transparent, empty. The boy turns away.

Had it been? I move through the woods, walking this memory, wanting to know, yet knowing. The pine path is the path of memory and the stone path too and then, yes, the cottage. It exists. I do not approach. It is enough.

As I walked back to the Lodge, I felt oddly peaceful. Passing the shore of the lake, I saw the late afternoon sun roll itself into a ball and begin to sink behind the tall spruces. Parked in front of the Lodge was a dark-green Ford station wagon. Ellen sat on the gray steps. As I approached, she looked up and said, "Hi."

"Hello."

"I tried the Chelsea. When you weren't there I guessed you'd be here."

"You drove all the way up here on a guess?"

"Let's just say I missed you. God, it's cold." Ellen crossed her arms and shivered. "Let's go inside."

She took over. Soon a fire blazed, food was heated, and a decision made. "We'll stay until tomorrow. I'm beat and I hate night driving." The firelight threw a giant shadow image of Ellen on the far wall. "Doesn't it seem funny to be here in the big house like this?" she asked. "It was always so sacrosanct. Your house too. Miss Jones never let us visit you there. When I see Ben Junior and Sally, and how independent and close they are, it really gets me how we had our separate bungalows and separate nurses and all. How Tammy and I envied you. Everything was special for you. They dressed you up in costumes and applauded every time you burped. Walmsey even took the temperature of your bath water with a thermometer. It was pretty ridiculous the way you were wrapped in cotton batting."

"We all were."

"Not Tammy and me. You were the royal prince. *His* only son. You were it." Ellen stretched her feet and pushed them closer to the fire. "They didn't really give a damn about us girls. Miss Jones took complete charge of us down there at Tam O'Shanter. One summer when Miss Jones was on vacation Tammy and I decided to run away. We stole some groceries from the kitchen and a canoe and we paddled away down the lake. We went a long way into another lake and even through some rapids. The second night we were gone Tammy kept telling me all these weird stories about kids being bitten by rattlesnakes and tarantulas. She meant to scare me but she managed to scare us both half to death. Well, the next day we paddled home. We carried the canoe around the rapids and we didn't even stop to rest or eat. We got back to Tam O'Shanter after dark and fell into bed. I didn't sleep though, because I kept thinking we'd catch hell. You know what?" Ellen's voice grew harsh. "No one even knew we'd gone. Three days and no one said a word. I've never been able to tell that story before. It's unbelievable."

"No, it's not," I said. I remembered walking to the boathouse and seeing that the canoe was missing. After that I went every morning and sat on the beach, staring out at the deserted lake. I was afraid to tell anybody, even Walmsey.

"They didn't miss us. Daddy Bert and Missy were there all the time and they didn't know we were gone." Ellen's voice captured the pain of an old wound re-opened. She turned her back toward the fire and spoke out into the darkened room. "What I really came here to tell you was that I've changed my mind. I'll sign your paper. After the way they treated you at that dinner, I began to understand what you meant. They have no right to dismiss you that way. You're a good person and you're important. Important to me. I was silly to dredge up those memories. I guess I did it because it's easier if you can remember the good moments. But there weren't many, when you come right down to it. What counts is you. What you said about wanting to handle it yourself, I understand that. I don't think you can, but I do think you're entitled to try."

"Thanks, Ellen."

"You were in Europe when Ben died. Your letter was very sweet."

"I was sorry I couldn't come home. I know you wanted me, but I couldn't."

"Shut up, Birdie, will you. I'm trying to tell you something and it isn't easy. When Ben first started going out with me, I couldn't believe that anyone that smart and attractive would really want *me*. I guess you couldn't exactly call me self-confident, and it didn't help to have Tammy the Beautiful as a sister. She said a lot of nasty things about why Ben was interested in me. I guess you never thought about it."

I had thought about it. I'd also heard enough innuendoes concerning the real reason why the brilliant Benjamin Billings had married Ellen Crowley, with her obsession for animals and clutter and childish chatter. Someone had even remarked to Missy at the time that Ben seemed "awfully concerned" about money. And Missy had replied, "He won't have to be concerned about it any more, will he, dear?" Ben had been the youngest partner ever admitted to Royceman Brothers and they'd said the Royceman Small Investors Fund was his idea. He was only thirty-two when he'd pulled off the Lambert deal.

"Ben was having an affair with a girl who worked in the research department of Royceman."

"He what? Did you know about it?"

"Of course I knew, because he almost never slept with me, only when he was tight. I knew he was *having* an affair but I didn't know who she was. One night we were in bed and I started kissing him all over, and Ben pushed me away, switched on the light, and told me about the whole thing. He said that he loved me but that I was not—I want to get it exactly right—I was not 'intellectually stimulating.' He said he didn't know what to do. He was really in terrible shape.

"The next day I called Daddy Bert and poured out the whole thing right there over the telephone. Daddy Bert told me not to worry, that he'd take care of everything.

"About three nights later Ben came home and he told me that Daddy Bert had fired his friend and had given Ben an ultimatum to shape up or get out of Royceman Brothers. Ben was pretty calm about it, and after he'd finished telling me what had happened, he said, 'You won't have to worry about it any more, Ellen.' And I replied, 'That's wonderful, darling, I'm so glad. I love you very much.' Then he went into the bathroom and stayed in there for a long time, and when he came out he kissed me and we went to bed. I watched him fall asleep and then I went to sleep myself.

"In the morning he was still fast asleep, but when I opened the door to leave the bedroom, Foxy dashed in and jumped up on the bed the way she does and began licking Ben's face. Only Ben didn't move. That's when I realized he was dead. I called Daddy Bert, who sent an ambulance right away. He met me at the hospital. Do you know how they determine if you're dead?"

I shook my head no.

"If your brain waves don't register—that's how they tell. The doctor called it 'electrosonic silence.' That's a very poetic term, don't you think?" Ellen began to cry. There was no noise at all, just tears coursing down her face. "Daddy Bert took care of everything. He arranged that the papers never mentioned suicide. He took care of everything all right."

After a minute I said, "I don't think you can blame him, Ellen."

"I don't blame anybody. Sometimes I wonder though what would have happened if I'd handled it myself. But I don't blame anybody, not even myself. I just wanted you to know what really happened."

We didn't talk any more after that. We just sat watching the fire burn down, and the next morning we drove back to New York.

11
___

*. . . (B) It is my absolute intent that the Royceman
Collection, as described in Article FIFTH, paragraphs 1
through 20 and Article SIXTH, paragraphs 1 through 8,
be housed in a suitable edifice constructed solely for that
purpose and that said Collection be opened to the
general public not later than twenty months after my
death. If this condition is not fulfilled the provisions
contained herein in favor of the Urban Museum shall
be null and void and the Royceman Collection shall,
upon expiration of the said twenty months, be
distributed absolutely to the National Gallery of Art
situated in Washington, D.C. . . .*

Excerpt from the Last Will and Testament
of Bertram Royceman

___

Held told me he was ready for my signature, but what
he'd prepared wasn't at all what I'd expected. Ellen had
been absolutely right. On the second page it stated that
my father had been incompetent ("senile dementia," it
said) when he'd signed his will just three—count 'em,
three—months before he died. It went on to cite Bartholomew Spencer Hayes's frequent visits to the hospital
and accuse him of using undue influence to secure the
Royceman Collection for his museum. It charged collusion between my father and Robert Royceman, assert-
ing that the "esteemed ambassador" had agreed to serve
as the Straw Man at my father's request.

When I finished reading, I said to Held, "This isn't
what we discussed. Where's the Straw Man challenge?"

Held blinked slowly, like a lizard. "It's in there. On page 3, where you see the number 5–3.3."

"But you said that was our case. We'd go after the Straw Man and the excess gift to charity and they'd settle fast."

"You're right, but if we objected only to the charitable disposition they'd know we were bluffing. We have to look like we mean business to make them settle. It must appear that we're out to break the will. That's the proper way to proceed.

"In this type of action it would be foolish of us not to object right now on every permissible legal ground, because later we can't go back and say we thought of new objections. Unfortunately, Bertie, there are only a few prescribed legal ways of breaking a will, just a few, and we have to use as many of them as we can justify if we want to look like we're not kidding around. To prove the incompetence of the testator is one. To prove undue influence is another. We'll go after the excess gift to charity too, but it wouldn't look right if we only did that. You know, law is a special field. It's like surgery. You have to trust the doctor."

"Not me. I want a cram course in the anatomy of a suit."

"Fine. Here's what I plan to do. First, as I said, we object on every possible legal ground so that we look convincing. Then we use everything in your father's will that works to our advantage. In studying the will, one thing that will pressure the hell out of Weisman is the time clause in reference to the collection. Your father specified that barring certain emergencies, like a building strike or an earthquake, the Urban Museum had to construct a building and get the collection on display within twenty months of his death or it would go to the National Gallery. Get that, Bertie. Twenty months, no matter what."

"Yeah, I remember. I was there when Weisman told him it was a lousy idea."

"Do you remember anything else?" asked Held, suddenly attentive.

"No, why?"

"Oh"—Held shrugged—"I just thought maybe you might remember something we could use. Anyway," he continued, "they'll settle because of that time clause. They've got to begin construction soon, but they can't with a lawsuit pending. Right now we're in a strong position to demand your paintings, the nine million, and an apology. I know all these other objections may seem extraneous but they're not. It's not common-sense correct but its legally correct to do it this way. It's very complicated. You can't be expected to understand."

Complicated. You can't be expected to understand. Complicated. I could feel a fist clenching and unclenching in my stomach. I knew Held was right. Lawyers use a language all their own. But I wanted to understand. This time, I had to understand. *Complicated. Sign on page 2. Sign next to the paper clip. Sign next to the penciled X. Complicated. Sign on pages 4 and 7. Sign four times. Complicated.* Just sign.

"Believe me, Bertie, there's no other legal way to do it." I knew Held was right. So I signed. With misgivings, but I signed. I remembered a Bertram Royceman theorem: "It's all right to deal with a thief as long as he's *your* thief."

"That's settled," said Held as he walked with me to the door. "How about coming out to the house for dinner tomorrow night? We'll celebrate. I'll send the car for you at six."

"O.K., I guess."

We stood beside the door. Held opened it. "By the way, there is one other thing. I don't want any more of your kookiness."

"Like what?"

"Like your giving the collection to the Urban. Luckily, that was just an exercise in ego. Weisman can't give the collection. You can't give the collection. No one can until that will is probated. No matter how many people make pretty speeches, the Urban's got nothing. I guess Weisman never dreamed we'd slap him with a suit. Just thought he'd ram it through. And remember, no more talking to Weisman direct."

"We're not exactly pals."

"I know, but from now on use me as a second. No conversation between principals. Understood?"

"Understood," I said. Although there was a lot that wasn't.

They are right when they say I am not cut out for Wall Street. The summer I worked at my father's firm I found it as strange as a season spent with some tribe whose culture was unfamiliar to me. What mysteries were contained in those white prospectuses, blue reports, stock certificates? I could never know.

Fear blocked my perceptions until the aperture of my consciousness was stopped-down so far no knowledge penetrated. I saw myself as one unit in a giant assembly line of robots in gray suits with black telephones attached to their right ears—robots seated before metal desks, their mouths opening wide to spew out a tattoo of metallic clicks and a constant flow of ticker tape. I hadn't thought about that summer in years, but I was determined that never again would I allow myself to be totally controlled and manipulated. I wouldn't waste dinner. Dinner, oh Christ, a whole evening with Mr. and Mrs. Edward Held of Greenwich, Connecticut. I wanted to beg off, but I wanted to talk to Ned too. Or did I? Maybe I'd phone and cancel. I was still considering that possibility at six-fifteen. Then I realized that the car would be downstairs. A ruddy-faced chauffeur in gray livery stood on the sidewalk, the rear-door handle in his white-gloved hand. "Don't bother," I said, walked around the car, and got in the front seat. The driver sat next to me and stared straight ahead. A network of broken veins engulfed his nose. "Let's go."

It would upset Tammy to see me in the front seat, just the kind of gesture she hated. I've never been overly fond of her. Tammy—who flushed Ellen's turtles down the toilet and told Missy, "They had some icky disease anyway." Tammy—who took a bill from Missy's purse and, turning to see me, said imperiously, "She owes it to me." Tammy—home from Foxcroft for Easter vacation, her voice racing with perverse pleasure. "The fox actually screamed like a person when the hounds tore into him. Later on, the field master cut off the brush and we all got blooded . . . Do you know how they feed the hounds? They take a whole dead horse, the whole thing, cut incisions in his carcass and toss him into the hound pen. It's really gross."

Tammy greeted me at the door. "Darling," she said, kissing the air just over my left shoulder. She was redolent with perfume, and wearing a white velvet caftan covered with Rorschach-like ink blots. Her fingers flashed hailstone-size rings, her hair was a gleaming sheet of pale-gold metal turned under in a lacquered pageboy. Ned was waiting in the living room. He wore a dark-blue velvet smoking jacket with a pale-blue silk scarf at his neck. The velvet kids.

Ned had three, and Tammy two, drinks before we sat down to dinner. The maid served the rare lamb, soufflé potatoes, and spinach from a triple-sectioned silver platter. Then she passed mint sauce in a silver bowl engraved with an elaborate coat of arms: four tiers consisting, in order of descent, of a helmet, two acorns, three oak leaves, one more acorn. I remembered it from childhood, when it had appeared on the back of Missy's gold hand mirror and on her cigarette case. "Isn't that the Ogden coat of arms?"

"It's ours all right," Tammy answered. "The Helds don't have a family emblem."

That was all it took to set them off. The thrust and parry of married bickering began. I felt trapped in a discarded draft of an Albee play. I'd seen this second-rate turgid little drama before, seen it almost daily during childhood, when the leading parts were played by my father and Missy. Later, Gina replaced Missy, bringing fresh banalities to the role of neglected wife.

Tammy (*brightly*): "Guess what, I'm going to Foxcroft this weekend. It'll be like old times. Addie's there now, you know. She's in the ROCs, that's the Riding Officers Club, the ten best riders and most outstanding girls in the school. I always wanted to be in that—"

Ned: "Four thousand five hundred dollars so she can sleep on a porch with no heat, and another two thousand for that damn animal. Her horse needs more shoes than an entire regiment, not to mention the vet bills."

Tammy (*breathlessly*): "We're both very proud of her. Ogden's away too. Ned and I rattle around here, although we're using the pied-à-terre in the city more and more. It's cunning really. I bought some chintz and made the curtains myself, and we've used some of Missy's Victorian furniture. We actually entertained last week."

Ned (*sarcastically*): "If you want to call it that. Frozen hors d'oeuvres in a living room that measures two by two. I told Tammy the only thing she can do with that apartment is to wrap the whole thing in a bolt of chintz."

Tammy: "I do want to spend more time in the city though. I feel useful there. I might even go to work. Once I was offered the job of jewelry editor on *Vogue*. I'd be very good at something like that. After all, if my sister can train to be a bookkeeper, I can do something too."

Ned (*fatuously*): "As far as I can tell, all Ellen did in that course was eat. She's fat as a pig. The trouble with all you girls is that you earn two dollars while your help eats up two hundred. That's feminine economics."

Tammy (*voice quavering*): "More lamb, Bertie?"

Ned (*interrupting*): "Why don't you ring the damn bell and let Mary pass it? That's what I pay her for, isn't it?"

Tammy: (*Starts to cry. Pushes chair back. Jumps up. Exits.*)

Ned (*Looks at retreating back. Reaches in pocket. Removes cigar*): "Too bad you don't smoke, Bertie. A friend of mine flies these Monte Cristos in from Canada. You're missing a real treat."

End of tonight's performance. Next show scheduled for tomorrow. Same set. Different props and wardrobe.

Tammy did not reappear that evening. Ned and I sat side by side on the living-room sofa facing the fire. Ned sipped a cognac and smoked. I hadn't come just to watch him play country squire, so I plunged right in. "Listen, Ned, it's important to me to understand exactly what's going on. Why couldn't we just knock out the Straw Man and then challenge the charitable disposition as we'd agreed. Why wouldn't that be enough to make them settle?"

Held puffed thoughtfully on his cigar. "It's too chancy. The decisions concerning the excess gift to charity have been erratic, to say the least, and only one of these cases directly involves the Straw Man." Held spread his hands in a horizontal gesture, the kind umpires use to indicate safe. "There have been very few instances of an excess charitable bequest and most of these, naturally, have concerned very rich people. It's ironic, Bertie, that our biggest problem comes from a Queens housewife named Mary Cairo who wasn't really all that rich. She drew a will specifically excluding her daughters-in-law and her grandson. When she died, her co-op apartment and her furniture were willed to her sister, but the bulk of her estate was willed to three charities. Well, Mary Cairo's grandson hired a lawyer to challenge the excess gift to charity. With me so far?"

"Yeah."

"As soon as a charitable disposition is in dispute, the attorney general, Louis Lefkowitz, in his role of guardian of foundations and trusts, gets into the act. That is, at least his people do. Fight for Sight was one of the charities and their lawyers got into the act, too. They all massed against Joseph Cairo's lawyer. Joseph Cairo won round one in the Queens County Surrogate's Court, but the Appellate Division reversed the decision and the Court of Appeals upheld the reversal. Joseph Cairo was denied the right to contest the charitable disposition.

"This is the way I size it up, and it's my personal opinion of course: What did it was all those great legal minds on one side, and on the other side, one poor lawyer from Queens."

"How does this apply to us? Who was the Straw Man?"

"That's just it, there wasn't any. Mary Cairo didn't have Weisman's sophistication. She just didn't want to leave anything to her grandson and daughters-in-law and she said so in plain language. She said she'd left them out 'for good and sufficient reason.' That's what stood up in court. The Cairo case became a landmark because if something as simple as that was permissible, then the Straw Man, which is a much more sophisticated device, seemed absolutely secure."

"I thought you told me we could get around the Straw Man and contest."

"I think we can. The Cairo case didn't sit well with some of our Surrogates here in New York. Cairo had prevented a charitable challenge simply by indicating that her intention was to disinherit her grandson and daughters-in-law. Now how to get around that? Bertie, our profession is like chess: for every move there is a countermove. The next case involving a charitable challenge was *Matter of Norcross*. Judge Samuel DiFalco felt that the crucial question was one of *intent*. Did the decedent intend to disinherit his kids and other potential heirs the way Mary Cairo had? Norcross had made it a point to state that he'd left his children out of his will because they were provided for elsewhere. Clearly, he did not intend to disinherit them. Therefore, DiFalco permitted the Norcross children to challenge the charitable gift.

"Also, a decision involving the estate of the painter Mark Rothko came down just one day before your father died. The executors of the Rothko estate tried to stop a challenge on behalf of the Rothko children, based on an excess gift to charity. They were overruled because Rothko had provided for his children elsewhere. The children were granted the excess, which should come to quite a lot.

"Well, that's you too. Your father left you a sizable amount of money outright and a trust fund as well. That shows his *intent* was not to disinherit you." Held gestured with his glass. "Want one?"

"No thanks."

Held walked to the bar, poured a cognac, and returned to the couch. "Now we get to the first case directly involving the Straw Man. It's called *Matter of Fitzgerald* and right this minute it's in front of Judge DiFalco. Get this. The decedent left her residuary estate to the Archbishopric of New York or, if it could not go to that organization because she'd left too much to charity, it would go to the person who was then the Archbishop of the Roman Catholic Archdiocese of New York. That's the Straw Man device, pure and simple. Well, an objection was lodged on behalf of her son, who has been incompetent since birth. Even though we're going to settle so it won't matter to us, I'll be fascinated to see how DiFalco decides this one. He ruled for the Norcross children, but will he rule against the Catholic Church in favor of an incompetent who is more than adequately provided for from various other sources and could never have a use for the money? It's a tough decision. You see how complicated all of this is and how dicey for us. Until there's a precedent set, until we have a decision ruling the Straw Man invalid, we simply must use other means to threaten Weisman."

Held walked to the bar and filled his snifter for the third time. This time he didn't ask me if I wanted any.

I was asleep when Weisman called. I groped for the phone, and when he began to shout, I held the receiver at arm's length. "I called to ask you if you are fully aware of what you are doing? Do you realize that by bringing suit you have lost your legacy? You will get nothing. The money your father left to you goes to Ellen Billings and to *Held's wife*. You have been tricked. Under these circumstances it would behoove you to make a modest, reasonable, out-of-court settlement immediately. Or else you're finished, Bertie. What Held is doing is unscrupulous, outrageous . . ."

"I'm glad you mentioned Ned, because I promised him I wouldn't talk to you." I reached over and pushed down one of the small round phone buttons. Then I listened to the dial tone. It's a soothing sound.

Missy sat on a flowered chintz sofa in the living room of a suite at the Sherry-Netherland. The coffee table contained a litter of papers, magazines, a silver bucket in which reposed an open bottle of champagne, and a tray with six long-stemmed glasses. "When Weisman called and told me, I thought, Not me, I'm not flying there for any funeral. I could just hear them: 'Rather long in the tooth, isn't she? Gina looks so much younger.' 'She *is* younger, my dear.' People can be so unattractive.

"Nicole DeRoussey told me about La Retraite and I sped there. Saved my life. You wear unbleached muslin and walk and walk and walk, and no liquor at all, just a little white wine. They do all sorts of wonderful things, wrap you in hot herbal blankets, and they have a maharishi who teaches meditation. He gives you your very own sound. Picked just for you. Every morning and night of my life I concentrate on that sound for at least twenty minutes. It's wonderful, you should try it. Birdie, do take off that drab coat and sit down. It makes me feel like a freak of nature to see you just standing there staring.

"What did I care if they were looking for me with their silly waivers and consents. Why look for me? He didn't leave me a red cent. Not that I expected he would. As long as you're taken care of, that's all I've ever cared about.

"This morning I was signing the register in the lobby when this absolutely sinister man with brown shoes walked over and asked, 'Mrs. Melissa Ogden Crowley Royceman?' and when I nodded yes he handed me this." Missy removed a paper from the clutter on the coffee table. Across the top was written in bold letters, CITATION. "Ned's coming to get this later, he'll take care of the stupid thing. I hate this filthy city. I came here just to see you and the girls, and it's the only place in this wretched hemisphere to buy clothes. I need them, I'm practically naked."

As Missy spoke, I heard *mother* vibrating inside my head. I couldn't concentrate on that breathy voice, like an excited child's, word plunging headlong after word. I studied her, trying to assemble the puzzle. Missy: skin concealed beneath layers of creamy pale liquid, blond hair cut short, eyes—ice-blue marbles—a sleeveless burlap dressing gown, an immense jeweled cross at her throat. I needed more pieces.

"Birdie, do sit down. I absolutely insist." She patted the couch next to where she was sitting. I sat down. Missy plucked the champagne from the silver bucket, filled two glasses, and handed me one. "I make it a rule never to drink at this hour, but this is a special occasion. Birdie, darling, I'm being married." She sipped the pale fluid. "His name is Roger Solomon, but almost everybody calls him Pappie. He's extraordinary—very simple, protective, great sweetness, three grown sons. He's in business—communications. Actually, he controls lots of papers and televisions in the Midwest."

Missy touched the jeweled cross at her throat. "He gave me this as an engagement present." She gestured at the wall. "And that." Above the couch hung a portrait of a stern man, balding, prominent nose, wearing a black frock coat with a white ruffled shirt. A network of small cracks fanned out over the dark varnished surface of the canvas. "Looks like it comes with the room, doesn't it? But it arrived last night with a special messenger who took down a perfectly adequate Audubon print and hung it there. Pappie sent a note with it saying it's our ancestor John Quincy Adams, painted in 1828 by Bryce Jones, whoever *he* was. Doesn't the old bird look like he's sucking a lemon? I don't know why Pappie went to all that trouble. His note also said he intends to hang it in our new library. He's building me a house in Grosse Pointe, you know. We're going to have an animal house just like the one we had for you when you were little. I hate the Midwest but . . ."

Missy leaned her weight on one elbow and looked up at the portrait. "Maybe we should build two libraries so I don't have to look at that disapproving old patriot. Second-rate too, not even Gilbert Stuart. Your father certainly ruined me for anything but the best. I guess that portrait is what I get for quoting John Quincy Adams to Pappie. I told him how John Q.'s final words were 'This is the last of earth. I am content.' I thought that was a nice way to feel. I mean, isn't it? After all, we're all heading in the same direction, there's no way back." Missy extended her arms toward me. "Look at these hands. Just look. See those blue veins, those spots, the wrinkles. There's nothing to be done. It all fades, Birdie. It all goes."

A high-pitched yapping came from the direction of the bedroom. Missy stood. "Back in a minute, darling." Next to me was a dark hollow in the flowered cushion stamped with the impression of her body. I slid my hand into that place. It was warm.

Missy returned, carrying a brown and white dog the size of a large mouse. "Lola darling, say hello to Birdie. Lola is the smallest papillon in the world." Missy held the dog in one hand and slowly raised the animal to her lips. She kissed the tiny black muzzle. The dog's pink tongue darted in and out in frantic response. "Yes. I love you. Yes. I love you. Yes. Isn't she something? You know how vicious small dogs can be. When I got Lola she used to attack my fingers until they bled. Then last year I almost lost her—pneumonia. I was up five nights straight. Since then it's just love, love, love.

"You know who saved your life, don't you, Lola?" Missy started kissing the dog again. "Yes. I love you.

Yes." At last she placed the animal on the couch. "Birdie, you haven't touched your champagne," she said reprovingly and, picking up her own glass, touched the rim to mine.

12

. . . *from an impeccable old Boston family, Bartholo-mew S. Hayes managed to attend not one but three prep schools—Groton, Choate, Hotchkiss—and finally Harvard University.*

In 1965 Hayes was a little-known curator at the Boston Museum of Fine Arts, specializing in the Mannerist School. One autumn afternoon he discovered a Caravaggio painting stored under some bedsprings in the attic of a Beacon Hill house. Hayes purchased the painting forthwith for a thousand dollars and one month later sold it to the National Gallery of Art for $750,000. Somehow this transaction captured the imagination of the American public and Hayes emerged a national hero.

Newspapers throughout this country featured his Cheshire grin as he stood in front of the painting, which depicted a languid Bacchus. Hayes himself wore an Edwardian velvet suit. "The greatest art find in American history and the greatest art historian," said Art Affairs Journal. *The New York* Herald Tribune, *in a tidal wave of enthusiasm, compared Hayes's discovery to that of the Rosetta Stone. The public's darling, at thirty-nine Hayes became director of New York's prestigious Urban Museum of Art . . .*

When Hayes became director of the Urban in April 1968, the museum had the aura of an exclusive nineteenth-century club, a club for Wasps, for old money, dedicated, as one of the trustees explained, "solely to the preservation and exhibition of our artistic heritage."

One of Hayes's first statements upon assuming office was: "This museum must change. No longer are we a series of living rooms where a few elite persons can

111

come and look at what their relatives gave to these rooms. We must reach out. We must expand into the community and bring art to the people."

His maiden voyage in that direction was the Art Mobile, made possible by a donation of $35,000 from philanthropist-financier Bertram Royceman. The Art Mobile consisted of a Buckminster Fuller dome placed on a flatbed truck. Under the dome the museum mounted an exhibition of painting and sculpture called "The Family Group." It arrived in the Bedford-Stuyvesant area on August 7, 1968. The temperature was 94 degrees. That day the Art Mobile dome was slashed in twenty-eight places and someone defecated in the lap of a figure in the Maillol sculpture "Mother and Child."

Hayes then issued a statement to the effect that unless the community contributed to the safety of the Art Mobile it would be withdrawn. Less than a week later, in a stunning example of penalizing the victim for the crime, he did just that.

It was then that the public began to see the first tiny leak in the inflated image of Bartholomew Hayes. This image finally burst in January 1972 with the advent of "Gateway to America," an exhibition that can only be termed a disaster, offensive to all minority groups in its prejudice and paternalism. The show abounded with photographs of Orthodox Jewish moneylenders, smiling black shoeshine boys, minstrels, and an especially startling study of a 300-pound black cook in a starched white apron. "For me, that's a most valid and enduring image," explained Hayes. "Just such a woman was my beloved cook when I was a child." His sister, Frances Duvernay-Hughes, disagrees: "My father hired French, Swedish, and Irish help, but he would never have a darky in the house." . . .

Excerpts from "Wasp Behind the Gateway" by Susan Rosen, *New York* magazine, April 24, 1972

Hayes's sonorous, nasal, Back Bay accent grated on my ears. ". . . a little intimate dinner for you," he was saying.

"I don't eat dinner."

"Then I'd love to see you any time. At your convenience, of course. I feel it's important to let you in on the secrets of our little family."

"O.K. then, eleven-thirty."

"Tomorrow morning?"

"No. Tomorrow night."

Hayes was seemingly unflappable. To my surprise he replied, "Splendid, quite good. Use the south entrance though. I'll be there to let you in."

I was curious to see his strategy. Use the same charmola he'd used on my father? Hayes stood in a pool of light in the doorway of the Urban, erect as an exclamation point, his Giacometti legs sheathed in blue worsted. Harold Linsky, the curator I'd met at that awful dinner, appeared as a frail shadow at his side.

Hayes clutched my arm, propelling me through the vast dim corridors of the Urban. He began a monologue in the same irritating tour-guide manner my father had used when showing his collection. Linsky and I walked in silence. "This is our famous Egyptian Wing. Daddies hate it but mummies love it." Hayes grinned.

He gestured at a life-size stone sculpture. "That's a superb figure, unique in all the world. I'm mad about the way it looks, but I deplore those curators who identify things in a way only a super-scholar would understand. The label says merely *Middle Kingdom*. What does that mean to you? It means nothing to me. I don't know how I can get my individual curators to include enough information. Even you, Harold; when a label simply reads *Stella,* I think it's a misspelling for a pre-Columbian monument. You should put the whole name, and the date, and the school of painting. Oh well, when you're the boss, the hardest thing in the world is to get people to pull together, not to go off and hide in their own esoteric little niches.

"Ah ha, here we go into our newly refurbished Great Entrance Gallery. It takes two full-time gardeners to maintain the islands of greenery in this area. Those four earthenware urns are seven feet in diameter. The fresh-cut flowers that you see are arranged biweekly. We have a little man who's a gem, Christos Faley. Twice a week he crawls out of bed at dawn and goes down to the wholesale market to buy those flowers himself. He arranges them in the restaurant kitchen. It takes him all day—a real artist. Saves us tons of money.

"Now let's turn right at the information booth and follow the yellow-brick road and—what's this? Shangri-La!" We emerged in a patio with thick stucco walls, Gothic pillars, and a red-tile floor. A round fountain bubbled in the center of this area. In front of one of the pillars a butler in a tuxedo stood beside a brass and glass bar cart.

I do not adjust easily to light and dark; my reactions are slow. I stood in the midst of an endless void of shadows and indistinguishable silhouettes, waiting for my eyes to accommodate me. After some time two model buildings, each resting on granite rectangular tables, emerged from the darkness. Hayes must have interpreted my silence and stiff posture as awe, because he finally shut up and just stood there looking proud. Then he murmured, "Oh yes, oh yes, oh yes." Another silence and then, "Brandy, coffee, tea, or me?"

"No thanks."

"Linsky?"

"Brandy, please."

"Sit. Sit," said Hayes, indicating a row of high-backed wood chairs. Carved squatting lions embellished the arms. Hayes made a clucking sound, his tongue rapidly vibrating against the roof of his mouth. "At long last you are here and it delights us to have you see the outstanding plans we have for your father's wing. You are the most important person associated with this project. The only male bearing the Royceman name."

Not a mention of my suit, the cocksucker. I must be scaring the shit out of him. It pleased me to see fear in another man. At one time I thought I'd cornered the market in that particular emotion. I turned my head and saw that one of the model buildings had begun to glow, seemingly from within. The light grew in intensity, although I could not locate the source. "The Royceman Pavilion," Hayes proclaimed dramatically.

The steel-and-glass model appeared to be perfect, even to thumbtack-size people on matchstick-size benches. Enclosed in a rectangular outer shell were four other rectangles, two large and two small. The small rectangles housed double-story, glass-roofed parks, complete with sponge-rubber grass and plastic trees. In this model you couldn't see what was inside the two large rectangles.

As if in answer to that question, the second model flooded with light, revealing a cutaway version of these areas. They were divided into two floors: on the main floor were several galleries. Above that, right here in front of me, were real rooms from my grandfather's house, only they were no bigger than the palm of my hand. I saw the Marie Antoinette bedroom, the library, even the dining room where I'd eaten all those Sunday lunches was duplicated in intricate miniature with the Tiffany ceiling and the Judith and Holofernes tapestry that had occupied so much of my childhood attention.

Hayes stepped forward, a lighted pointer (the kind they use in school lectures) in his hand. My God, I thought, he's going to do a number on me. He tapped the cutaway model. "In addition to an upper floor of perfectly reproduced rooms from Royceman House, we have a main area consisting of some twenty modern galleries. The walls contain glass shelves for the many objects of the Royceman Collection." Hayes moved the pointer. "As you see, we have constructed free-standing glass walls and rectangular glass columns with shelves, thus allowing for complete, in-the-round vision."

The pointer darted about the model. "You're wondering how the paintings and objects in the Royceman Collection are reproduced here so exactly? We used a newly developed photographic method to accomplish this. Actually, they're one twenty-fourth normal size. The scale is one half inch equals one foot. Splendid, aren't they? I think so."

Hayes had a habit of answering his own questions. "Bertie—I may call you that, may I not—you can't imagine how difficult it is to get anything built in this city. It simply takes forever. Twenty months seems like a long time, doesn't it? But it is barely enough. We wouldn't want the Royceman Collection to go to another institution, would we? Certainly not, when we consider how much it meant to your father to have it here. I thought your presentation speech was extremely clever, really."

Hayes placed the pointer on that part of the glass-and-steel rectangle that jutted into Central Park. "It's hard to believe, but there are some people who think we shouldn't be here at all. Although our charter enables us to do whatever we choose with the land we stand on, including using it for expansion, this land is technically owned by the city. Also, we are forced to use city and state funds for maintenance, so suddenly everybody thinks they own us. If I could, I would run this institution purely on private contributions. That would be sheer heaven.

"We live in perilous times, Bertie, when the least little thing can provoke an attack from a dangerous and volatile public. Do I underestimate them? Oh no. Look at the way they destroyed me for 'Gateway to America,' which, incidentally, I still believe to be the most liberal exhibition ever presented at an American institution.

"Yes, public opinion is becoming a force in this city. We must accept that fact. Tomorrow we're putting these models on display, and in a week or so we plan to hold a public hearing so that every busybody in this city can voice an opinion about our plans. You should come, Bertie. It's quite ridiculous. Every fool comes out of the woodwork and demands to be heard. I listen to them. I bare my soul to them. I say, 'That appears to be an excellent suggestion.' Or, 'We'll certainly take *that* under advisement.' I have infinite patience. Yes, you should see it.

"But rest assured, no one will change so much as one brick of the Royceman Pavilion. Yesterday we signed a rather lengthy contract, twenty-seven pages to be exact, with the three executors of your father's estate." Hayes pressed his finger to his lips. "Hush, hush. Top secret. Classified. I mention it only because we are in the bosom of the family. We have settled every facet of this project: building, display, maintenance—everything. No detail overlooked. The wing will be constructed exactly as you have seen it tonight. You are assured of a fabulous family monument."

"What executors?" I inquired blandly. "It is my understanding that the will has not been probated."

The pointer slipped down through Hayes's fingers, causing ugly shadows to cross his face. "Quite right," he replied. "That's why I asked you here this evening. I want you to understand how important this is, both to us and to you. I want you to share in our great vision. Think about it, Bertie. Think carefully about what part you are going to play in this art continuum. It's your decision. Decide for your heritage."

Hayes touched a button on the pointer, the light clicked off, and simultaneously the models receded into the darkness. I could not see Hayes but heard his voice. "It's men like you, Bertie, who can make this institution strong. Right, Harold?"

I'd forgotten Linsky's presence. During the entire demonstration he had remained silent. His insubstantial body emerged into the light. "I'm glad you came," Linsky said. He sounded sincere.

Hayes, clearly disappointed at this mild reaction, said in a jovial tone, "Why, Harold, what eloquence."

"I hardly think there's much to add to your presentation," replied Linsky evenly.

"I have something to add," said Hayes. "I'm pleased and proud to welcome another generation of Roycemans to the Urban Museum of Art."

I tell you, Hayes was really brown-nosing me.

13

... After the "Gateway to America" exhibition, Bartholomew Hayes joined the ranks of museum directors in trouble. His insensitive paternalistic attitude toward the public brought unanimous criticism. His display techniques were branded "carnival flamboyance." Increased attendance figures [during the "Gateway to America"] engendered the comment, "Twenty-eight thousand in four hours—that's a circus, not a museum." ...

Hayes openly sought to succeed Roger Stevens when he stepped down as chairman of the National Endowment for the Arts in Washington. Hayes's position as director of the Urban was to serve as a stepping-stone toward that goal.

In the abstract, the "Gateway to America" exhibition was a logical move for Hayes. Its purpose was to prove him a forward-thinking friend of minority groups, in tune with the times, and, as he stated, "relevant to the needs of the people." What it really proved to New Yorkers was that Bartholomew Hayes was totally out of touch. ...

Private and political criticism have seemingly disqualified Hayes as a potential candidate for Washington. Two years ago he stated, "I only want this job for four years. After that it becomes a kind of sinecure." Today he says, "I expect to be in this job for my entire career. It's a big one. My goal is to build the Urban into the most important and encyclopedic museum in the world." ...

Politically out, no longer the hero, Hayes has turned with a will to the traditional director's job of fund raising. His talent in this field is phenomenal

*and accounts for the massive overhauling of the Great
Entrance Gallery at a cost of $2.5 million. He an-
nounced at a trustees' meeting last week that upon
the demise of Bertram Royceman, the Urban Museum
would be the recipient of the Royceman Collection.
The collection is valued at approximately $95
million . . .*

Excerpts from "Wasp Behind the Gateway" by
Susan Rosen, *New York* magazine, April 24, 1972

———

We walked down Fifth Avenue. I noticed that Linsky
was even shorter and slighter than I was. "How come
you were there tonight?"

"Command performance."

"Got a joint?"

"No, but there's some at home, and Michael's waiting
with a late supper if you'd like to join us."

"Michael?"

"My roommate."

"O.K., but let's walk. I want to empty my head."

After a few steps Linsky asked, "How did you like
Barrymore's act?"

"Who, your boss?"

"Who else. He's scared. He doesn't want to lose out to
the National Gallery."

"He won't but don't tell him."

"Not me. I adore seeing him squirm. He can't understand it. He charmed Adele Laskoff into giving the
money for the Great Entrance Gallery and your father
into donating his collection, and he's working on the
Swazey Collection of Primitive Art. So he decided the
same razzle-dazzle would work on you."

"It didn't."

"You don't have to tell me. Sometimes I wonder what
will happen to Hayes. He knows how to deal with what
he refers to as 'our class,' but there ain't many of
them left. If he pulls tonight's act at that public hearing,
he'll be in a lot of trouble. He needs 'the people' for

attendance records so he can ask for a lot of city, state, and federal money, but he holds them in contempt. He doesn't understand why they think they have a place in *his* museum. Did you see his 'Gateway to America'?"

"No."

"For openers, the catalogue introduction stated that Jews, blacks, and most certainly Puerto Ricans were not *as yet* socially acceptable in this country. He let that be printed."

"How could he?"

"Experts. Experts," sighed Linsky. "He hired a Jewish and a black consultant, both of whom bent over backward not to give their people a break. It's a common phenomenon. After all hell broke loose, Hayes dimly apprehended that 'the people' are rather more influential than he'd suspected. He called me into his office and asked if I could arrange to introduce him to some prominent Jewish clergymen. 'It might be valuable for me to absorb their ideas,' he told me.

" 'Do you want Reformed or Orthodox?' I asked.

" 'I don't know which,' he snapped. 'Just arrange a market sampling.' "

Linsky's apartment was located in an old building on Broadway sandwiched between two movie theaters. The marquee of the closest one read, PLEASURES OF THE FLESH and SELECTED SHORT SUBJECTS.

The door to the apartment was opened by a young man of about twenty-five. He seemed twice as tall as Linsky, his naked torso disappearing into a pair of Levi's. A mass of wiry red ringlets framed an oval face with a tiny pug nose and a prominent cleft in the wide chin. "I've brought us a visitor. Bertram Royceman, Michael O'Keefe."

"Try Bertie," I said.

"I'm glad you're here, Bertie." O'Keefe extended his hand. "I've made the greatest Bolognese sauce and I'm starving. I used to be macrobiotic, but now I'm simply good."

The apartment was decorated in Victorian Whorehouse. Lamps were everywhere: Three nude bronze nymphs stood back to back, their arms stretched up to support a pleated shade. Another lamp, executed in green-tinged bronze, was a nymph holding a horn which housed a light bulb. A third lamp sported a dancer whose dress swirled, starting at her feet, around her body two or three times, ending in a billow of bronze over her head.

I took all this in quickly. Over the couch hung a print of a girl in a sort of Turkish costume. Her headdress, which covered the entire upper half of the picture, consisted of a turban from which sprang peacock feathers encrusted with jewels. "You should see that when you're high. Those colors are something else," remarked O'Keefe.

The dining-room table was made up of hundreds of tiny glass squares. We ate and drank and smoked, and Michael and Harold carried the conversation until I felt more relaxed than I had in a long time.

Harold stood up and disappeared from the room. He was back a minute later, clutching a fireplace poker. He gestured with a stabbing motion at an orange enamel pot of spaghetti on the table. "That's a superb pot, unique in all the world. I am mad about the way it looks, but I deplore those curators who identify things in a way only a super-scholar would understand. The label says merely *Spaghetti Krater*. What does that mean to you? It means nothing to me. I don't know how I can get my imbecile curators to include enough information.

"That," he said, gesturing again with the poker, "is a Soave Bolla bottle of wine. Not unique, but splendid. It was donated to my museum by a well-endowed lady of sixty-five with very damp pants. I blew in her ear one autumn afternoon. I am very competent with older ladies. This," he said, gesturing yet again, "is Michael O'Keefe, a talented artist, a revolutionary, a superb lover and cook, and a deplorable cleaning man."

Michael plucked the poker from Harold and pointed it at him. "This puny oddity is Harold Linsky, my curator of contemporary art. Unfortunately he is a Jew and a faggot, but he has quite a following and can come in handy. One look at Harold here and they drop their lawsuits, not to mention everything else. We ask him to put in an appearance whenever we receive young deviates, Jews or beatniks. We soften them up and hope that Harold will take over and clinch the deal."

"Is that true?" I asked, laughing. "Is that why you were there?"

O'Keefe cut in. "You bet. How can you resist that smile. That brain. Oh, oh, oh, irresistible." O'Keefe lowered his voice to a confidential whisper. "If you *do* decide to settle, promise me you'll tell Harold first so he can claim credit. He'll get a raise and a promotion."

"Stop that," said Linsky.

"Hayes hates you, but he's stuck with you. You're his albatross." O'Keefe's lips parted in a half-smile. "Remember how he tried to get rid of you when we were at the Biennale showing my work? The minute we left town . . ."

"It's my story," Linsky cut in. "Bertie, do you know Frederick Headly, the avant-garde collector?"

I shook my head no.

"Well, last spring Headly asked me to exhibit his newest acquisition, which he would then present to the Urban. It was called '747' and consisted of a hundred separate canvases covering every aspect of the Boeing 747. It measured 40 by 75 feet. It was junk and I refused it.

"When Michael and I got back from Venice at the end of the summer, there it was, hanging in the new Entrance Gallery. I was so upset I couldn't even speak to Hayes. He makes me Curator of Contemporary Art in one breath and then cuts my balls off in the next. I went home and wrote him a letter of resignation."

"Let me tell what happened next," interrupted O'Keefe. "Everybody rallied round Harold and two of the most prominent trustees threatened to resign. About a week later Hayes called Harold into his office. He had the letter of resignation in front of him and he said, 'It has come to my attention that you are regarded as an institution around here.' Then he tore up the letter, right in front of Harold."

"He's never interfered in my department since," added Linsky. "I'm planning a show of fifty contemporary artists and he hasn't even asked to see the list."

"Will you be in that show?" I asked Michael.

"Not me. I won't cater to that materialistic establishment. My art is dematerialized. There is no object produced. As soon as you produce an object you are the victim of the money establishment, a commodity in the business of art. The museums, collectors, and dealers all profit from your work, but the artist is the forgotten man."

"Only you just said you'd exhibited at the Biennale."

"That was a documentation proving that my work exists."

"Like what?"

"Photographs, maps, written descriptions, receipts, letters, that sort of thing."

"I'd like to see them."

"Not now."

"Why not?"

"Because we're high. I don't want to do it that way. Come tomorrow."

"Michael, don't expect me to sit through your little Show and Tell. I've seen it," said Linsky. He sounded annoyed.

O'Keefe smiled. "That's just fine with me. Bertie, why don't you come up and see my etchings while Harold is at work?"

"Cut it out. I'm not in the least worried that your dubious charms will affect Bertie."

"You're not? Not even a teeny-tiny jealous?"

"It's the work and you know it. He has no place in your damn activist work."

"Well, that remains to be seen, doesn't it? Will you come tomorrow?" O'Keefe asked.

"Not if it makes waves."

O'Keefe adjusted his silver belt buckle. "Actually, the reason Harold's so uptight is that I haven't told you about my latest project. It's a cooperative. I'm a member of the Art Workers and our group's big project at present is to find a way to prevent that disgusting enshrinement of high art where dollars are worshipped, the Royceman Mausoleum."

"I think he's got it," murmured Harold.

"If that's it, it's O.K. I'll come." I liked O'Keefe's raving better than Hayes's cajoling. Perhaps the grass made me feel that way. Sometimes I wonder why I like to smoke when I'm not into a lot of other things. With grass, people are always on the other side of an invisible wall, which is the way I want it. Also, smoking decreases my anxiety, although I didn't feel anxious with Linsky and O'Keefe. And homosexuality doesn't bother me. I don't see why people care. It's never appealed to me, though.

My first time was during an Easter vacation. I was sixteen. A new maid, quite fat, with moist pneumatic skin, climbed into my bed. She rubbed me down and polished me off with the same vigor I later saw her devote to the family furniture. I use this to illustrate my belief that sex is a service business.

O'Keefe passed me a tiny white stub clasped in a bobby pin. "We must all protest this private monument on public property, even you."

Then Linsky raised his glass of white wine in a salute to me and said, "I have brought you into the camp of the infidel."

14

*Concept art has no end product but is a stated idea
usually recorded by either a description or
a photograph.*

—Edward Ruscha, 1970

*The world is full of objects, more or less interesting, I
do not wish to add any more. I prefer, simply, to state
the existence of things in terms of time and/or place.
More specifically, the work concerns itself with things
whose inter-relationship is beyond direct perceptual
experience. . . .*

—Douglas Heubler, 1970

*Art is defined by context and completed by the
response of the spectator.*

—Marcel Duchamp, 1910

I like things simple. They rarely are. I don't bother with
what I can't understand, but if I make the effort to
grasp something, I want to know it all. That way maybe
I can control it. I never want to live in a place where I
don't know what's going on in every room and in every
dark corner. I will never understand how my father
could live in one house and let two others go unoccu-
pied, knowing that people could touch all his thing and
he would never know.

In my room at school each object was where it should
be. When I went to sleep at night I'd wind my wristwatch twelve turns and place it on my night table exactly perpendicular to my Kleenex box. The edges of my

books were always even on the left side. I knew everything.

I mention this because now I was involved in trying to comprehend things larger than any room I'd ever occupied. Not that I was sure I could keep it all organized and clear, even for myself, but I had to make the effort. That's the way I operate. I hate people who create a whole mysterious vocabulary to keep you in awe of concepts that have simple explanations, or not so simple explanations, but *can* be explained. Lawyers do that, and people on the Street, art people too. They confound you with all that complicated documentation.

We exist through media. Media confirms existence.

Success and failure, life and death, are represented in terms of media utilizing symbols. Most people are controlled by these symbols. Some control. My father understood that. He manipulated symbols to achieve status, wealth, prestige.

Take paper. Symbolically it encompasses everything. Checks, bills of all denominations, induction papers, discharge papers, car insurance, dog licenses, death certificates, bank balances in all forms: savings, checking, loan, business, household, joint, separate, numbered in some foreign country. The contents of hidden vault boxes: forbidden letters, stock certificates, pawn tickets, wills—with red wax seals, written, printed on yellow paper, on white bond typing paper, on copy paper smelling of acid—flaking, peeling, rotting, embedded in plastic.

Newspapers, magazines, pornographic books, soft cover, soft core, hard cover, hard core, love letters, ante-nuptial agreements, alimony payments, custody suits. Birth certificates, diplomas, mortgages, social security, federal income tax, Blue Cross, Blue Shield, Red Cross, Save the Children, the Bible.

To tell the truth, I was ready for the Royceman Transfer and it was ready for me.

I'd come to see O'Keefe's work and we were sitting on the floor while he showed me the pages of an enormous black vinyl notebook. "Here are thirteen photographs of the same piling in the Hudson River. I photographed every hour from 8:00 a.m. to 8:00 p.m. Notice how the water level changes at different times of the day and the last two photographs are practically black due to the hour."

O'Keefe turned to the next page. "I love this one. It's a rendering of the New York Stock Exchange as it exists, and right here next to it is one of the Exchange if it were transferred to Atlanta, Georgia. In my mind I just picked up the whole thing like King Kong and plunked it down in the Athens of the South. I've done several of these works. I call them Transfers. Look at this one." He turned the page. "This is called Everest Transfer. It's a map of the Mojave Desert with a scale drawing of Mount Everest superimposed on it. Doesn't it blow your mind? I ask you, will you ever be able to think of geography the same way again now that you've seen Everest in the middle of the Mojave Desert?"

O'Keefe flipped the page, then quickly flipped again. I caught a flash of an exploding building, cracking apart at the moment of impact, dissolving into fire and rubble. "What's that?"

"Oh, I don't really consider that art because it was just luck." O'Keefe turned back and showed me the photograph. "I was in New Haven and walking by this building when the damn thing exploded. I photographed it at exactly the right moment. The photograph has real dynamism, doesn't it? But I can't take credit for it. Here's one that's all mine, my most successful project so far." O'Keefe reached for the notebook, then returned it to me. "See this, I took a load of ticker tape from the floor of the Exchange, piled it in a truck, and dumped it in a grave I'd dug at the Trinity Church cemetery. I call it Wall Street Funeral. Eerie, isn't it?"

"You're serious about this stuff?"

"God damn right." O'Keefe looked up angrily. "What am I supposed to be, a second-generation Minimalist, or Op or Pop or Hard-Edged? It's all a bore."

O'Keefe closed the book. "Bertie, I don't expect you to get it all at once. When I met Harold I was really out of it myself. You know what I did? Shell constructions. I glued shells on fucking formica. That, and ran an elevator at the Urban to keep from starving. That's where I met Harold. One day when we were alone in the elevator he reached out and touched my arm very gently. That was all, but I thought it was the appropriate time to ask him if I could come up to his apartment and show him my work. I brought my stuff here. Harold looked at it and said, 'You're nowhere.'

"Harold educated me. The first thing he told me was, 'Find something unique. It's the only way into the game.' After a lot of experimenting I came to concept art. With it, I'm breaking new ground and I'm not imprisoned within the walls of a museum. I'm good and I'm important. Harold says I could become so well known that the Urban would acquire the sites of my projects the way the Smithsonian owns great archaeological sites. Get that, O'Keefe up there with the Pharaohs."

Michael began pacing around me in a circle. I had to shift position to keep him in my sight line. "I want you to understand what I'm trying to do. You'd get it if you were into yourself. Have you ever been psychoanalyzed?"

"No, why?"

"Why not?"

"I like to work things out for myself. My father used to say that going to a psychiatrist showed a lack of self-discipline. I agree."

"Ever dropped acid?" O'Keefe shrugged. "Forget that. I know the answer. If you had, you'd know what I'm talking about. You'd know that environment is not stable, that color is motion, that we're all seeking inner knowledge. My work helps you understand your inner self and all that surrounds you by expanding your perceptions. It's quicker than psychiatry, as good as acid."

O'Keefe bent down and picked up the vinyl notebook. "What this contains is simply proof that my work exists.

The idea is the art. The art is the idea. Documentation is of prime importance because the only way to show that there is any art is to express it in the form of media."

"But good God, Michael, doesn't all that documentation get to you? I feel engulfed by it. My family must be the most documented people in the world, expressing themselves through wills, agreements, contracts. Photographed. Written about. And, Jesus, just think of all the stuff at Royceman Brothers: eighty years of stock certificates, ticker tape, research reports, prospectuses, the five-day-a-week output of ninety secretaries. My life is expressed in the form of fucking media, all right. I could never reach my father because it came between us and kept us apart. I'd like to take all that shit and throw it in one gigantic pile. You'd see a mountain higher than Everest if I could do that."

Michael was staring at me and I felt a peculiar sinking sensation because I'd let myself go. "I didn't mean to get into that."

O'Keefe picked up a cigarette. He didn't light it but began tapping the end against the surface of the table. "It's perfect, you know. Can you get your hands on any of that stuff?"

"If I wanted to, I could. There's my Standard Oil stock and my trust agreement and . . ."

O'Keefe interrupted. "I mean lots of it."

"I don't get you."

"Media—paper, ticker tape, reports, everything you just mentioned. That should be our protest. How's this? We'll drive down to Royceman Brothers every night and collect everything they throw out. We'll store it, and after a couple of months we can transfer all that stuff to the back of the Urban where they want to build your father's wing. We'll drop it on the building site to demonstrate the incredible flood of Wall Street debris that is responsible for that wing. Have you ever seen the Sheep Meadow after a concert?"

"No."

"It's a sea of debris—paper and crap everywhere you

look—and that's after only one concert. Imagine what this will look like, there'll be tons of stuff, and it won't be random but by design. It's fabulous. We'll call it the Royceman Transfer. Bertie, I love it that it came from you."

"Come off it."

"No, it's your image of a mountain of media that's going to become a reality. You pinpointed an act that is the logical fulfillment of three generations of art collectors. For your grandfather, Italian Primitives were fine. For your father, a collection of Impressionists that multiplied in dollars two hundred times over. But for you, the role of patron to the new art is the only right one. A clean slate. You'll sponsor this project. It won't cost much. Just truck rental and storage. I'll talk to the Art Workers and get them to collect the stuff. I'll give you the receipts for the rental of the trucks and photographs of the Transfer as part of the artistic exchange."

"It's crazy."

"No, it's not crazy. It's the consummate social protest."

"They won't settle," said Held. He looked down at the red tablecloth. "I don't know why you picked this place. It stinks of urine and Lysol."

"It's an easy walk."

"It's a dump."

We'd met at three that afternoon. There were no other customers in the restaurant, only two waiters and an emaciated gray-haired man in a blue-striped apron drawing a broom through the sawdust. Held took a swallow of his bourbon and reached into a round brown crockery bowl in the center of the table. "What kind of nuts are these?"

"They're chick peas."

"What are they?"

"They're a legume."

"A what?"

"Forget it— They won't settle?"

"No."

"But you said it was certain. Two weeks, you said."

"I know. It should have worked, but I miscalculated. It may be a good thing. They had their chance. They blew it. We can break that will with a clear conscience."

"Ned, don't try that. If you want to get anything at all, we'll do it my way."

Held ran a finger in rapid circles around the rim of his glass. "The real reason they won't settle is because they don't feel threatened. They don't feel they're dealing with an adversary of any stature. Weisman called you a piss-ant."

"Cut that shit. Just tell me straight what we can do."

"You can't do anything. I'll do what I'm doing. The DiFalco decision takes on a real importance for us now. If he rules the Straw Man invalid and grants the mentally retarded child the right to contest, as he did the Norcross children, we're in great shape. It'll be obvious to Weisman that he can't afford to fight us in court because we'd be sure to win. With that precedent going for us, we'd automatically get over forty-seven million and he couldn't do one damn thing about it. Once you're permitted to challenge, you win. That's all there is to it."

"When does DiFalco decide?"

"I don't know exactly. Soon. We should know within a month. If only it were February or March instead of November. We'd be that much closer to the deadline and we'd know where we stood with DiFalco. See how right I was to object to everything? Every month that goes by we get stronger. Twenty months is all the time they've got. I'm using every legal means we can justify to block construction."

"I might be able to think of some other ways to pressure them, to block construction."

"Like what?"

"Did he really call me a piss-ant?"

"That was the mildest of what he called you. At least piss-ant is hyphenated."

"I told the Art Workers my idea for the Transfer, and they responded," said O'Keefe. "But then they decided to have another meeting to see if anyone could come up with a better alternative."

"I hate committees," I said, with the absolute authority of hearsay. (My father had a theorem about them too: "When the committees are through—do it yourself.")

"Come with me."

"I want this protest to go through, but I don't want them to know who I am."

"I'll introduce you by your first name."

I admit I was curious. The meeting was in a building at 180 Bowery that had once been a bank. As we entered the room, I saw a line of tellers' cages, one after another, down the entire length of the back wall. The brass mullions of the cages gleamed in the bright light. I rubbed my eyes and felt a slight pulsing in my left temple. There were forty or fifty people in the room, drinking and talking. Opposite me stood a redwood picnic table covered with bottles of liquor, glasses, and a wooden board containing perhaps five kinds of cheese, a butcher knife, and loaves of French bread. An immense man with a Vandyke beard picked up the knife, hacked at the bread, and crammed a piece into his mouth. His enormous hands were filthy, his fingernails rimmed with black. He saw me watching, gestured at O'Keefe, and then walked over to us. "Who's your friend?"

"Bertie," answered O'Keefe.

"I'm Torval Einsig. If there's anything you want to know that glamour puss here can't tell you, ask me. It's good to get some new blood around here. What's your work?"

"Conceptual," O'Keefe answered for me.

At that moment a corpulent girl, with long stringy blond hair, wearing faded-orange velvet pants (which caused her ass to resemble a plump apricot) and a crocheted fishnet top, appeared at Torval's side. She directed her conversation to him. "My boss is dying to meet you. I promised I'd bring you over."

"He's here?"

"Just over there." She pointed.

"He can't walk across the room?"

"He doesn't have to, he's the boss."

"Not mine. Fuck him."

"He wants me to do a profile on you for the paper."

"Why me, Rosie-posie?"

"Because you're our great leader."

"You think it's shit to be president."

"I think it's fine." She reached up and took his arm. He did not protest as she steered him away from us into the crowd.

"The fat charmer who so graciously ignored us is Rose Thomas, a dyke art critic," explained O'Keefe. "She's the one who took off all her clothes and jumped into the Whitneys' fountain in Southampton last summer to protest their party for some South African dignitary. You'd think with that body she'd stay covered up, but she deludes herself into thinking she's absolutely gorgeous."

"Who's Torval Einsig?"

"That big mother is president of the Art Workers. He's a true primitive, a product of great American institutions—orphanages, foster homes, reformatories, jails. He's a Destructivist. His work is similar to mine, only for Einsig *disintegration* is the essential part of creation."

With this bit of jargon O'Keefe tossed his mane of red curls. His manner and dialogue could have been courtesy of an old Cary Grant movie. Also, I was catching on to his pronouncements, which resembled popovers—they appeared impressive but on examination lacked content.

Before I could comment, a stocky man with a bald polished-ebony head clapped O'Keefe on the shoulder. He smiled at me, revealing an expanse of brilliant white teeth in Dentyne gums. "Gentlemen," he said.

"Hi, Booth," replied O'Keefe. Then, indicating me: "This is Bertie."

"Hello, I'm Peter Booth. Michael, let's start the meeting. I didn't come here to socialize and drink bad booze."

"I'm for that, but get Torval to do it. He's so pleased to be president."

"Why wait?" Booth promptly inserted a finger into each corner of his mouth and whistled. The simmer of conversation ceased. "Let's begin," Booth shouted. "Everyone sit down. Now."

"I'm supposed to do that," protested Einsig.

"Then do it."

"Sit down," bellowed Einsig.

It was musical chairs. Forty people or more all headed for the few wooden chairs in the room, jostled each other, doubled up, and when there were no seats left, those remaining settled on the floor like so many rag dolls.

I whispered to O'Keefe, "Let's stay at the back of the room, I want to observe." From that position the only face I could see was Booth's. It's strange to see people speaking away from you. Their voices seem to float up from nowhere.

"Let's pick a project chairman," said a male voice.

"Chairperson." The net top and strident voice belonged to Rose Thomas. "Chair*person* not chair*man*. Women do exist."

"That so?" commented a deep voice. "That's the oldest news in town."

"You a woman?" another voice asked.

"Cut that," said Booth. "Let's have nominations."

"We don't need them," said Torval from his place on the floor. "I'm still president, so if there's any trouble I'll get in there. Let's just talk." There was a clamoring as three or four people began to do just that.

"One at a time," yelled Booth. "I've got something to say first myself. We're all here to get our shit together and decide what to do about the Royceman Wing. Last week we heard Michael O'Keefe's proposal for a protest, but it doesn't touch on the basic issues. I ask you, do you see a black artist represented in that lily-white collection? Not one. We must speak out against that."

Rose Thomas cut in, "Women are the real niggers, Peter, and don't you forget it. Is the curator of the collection a woman? No. Are there any women represented in that collection? Only Mary Cassatt, Louise Nevelson, and Helen Frankenthaler. Three, to thousands of men. Women need representation if . . ."

As Rose Thomas talked I wondered, Is it about art or issues? I could not imagine my father looking at a painting and asking himself if the artist was black or a woman. His only interest was in the work itself. For him there were no other considerations. Should there be?

"My idea is to invade that director's office and demand . . ."

"Shut up, Rose," Booth instructed. "That's enough."

"Who says, you prick?"

"I say, you cunt."

"Listen, Booth," said a silver-haired man. "Do it in some order. It's shit this way."

"You're right," replied Booth. "I just want to say our protest must speak out for the black man."

"You said that already," interjected Rose Thomas.

"Well, I'll say it again. Who's next?"

"Me," answered Rose Thomas. "I want us to lay siege to Hayes's office and not move until he hires more women and includes more women artists in his exhibitions. Look how well it worked when our sisters did that to the editor of the *Ladies' Home Journal*. They got to edit a whole issue, and they wrote articles, and got paid for them too."

"Is that it?" asked Booth.

"Yes."

"Next."

A fragile girl with Botticelli hair raised her hand as if in a schoolroom. Booth gestured; she stood, hesitated, and then spoke in a soft voice. "I have only one point, but I think it's a valid one. We are a city of five boroughs and four of them are starving for the artistic experience. Most of the art is concentrated in one small part of one borough. I see no reason why another collection should go to the Urban. The Urban is an octopus reaching out to grab everything in its ugly tentacles. This collection should be in Queens, in Staten Island. There's an empty Customs House on Bowling Green, it should be there. Some place, any place where it is needed."

She held up a white paper and waved it. "Instead of spending months collecting paper, we can do the same thing with one little piece. I've prepared a decentralization petition. I want to circulate it right after this meeting, and after you sign it we'll send it to the board of trustees of the Urban."

There were small gusts of laughter. I felt sorry for her. Her appeal seemed reasonable. It even made sense to me, a lot more sense than sitting around Hayes's office.

A young man in a patchwork shirt jumped to his feet. "They won't even read that petition. They'll toss it in the nearest wastebasket. What we should make them do is sell that collection, the whole thing, and distribute the money to the poor of every race and color. My idea is to force them to do that. Maybe we could get in there with black, yellow, and red crayons and fix up some of those pure-white paintings."

"Or a knife," Torval Einsig called out.

For a moment the room went silent. Big talk, loose talk, fantasies, I thought. Einsig was like a naïve child expressing rage, and yet improbably I caught a flash of the people in this room wildly dashing down the long marble corridors of the Urban armed with giant crayons, scribbling frantically on the paintings. In my mind's eye I saw my Ingres, my pristine countess, with brutal smears of red cruelly defacing her gray silk shirt, with a knife ripping through her pale hand, slicing into the fragile fingers that clasped her fan. A ridiculous vision—what artist would consider destroying the work of another?

A female voice was saying, ". . . and you're always suggesting such hostile things. I think it's time we tried *love*."

"She's crazy. Next she'll suggest we kiss Hayes's ass."

"Or his ring."

"How about his blue bloody balls."

"He hasn't got any."

"He's got three, like a pawnbroker."

I saw Torval Einsig lumbering to the front of the room. He stared at the group until they were completely quiet and then he said, "You're getting your rocks off, but that's all. I'm taking over. Let's sort out these ideas and see where we're at. Who's for the love protest?" There was no reply. "Who's for the decentralization petition?" Still no response. "Who's for camping out in Hayes's office?"

"Does that protest include black issues?" asked Booth.

"It could," replied Torval. Hands began to shoot into the air, a lot of them.

"Wait a minute," O'Keefe shouted and started moving. "What about my idea for the Royceman Transfer?"

"That's last week's idea," someone said, laughing.

"No one's even mentioned my idea and it's much better than Rose's."

"Not so," Rose Thomas shouted. "Mine will give a lot of press coverage. The *Ladies' Home Journal* protesters were in the papers for a week—*nationwide*."

"What about the bread?" inquired the man in the patchwork shirt. "It doesn't cost anything to camp out. No truck rental. No complications."

"I've got someone who'll put up the dough." O'Keefe sounded desperate. He looked at me and spread his hands in a gesture of supplication. I shook my head no. "But I can't say who it is right now." There were hoots and groans.

"That's enough," said Einsig. "Those interested in the camp-out sign up with Rose Thomas right after the meeting. Those interested in the Royceman Transfer sign up with O'Keefe. We'll meet again next week to see which one we want to do. And next week we won't try any substitute presidents."

"And remember, we need a big idea with impact," Peter Booth added.

A new voice cut in. "I don't think two committees are the way to study anything. I think . . ."

Everyone was talking, but who was listening? I needed to get out. I felt those sounds would go on endlessly, filling the air with the hum of expressed ego.

I moved along the wall to the door, then into an adjoining room. What once must have been a bank office now served as a living room. The only evidence of its former life was a gray steel safe, with a gleaming silver dial on the door, which served as a table. Several people were drinking and talking quietly. I leaned against the wall. I noticed a girl standing under a canvas on which was printed as if by a huge typewriter:

```
Red (red) adj redder, reddest,
n--adj 1. of a spectral hue
beyond orange in the spectrum.
2. Ultraradical politically--n
```

The girl's tiny white face was engulfed by a corona of black curls, springing Medusa-like from her head. She was smaller than I was, fine-boned, and wearing an old-fashioned satin floor-length dress with a pattern of Monet-like water lilies. From beneath the dress I caught the gleam of bright emerald-green boots.

The girl carried a plastic glass of liquor in one hand and the strap of an enormous, sequined puff purse in the other. Her regular features belonged on a college campus, but her wild dark curls and that dress lent a look of exoticism. She saw me staring. I turned away, but on the periphery of my vision I could see her walking toward me. She stopped in front of me and said in a deep, well-modulated, unaccented voice, "I saw you the minute you came in. You didn't see me. I've been watching you. I love men with skinny hips. Would you like to fuck me?"

"Stop putting me on."

"I'm not putting you on." She took a sip from her

glass. "It's funny, people accuse me of that when I really don't even know what a put-on is. I'm just too frank, I guess." She shrugged. "Anyway, it would have been fun."

"What?"

"To have you fuck me. I'm very good and very obliging. I do almost anything. I suck and I come easily. The only thing I don't go in for is groups. It's a little too impersonal, don't you agree?"

"Just a minute. This is crazy," I said. But even as I said it I could feel the desire beginning. I felt a growing power and this ridiculous mop of a girl turned me on. I saw her naked, manipulating me. Slut, whore, I thought. That excited me too. I could smell the alcohol and the female odor.

A Bertram Royceman theorem: "Say yes—you can say no later." Then a thought: in some ways, I was not unlike my father.

15

. . . The Urban also acquired an untitled Sam Francis, painted in 1954. It was purchased through the Lowell Fund for $65,000.

After the acquisitions meeting, Director Bartholomew Hayes remarked, "This Sam Francis is a particular favorite of mine, a gem. It was executed at the precise moment this artist reached the height of his powers."

Excerpt from *The New York Times,*
November 21, 1972

"I like beginnings best," she said. "Beginnings are beautiful, middles are O.K., and endings are endings." She sat on my bed, removed those emerald-green boots, and then pulled her dress over her head. She was naked underneath. I remember thinking, It's November, she'll catch her death of cold.

Doing it was not as good as the promise. I entered her quickly and anxiously, drained fast. It was altogether ordinary. As soon as it was over she asked, "Are you hungry?"

"No."

"I am. Can I raid the icebox?" Without waiting for an answer she got up and walked across the room. She had a straight, thin body with tiny breasts; her ribs showed. She called from the kitchen, "Don't you eat? There's nothing here but Tab and that's guaranteed to have no nourishment whatsoever."

"Sorry."

She came back, rambled in her huge sequined purse, and came up with a jar of Skippy peanut butter. Then she walked to the bed, sat down, opened the jar, dipped her finger into the peanut butter, removed it, and began to lick at the mess. Between licks she said, "I'm Brenda McLain. What do I call you?"

"Bertie."

"What?"

"Royceman."

"Imagine." She began to giggle. "I've just been fucked by Mr. Rich, Rich, Rich."

"Maybe that's why you wanted me to fuck you?"

"Could be, if I'd known. Which I didn't. Mr. Rich, Rich, Rich, and also Mr. Insecure. I told you I like men with skinny hips. I also like it that you're shy and the way you show it is by holding yourself apart from people." She stuck her finger back into the peanut butter. "Want some?" she asked, gesturing with a finger full of peanut butter.

"It's revolting to watch you eat that stuff."

"I know, that's why I'm doing it," she answered, crossing her naked legs. "It's important to me to see a little affect. You know, the first sign of mental disease is lack of affect—when you don't react to things."

"I react to that all right."

"Yes, you do." She grinned. She had toothpaste-ad teeth. She screwed the lid back on the jar.

I reached up and put my hand in that dark cotton-candy mass of hair. "I hate all that Brillo. I can't find your face."

"I like it this way. One summer at camp I didn't comb it for eight weeks and when I got home they had to cut it all off, it was so matted. Did you ever see Ingrid Bergman in *For Whom the Bell Tolls*? That's what I looked like. When it grew back my mother dragged me to the hairdresser to have it straightened. She did that for years, but it's natural now. I let it grow back when I was at the Sorbonne."

"You, at the Sorbonne?"

"Mais oui. You don't have to sound as if you'd been poleaxed. Sixty-eight, my junior year. Of course I had three strikes against me: I was a Durant scholar—that was like Phi Beta Kappa at my school—Catholic, and a virgin. It's a lousy parlay if you want to be on your own. I got so depressed I never went to classes. I sat around the Deux Magots drinking and moping. I made it for the first time that spring during the student strike, in a car someone had hoisted onto the sidewalk across from the Madeleine. It was better after a few lovers. Now I think all that restraint and proper education and Virgin Mary hypocrisy is for the birds. Although I still believe Jesus was pretty groovy. You're Jewish, aren't you?"

"Half. One time I wrote Judeo-Protestant under Religious Preference on a school application. I got accepted anyway. I can trace my ancestors to Independence Hall on my mother's side and to the Frankfurt ghetto on my father's. The blood ran thin in my mother's family though. They're almost all remittance men who've got nothing left to bank but their heritage. My father's family are the tough ones—business tycoons, statesmen, earthshakers. But my father was pretty ashamed."

"Of what?"

"Of not coming from what my mother came from."

"Was that important?"

"To him."

"That's something." She rubbed her thigh. "It's all scrambled eggs to me. In New York everybody is Jewish, especially the Wasps and Catholics. I don't get it. Wall Street either." She crossed her eyes. "Ask me about turning the mileage back on a used car and I'll show you something. But Wall Street! You know those electric signs that flash the Dow Jones averages, like 7.47 or 6.13? When I came to New York I thought they told the time—the wrong time."

I kissed her then. "Hey, cut that out, I'm a mouth breather. Tell me, what's the difference between the New York and the American Stock Exchanges?"

I kissed her again.

"Which board is the Big Board?"

And again.

"Why do most people prefer common stock to preferred stock? Answer that."

"I can't, all the juice has drained out of my brain." I took her hand and pressed it against me. "To here."

"This time I'll suck your cock and it'll be better," Brenda announced. And it was.

Afterward, she touched my shoulder and asked, "What were the likes of you doing at that meeting?"

"I came with O'Keefe."

"O'Keefe, that hypocrite. He's got Linsky wrapped around his little cock. Harold Linsky may be a powerful art curator, but with O'Keefe he's just a desperate lover trying to hang on. I'll bet O'Keefe pressures Harold into giving him his own one-man show at the glorious Urban. Then Michael O'Keefe will be just another member of the Establishment himself. Then he'll drop that revolutionary pose."

"Maybe so, but I'm thinking about sponsoring his protest."

"Wow, if you'd announced that at the meeting, there would have been a riot. 'I'm Bertram Royceman and I'd like to sponsor the Bertram Royceman protest.'"

"I couldn't do that."

"I guess not, but I would have loved to see their faces. Why would you want to help them protest?"

"To show certain people they have to deal with me."

"Whatever that means. I guess you've got your reasons. I wouldn't do it. The Art Workers are a rough bunch, once they get going. They sit around and talk and talk and it seems almost funny, but all the time the pressure is building, until it explodes into something terrible. Look, last year twelve of them stormed the book shop at the Museum of Modern Art. They set fire to some of the books, and your pal O'Keefe stood on the counter and urinated on the cash register. They said later that the protest was to get museum officials to recognize artists whose work couldn't be displayed by conventional methods, but that was an afterthought. Anyway, I ask you, how can you negotiate seriously with someone if you know that they've peed on your cash register? I've had it with the Art Workers."

"You seem to know them very well."

"Sure, I'm an art tart. I like to fuck artists. I used to be with Torval Einsig, he's numero uno with that bunch. I lived with him until recently."

"How recently?"

Brenda wrinkled her forehead as if thinking very hard. Then she tilted her head to the side, stared out into space, and said, "Until tonight."

We never discussed Brenda's moving. She just did. Ropes of enormous glowing pink and gray fake pearls and strings of Indian beads dangled from the frame of my mirror. A large-brimmed vermilion felt hat, with a bunch of plastic cherries pinned to the crown, reposed on top of my oak chest. Brenda didn't bring any clothes; presumably they were still at Einsig's. "That was a pretty abrupt departure," I observed.

"I'm on the mercurial side—no longevity. I'm Gemini on the cusp of Cancer," she added, as if that explained everything.

Her first day in residence Brenda went out and returned with two shopping bags, one full of groceries and the other containing a tape deck and cassettes. She tipped the bag and the cassettes cascaded onto the bed. "I brought us some basic staples. Basic Bob—Dylan, that is—Roberta Flack, Kristofferson, Paul Simon, the 'Concert for Bangladesh,' Dory Previn, the Stones, Carole King. I can't exist in a place with no sound."

We listened to the tapes and Brenda sang along while she molded dough into empty round coffee tins to produce succulent loaves of bread. "Blue Moon, I saw you standing alone," she'd sing, as her fingers deftly pumped the pale-yellow mass.

I'd rarely used the tiny kitchen which came with my rooms. Suddenly it blossomed with implements: a spice rack, a garlic press, a pepper grinder, a wok, a set of tempered-steel Sabatier knives.

Nothing changed, but some things changed. Imperceptibly. It was nice to wake in the dark, to touch her, to hear the music, to move to the schedule of our bodies. We lived at random—waking, making love, eating—not by the clock but by our moods.

In addition to my newly equipped kitchen, the top dresser drawer of my chest now held jars of peanut butter, grape jelly, saltines, tea bags, and an immersion heater. You could actually lean out of bed and grab the food. "That drawer is my security blanket," said Brenda.

Brenda seemed completely open, everything bubbling up through the surface. I could never be that way. She managed to be open but not a receiver of pain. I found that incredible.

"Einsig is looking everywhere for you," O'Keefe said in an ominous tone.

Brenda placed her elbows on the stained pink formica table, interlocked her fingers, and rested her chin on them. "Just tell him to look at the Chelsea." She sipped her hot chocolate, inserted her spoon in the mug, removed a glob of Reddi-wip, and transferred it to the black ashtray in the center of the table. "I don't go for terror tactics, you know."

We'd met at Riker's on Fifty-seventh Street and Sixth Avenue at midnight. The only other occupants were two hookers, both in identical white boots with mile-high lacquered hairdos. One was devouring a tower of pancakes that rose from a pool of viscous brown syrup. They sat at the counter under a harsh fluorescent fixture, outlined with a collar of tinsel implanted with clumps of red-plastic holly berries.

O'Keefe sipped his Coke through a candy-striped straw. "I had to see you tonight, Bertie. I desperately need your help. Last night we had another Art Workers meeting. This time they talked for four hours. At the end a majority voted on including Vietnam in any protest. It's endless. I had to do something, so I asked the *real* Art Workers, eight people who care, to come to the apartment tomorrow at three to get something going. This group is small enough to *act* instead of *talk;* only to make it happen I need to tell them *who* you are and that you'll give us the money for the protest."

"That's what I want too. Brenda and I will be there at three."

"You go, I've had enough of that stuff." Brenda put her saucer on top of her hot chocolate mug. "Let's get out of here. I saw a cute bar across the street."

"We can't," O'Keefe protested, "I promised Harold we'd meet him here. I don't know what's keeping him. He had a trustees' dinner but it started at eight. I went to see *Deep Throat* to kill time."

"*Deep Throat,*" exploded Brenda, "that's disgusting."

"I loved it. It's a camp," said O'Keefe. "Have you seen it, Brenda?"

"No, and I don't want to."

"I don't see how you can criticize what you haven't seen."

"You don't? Well, I want to tell you, we live in a lousy country. Everyone looking for a reason to justify their dirty thoughts. That film's making millions because it's fashionable and acceptable. It's playing at good theaters and men with briefcases under their arms go with their wives, the kind of women who wear Cartier tank watches."

"It was a pretty classy audience at that," replied O'Keefe. "Most of the guys who masturbated kept the *Times* on their laps, not the *News.*"

"Tell me, Michael, have you ever gotten hepatitis from putting it up Linsky's asshole?"

"Brenda, you talk real tough—for a prude."

"That's the last thing I am, it's that I find pornography dehumanizing. That's why I avoid group sex and all that stuff. Of course, the worst are Webster and Warhol films because they're *art*. If you're seeing a dirty movie that's made by an artist, you can indulge your filthy, secret, voyeuristic instincts under the guise of artistic merit."

"Andy Warhol doesn't pretend to anything," said O'Keefe. "He told me he just wanted to be the Walt

Disney of the Porns. He doesn't rip people off. They rip themselves off."

"Ralph Webster's a rip-off though. I know. I met him when I was having dinner in Max's Kansas City and he asked me to be in his film *Kiss and Caress*. It was supposed to be four hours of people kissing and caressing. My scene was going to be shot outside, near the Bronx Zoo. While I was waiting, one of his regular superstars, Rochelle New, started in with four guys. There was a large crowd watching: lots of mothers with little kids and lots of schoolchildren. These guys started kissing Rochelle and sort of rubbing her all over. Then one said, 'Let's kiss her cunt.' She began to yell, 'Not here, not with all these kids watching.' Nobody listened. They pulled off her jeans and two guys held her while the other two pulled her legs apart and kissed her cunt.

"Webster had an Arriflex camera and he knelt over them saying, 'Beautiful, fabulous, fantastic,' and she kept screaming about the kids. It's all right there in the movie. What got me was that no one reacted. No one at all. All those kids and mothers just stood around watching. I guess they'd been told it was *art*.

"I even went to the first screening of *Kiss and Caress*. The invitation specified black tie and it was for the trustees of the Museum of Fine Arts. Afterward, they had a champagne reception and people came up to Rochelle New and treated her as if she were Garbo, as if it had really been *art* instead of just fucking and sucking."

The plate-glass door swung open and Linsky entered, blinking in the fluorescent glare. He sat next to O'Keefe.

"For Christ's sake, Harold, we've been waiting hours."

"It took a long time. It was the ball of Louis XVI the night before they stormed the Bastille."

"Do tell," said O'Keefe.

Linsky signaled the waitress. "One coffee, please, black. First off, these meetings are usually awful, but this was the worst. Those ignoramuses dig eighteenth-century furniture and Renoir, but they don't know beans about contemporary art. I've wanted to buy a Sam Francis for the Urban for two years. The problem was enormous because Hayes had literally never heard of Sam Francis. What's more, although the curators are the professionals, we can't acquire anything without trustee approval. I wouldn't give up though. I kept badgering my friends on the board and finally, miracle of miracles, I was preselected."

"Preselected?" asked Brenda.

"It's Hayes's crazy idea. If there's one million two hundred thousand to spend on acquisitions, he insists that the curators meet with him to select exactly one million two hundred thousand dollars' worth of objects. Hayes thinks that the trustees will approve our selections because there are no alternatives. It doesn't work though. They still turn down objects they don't want or understand, which is a lot, believe me. All that the preselection meeting does is make the curators who have their objects knocked out hate the ones who are left.

"After we're preselected, we rehearse our presentation like a high-school play. Hayes instructs us not to make it too erudite or technical. 'The trustees must be fed simplifications,' he says. Also, our objects get spruced up like a whore in the parlor. Even before we acquire an object, Hayes spends money on potential acquisitions. He gave Schlitzer twenty thousand to have a calix krater restored before it was presented. He said you couldn't ask the trustees to pay eight hundred thousand for a box full of fragments. He gave me two thousand to have the Sam Francis cleaned, relined, restretched, and reframed.

"Tonight was to be my big night. I think all the other curators were just as uncomfortable as I was, having dinner with all those frozen-faced department-store dummies. After dinner, we went into the Acquisitions Room, which has a platform at one end. First they brought in Schlitzer's krater. It looked spectacular, as new as if it had been painted yesterday, which it probably had been, with all that overpainting. The trustees voted a unanimous yes. I thought that was a good sign.

My Francis was next. Four museum attendants carried it in. It's big, 17 by 24 feet. They set it up there on the platform. I looked at it and almost died. It was upside down. All those paint drips running up the canvas toward heaven."

"You're making it up," said O'Keefe.

"No, I swear. It's too delicious to invent."

"What did you do?" asked Brenda.

"Started to run down the aisle, but that old buffoon Gifford Fitz-Douglas grabbed my arm. 'Good choice,' he said, and the gray-haired lady next to him nodded and smiled.

"I couldn't believe it. One by one the trustees began expressing approval. I can't let this happen, I thought. Then I said, 'It's upside down.'

" 'What?' asked Fitz-Douglas.

" 'It's upside down,' I repeated.

"There was this awful silence. Hayes just sat. At last he stood up, ramrod stiff, and clapped his hands. Four attendants appeared from nowhere and turned the canvas right side up. After that there was another silence. It seemed to go on forever. Then Fitz-Douglas announced, 'Well, it looks good that way too.' And they bought it."

"Is that all?" O'Keefe started to laugh. "All that proves is those trustees don't know which end is up."

"Don't be flippant," said Linsky. "They are the guardians of our artistic heritage. They are the mighty pocketbooks and we revere them."

16

SON PROTESTS FATHER'S PAVILION

Torval Einsig, president of the Art Workers, a New York–based group of radical artists, today announced that members of his organization were planning a protest against the proposed Royceman Pavilion of the Urban Museum of Art. He would not reveal the nature of the protest but said that the financial support needed for this project will come from Bertram Ogden Royceman, son of the donor of the proposed pavilion.

Bertram Ogden Royceman lodged an objection to the disposition of his father's estate in the Surrogate's Court of New York City, October 30, 1972. . . .

Excerpt from the *New York Post,* December 5, 1972

Brenda insisted we go: "This is my day." I hadn't been to the Hayden Planetarium since Walmsey had taken me as a child. Walking past the front steps of the Museum of Natural History, we saw a man exposing himself. He stood under a rust-streaked green bronze equestrian statue, holding his penis in his hand and jiggling it up and down. Eyes turned away, protective hands clutched at children, people were repelled as if by a negative magnet.

Not Brenda. She marched up the steps and stood in front of the man. "Stop that this instant," she commanded. "You'll be arrested, you dope." The man opened his mouth in a soundless cry, stuffed his equipment back in his pants, and fled.

Brenda began looking for the "Moon Rock," but couldn't find it. A gray-suited attendant told us, "It ain't here no more. It travels." We looked instead at a meteorite called "The Woman." (I don't know why it was called that, since it looked like an enormous piece of brown Swiss cheese.)

Along one wall a series of scales told you what you weighed on different planets. The front of the Sun scale had a bright-yellow light, the Moon scale had a blue light, Mars was red, and so forth. I weighed 21.7 pounds on the Moon and 3,770 pounds on the Sun. I don't remember what I weighed on the other planets.

We entered the sky dome and settled into the blue plush seats. The twelve signs of the zodiac were projected around the circumference of the circular dome and above them a sky full of stars. Brenda reached for my hand and squeezed it. "That's my sign, right across from us, the twins, Gemini," she whispered. "There's the North Star. That bright one straight up from the end of the Big Dipper. Make a wish. Quick."

"You're kidding."

"No, I wished."

"They're not real."

"Who says? Who knows what's real?"

Brenda might be right. I'd just sit there in that artificial night under that electric galaxy and who knows?

At three I could fly. I'd stand on one of the twin beds in my room and fly to the other, some distance away. I always did this with the door closed. I believed I could also fly around the room. At four I lost my power. Then I remembered Red Cloud Jones. At five I was sure I could reassemble molecules. The first time I saw him I felt that if I could do it correctly, he'd disappear. I'd taken the path that led from Bird's Nest to the Lodge. The tall trees marked a roadway of night sky. There was a full moon, brighter and rounder than the electric one I now observed. The stars were barely visible in that strong light. He appeared on the path about ten feet in front of me. He wore a leather loincloth, brightly beaded, and his skin had a wet glow.

Then I saw his hair. It was bright red in the moonlight and was topped by a feathered headdress which flowed up and out and cascaded down his back. He lifted three fingers of his left hand in the air, in a gesture to me. I wondered how I had conjured up this particular vision.

I saw that Indian again the next afternoon as I walked back from the lake to Bird's Nest. This time the apparition made the same gesture and smiled. I decided to stay indoors close to Walmsey, but she insisted I remove our bathing suits from the line. I saw him sitting on a tree stump near the back screen door.

The next day it was raining and I managed to stay in all day. Dinner was at the Lodge, and when I arrived he was standing behind my father's chair. "This is Red Cloud Jones, chief of the Saranac Indians. We asked him here to amuse you," said my father. "But I see you've been ignoring him."

"How!" said the redheaded apparition, raising his left hand in that familiar gesture. "You want be big chief like Red Cloud?" I just made it out of the room. After I threw up, Walmsey brought me back to Bird's Nest and put me to bed.

Who knows? Red Cloud had been real, for sure. A machine-made galaxy was not. But molecule for molecule, this manufactured sky seemed as real as, realer than, a redheaded Indian, a talking bird, a plane in the heart of the lake, a grotesque doll cast in the form of a once-powerful grandfather.

My father's molecules, how do I assess them? Was one of his equal to two of mine, or ten, or a hundred? How do you determine the ratio? How many millions of molecules compress to create an elevator, and Missy and Tammy and Ellen? There must be molecules in the rubber gasket and in the metal painted to resemble mahogany. The people were molecules too. Only molecules. Doors shut. This existed. It closed me. Shut me as those doors shut. Irrevocably. Descend. Gone. Cut. There is one thing I absolutely know about what is real. Real hurts.

I heard an orchestra playing *Swan Lake* and the narrator's voice straining to be heard over the music as he spoke of "the dawn of what we have come to regard as civilization." I felt Brenda's hand searching my lap. She unzipped my fly and began to stroke me.

"Thank you for bringing me." She kissed my ear. "I just love being close to nature."

O'Keefe made it sound like a big deal. He leaned against the living-room mantel (definitely playing Cary Grant), I by his side, and said, "I want you to meet the person who conceived the Royceman Transfer and who will give us the money to make it a reality." He executed a brisk half turn and pointed at me with one finger. "May I introduce," he dragged out the name, mouthing it as slow as taffy, "Bertram—Royceman—Junior."

There were eight Art Workers in the room and I must say they looked surprised all right—astounded. "Please, just Bertie," I blurted out. It seemed so pretentious, more like tea at the headmaster's than a radical meeting. I wanted to explain that I was not now, nor had I ever been, a Junior, only I didn't think I should get into that, especially with strangers. Mostly I wanted to get the hell out of there, but I didn't move. It had to be done.

Rose Thomas sat in a straight chair facing us, wearing a silver miniskirt, her legs spread wide, exposing a dark thatch of wiry hair. After a few seconds she said, "You made that sound like the Second Coming."

"As if you'd ever had a first," Torval Einsig remarked. His enormous body occupied the entire couch.

Peter Booth appeared at my side. His large black hand grabbed mine. "You're doing a good thing. You're going to be a star."

"Everyone stay seated," O'Keefe ordered, clearly relishing playing leader. "We are about to make final plans."

"Forget it." It was Einsig who had spoken. His voice sounded smug.

"Come on, Torval, cooperate."

"It won't work, Michael. You listen, for a change. Amos Barth and I did a trial run. We took his pickup down to Royceman Brothers last night at seven. We figured it would be the right time—after work but before the garbage men would pick up the stuff. Only there wasn't any. That place is so damned fancy they keep the garbage in a special room with a brass plate on the door reading REFUSE ROOM. They're too highfalutin to throw their junk in the street like everybody else."

"Is that true?" Michael asked me.

"I don't remember."

O'Keefe turned toward Einsig. "If it is true, you could have thought of something, Torval."

"I did. I only want to help. I knocked on the door, a guy opened up, and I told him Barth and I wanted the stuff to reprocess it. I slipped him five bucks. I'm sure your friend will be happy to dip into his shekels to pay me back for that. The guy said it was all right with him since this is his last week. But what do you plan to do after this week? You would have to pick the Fort Knox of garbage. That's it. You've had it."

Einsig had summed it up, and he looked complacent and self-satisfied. I found myself saying, "Don't worry about any of that. I'll take care of it."

"How? Mister — Bertram — Royceman — Junior?" asked Einsig.

"I said I'd take care of it. I'll let you know how."

End of discussion. Suddenly people began popping up, as if by moving about they could dissipate the tension in that room. O'Keefe stayed close to my side, monitoring my conversations.

Then Einsig was standing beside me. In his red and black flannel shirt he resembled a burly lumberjack. "Listen, I'm glad you're going to work it out for us so we can do this protest. Fits right in with my ideas. We've got to destroy the golden calf, right? Who's got a chance when all those objects are worshipped—worth millions. We'll never come into our own until we get out from under them. They should be burned, blown up, slashed to ribbons . . ."

O'Keefe cut in. "Torval, I think you and Bertie have a lot in common. You're both protesting a powerful father—Bertie's, real; yours, the art tradition—whose image must be destroyed if you are to function freely."

"Stop with the lecture. I never liked school."

"There are a lot of other people here waiting to talk to Bertie."

Einsig moved between O'Keefe and me. "I hear you're with McLain. Don't think I mind. McLain's a good fuck, but she don't know shit about life. Those anemic sorority girls always run back where it's safe. They want kicks with gold plating. How come she's not here today? Afraid to see me? You tell her not to be scared. I don't care what little rich boy she blows."

"That's fortunate for me. This little rich boy is pleased to have your seal of approval."

"Not much fight in you, is there? That's right, I forgot, you people are into money, not fighting."

"I believe you're the one who emphasized money." I reached into my pocket and handed Einsig a five-dollar bill. "Here are your shekels. Now, if you want a fight, I'm ready. Your choice of weapons, of course. What'll it be—sabers, pistols, paintbrushes at dawn? I've got it, I'll use a slingshot."

"Cut it out." O'Keefe was back between us. "Cool it, you two."

"Good with me," said Einsig. "I shouldn't waste my energy talking to Mister-Bert-Rum-Tiny-Royce-Mean-Junior-Millionaire." He turned abruptly and moved away. It seemed that I had acquired an enemy.

17

The Urban Museum of Art has scheduled a public hearing to present plans for the proposed Royceman Pavilion. The meeting will take place in the Franklin Theater on the main floor of that institution, Friday, December 11, at 7:30 p.m. . . .

Bartholomew Hayes, director of the museum, stated: "We live in an era of public participation and trust in the great cultural institutions of this nation. It is our solemn duty to fulfill the obligations of that trust. Therefore, we intend to throw open our doors to the people of New York City. We ask their advice and their involvement."

Excerpts from *The New York Times,* December 2, 1972

It had been his instrument. I had watched him sitting at the gleaming desk in the Impressionist Room, hunching his right shoulder to secure the telephone between ear and mouth, hands free. I had sat in his hospital room, quietly, in a green leather chair by the window, while he sent his voice out. I had thought it merely an interruption, an invasion of privacy. I had not considered the instrument itself. How perfectly it suited.

Protected, uninvolved, anonymous, I could sit at that scarred, square, wood table in that tiny, dim kitchen and project my voice to all the people in all the rooms—bedrooms, offices, libraries—rooms where people talked as they sorted their mail, sipped coffee, masturbated. No exposure for them. No exposure for me.

Seven stabs of my fingertip and "yes" and "I under-

156

stand" and "I agree" and "yes" and "yes." Saying yes.
To me.

"The Equal Opportunity Office?"

"That's right," I answered in what I assumed passed
for a business voice. (It was as close to my father's
tone as I could remember.) "I'm Raymond Cortes, and
as I was saying, according to our records, a Peter
Booth applied for the job of refuse room administrator
and was turned down. Mr. Booth is black."

"I don't remember that at all. I see everybody. Can
you hold a minute while I look up the records?"

"Of course."

Brenda kissed me on the top of my head and slipped
a tray in front of me. It contained two plates of scrambled eggs and bacon, a pot of coffee. Two cups.

"Mr. Cortes?"

"Yes."

"We have no record of a Peter Booth. You must have
the wrong firm."

"This *is* Royceman Brothers?"

"Yes."

"And you are who?"

"Atkins. Saul Atkins. Personnel."

"I am correct, Mr. Atkins. Booth did not file an application. Bluntly, he felt so rejected because of his
color that he simply left without protest. However, it is
my job to protest for Peter Booth. You may reject him
but the laws of this country do not. Am I clear? We
have legal recourse to deal with bigots."

"Just a minute, we employ blacks here. Lots of
them."

"I have your complete employment records in front
of me. I consider the proportion to be pitifully poor."

"We employ qualified people, regardless of race."

"Peter Booth is qualified."

"He didn't apply. There's no record."

"Let's get to the discussion at hand, Mr. Atkins. Is
the job of refuse room administrator vacant?"

"Oddly enough, it becomes vacant in a few days, but we never told . . ."

"And have you filled that vacancy with a Caucasian?"

"We haven't filled it."

"Then if Booth applied, he would be eligible for the job."

"What are his qualifications?"

I poured coffee into my cup. "A bachelor of arts from Yale University, a master's degree in art history from Columbia University, a . . ."

"Forget the question. Just send him down. We don't want any trouble with you fellows. If he can pass the physical, he can have the job. You want to know the salary?"

"No. I am sure it will be the same as that of the former Caucasian refuse administrator."

"Of course. Booth?"

"Peter Booth. I'll send him down tomorrow. Is three convenient?"

"Fine."

"I'm glad we've been able to resolve this matter so amicably, Mr. Atkins."

I hung up, took two quick gulps of coffee, and dialed that familiar number.

"Gina?"

"Who's this?"

"It's me, Bertie."

"Oh hi, Bertie, how are you?"

"How are *you?*"

"I'm fine, really fine . . . sort of."

"Gina, I called to tell you that I'm pretty sure I can get those guards out of there. I want to come right over."

"Oh Bertie, not right now, O.K.? I haven't been feeling exactly great. The doctor says I should be very quiet."

"If I can get them out of there, it'll be quiet."

"That's marvelous, but the doctor tells me I'm not to upset myself. He made me promise to leave things exactly as they are for a while."

"One phone call is all it should take."

"I'll tell you what, I'll ring you the second I'm up to it. You could come up for a square meal at the same time. You've always looked like you could use one, you know. Well, so long, dear, it's good to hear from you. See you soon."

The phone clicked. She'd hung up. Brenda called from the kitchen, "I hope you own stock in AT & T."

"Hey, come here," I yelled. I put a forkful of eggs in my mouth; then, looking down at the yellow pad in front of me, drew a line through the note which read *Get man in garbage room.* "Hey, come on."

Brenda walked across the room. She was wearing a black turtleneck sweater over jeans. She looked good. She sat opposite me and poured herself a cup of coffee. "While you're making all those calls, why don't you call the eye doctor, you're out of drops."

"I feel much better."

"Still sensitive to light?"

"A little."

"Then you should."

I shoved a black loose-leaf notebook across the table. "What do you think of this?"

Brenda opened the book.

"It's an organizational plan for the Art Workers. I did it this morning. It's broken down into jobs: drivers, refuse-loading detail, refuse-unloading detail waiting in Garden City."

"They'll never do it."

"I figure to pay them, twenty dollars a shot."

"They'll do it! For twenty dollars they might even retain some sanity. You might even make pussy cats out of them."

"My father had a theorem: 'What a man will do for love, he'll do more efficiently for money.'"

"Well, that's exactly what he got. That's where feeling goes when you can't deal with it—into efficiency. I spent too much time being efficient. Always for other people. One day I said, 'Brenda, it's time for you,' and I've drifted ever since."

She put her cup on the table and moved behind my chair. I felt her arms around my neck, my head pressed against her diaphragm. "I have a theorem: 'Anything worth doing is worth doing wrong.'"

"Doesn't that bother you? To make a mistake."

"Sure. About once a week I think that if I make another mistake they're going to ship me back to Utica. Utica is needlepoint in the afternoon, seven kids, booze in your coffee, antimacassars on the chairs, and a cross over your bed. It terrifies me. Sometimes I see myself back there being an automaton. In my whole life, my mother's looked at me with only two looks: one meant keep your mouth shut, and the other—cross your legs. I'm afraid, but I used that fear to break out. I believe there's only one real sin—closing off."

"I can't stand that turmoil."

"I prefer turmoil to lack of feeling."

"I don't."

"I know. That's the challenge." Without moving her arms Brenda pivoted her body and sat on my lap. Then she kissed me. I carried her to the bed and we made love for a long time.

"I bought you a present," Brenda said. "I hoped you'd find it, but you've been so busy wheeling and dealing you haven't. I'll give you a hint. This minute you're very hot, burning."

"I hate guessing games. Tell me."

"Under the pillow."

I reached under the pillow and removed a small brown corrugated cardboard box. I shook it. It made a rattling sound.

"It's a kit, a model of a clipper ship. I forgot the glue."

When I woke, the clock read five-thirty. Brenda was propped up on two pillows at the far end of the bed reading, holding her book at a slight angle to catch the modest light from the bed lamp. I kept my eyes almost shut, looking out at her through a tiny shaded slit. Brenda, I reflected, fit into whatever place she occupied.

She didn't irritate me. I wasn't constantly cleaning up, trying to scrub and polish her out of my life.

Brenda was different from the others: the girl in London, her high title matched by the odor of her body. I made her take a bath before we fucked. The redheaded Amazon, so strong she carried *me* to the bed. The aggressive reporter who came to interview me, taking me for one of the collecting Roycemans, and stayed two days and three nights. In and out. In and out. Nothing in common save this: they came to me. Appeared and were used.

I reached out and tapped Brenda's hip with my foot. "Hey, get up. I want to go to that meeting at the Urban. If we start now we'll have plenty of time to walk."

Brenda put the book on the bed table. "Let's stay and smoke."

"We've been in bed all day."

"I'm a growing girl. I need my rest." Brenda rolled over onto her stomach in a maneuver that brought her close to me. She ran a finger down my spine. "This room is our magic capsule, with particles of air, light, and comfort pumped in, just for us. Everything works— you, me, everything."

I sat up, putting my feet on the floor. "I've got to go."

Brenda crossed her hands on the pillow, palms down, and rested her face on them. All I could see was that black mop. "I love the smell of this bed," she mumbled.

"Please come with me. I was just thinking that I'd rather have your company than fuck with anyone in the world."

Brenda turned her head. "And I'd rather talk to you than fuck with anyone in the world myself, but I'm glad we can do both. O.K., I'll come."

I dressed, went into the kitchen, and carried the tape recorder back to the bedroom. I placed it on top of the dresser, ejected the Kris Kristofferson tape, and inserted a blank cartridge. I opened the top dresser drawer. There, next to the jars and boxes of food, was a red nylon-mesh shopping bag. I put the tape recorder and the black loose-leaf notebook in the bag. It was more comfortable, easier to carry, less conspicuous. I slipped a small white pad and a yellow pencil in my jacket pocket, then my shades. I pulled a wool knit cap low on my forehead. That completed the arrangements for my business meeting.

The walk uptown was fun. Brenda does not walk, she lopes along on a slight diagonal. You don't even know it (I don't think she does either) until you find yourself nudged closer and closer to the curb. About every seven blocks I'd catch myself on the brink of the gutter, stop, and push her over toward the buildings. At these times she'd clasp my waist and sometimes we'd kiss, clouds of white vapor between our faces. Once she said, "I can feel every rib. You have three too many." And I countered, "Do you think you'll like walking when you learn how?"

Icy twilight became night, yellow streetlights revealing mica pavements. "Here's the route," announced Brenda. "Up Park, into the Commodore Hotel, down into Grand Central Station, up into the Pan Am lobby, out onto Park again, over to Fifth to see the Christmas windows and do a little eye-buying."

"How about straight up Madison?"

"Come on. At least we could cut over to Fifth and jog up."

"No. I promised O'Keefe we'd pick him up at Schrafft's."

"Three's a crowd. Do you think he dyes his hair?"

"I have to give him the notebook and tell him the plans."

"*Have to* is the most obscene phrase in the English language."

At that hour, looking through the extreme curve of Schrafft's plate-glass window is like peering into a distorted crystal sphere in which aged females are trapped: ladies in dark clothes, seated in twos and fours at tables, drinking glutinous soup and masticating toast. Toast at dinner? Still more of these women are seated single file at a counter parallel to the window. I could see

O'Keefe's back at the far end of the counter. I rapped on the glass; he turned, dropped a coin on the counter, and a minute later the revolving door discharged him onto the sidewalk. ·

"Good evening, pals," O'Keefe said. "You realize my neck may be permanently damaged from craning around waiting for you to appear. I've experienced one of the great culinary mysteries of the world. I've just consumed a sandwich—tuna, chicken, or ham—I'll never know which. I am sure it was on cheese bread. Yes, definitely. Let's take a cab, it's freezing."

"This is spring weather for Utica," Brenda said. "It's only four blocks."

I took Brenda's hand. "We like to walk."

"I absolutely must insist on a cab. I have to keep my friends warm." O'Keefe patted a bulge in his jacket pocket. We kept walking. "Don't you want to know who my friends are?"

"Lilliputians?" asked Brenda. "Angels on the head of a pin?"

"Guess again. Let's play Twenty Questions. Is it animal, vegetable, or mineral? Animal. Is it smaller than a breadbox? Yes. As a matter of fact, it lives in a breadbox. Guess."

We were both silent.

"Guess."

"We hate guessing games," said Brenda.

"All right, spoilsports, you'll see soon enough anyway. We're going to create a little to-do tonight, just to keep our muscles flexed. Not a sophisticated demonstration like the Royceman Transfer. Thanks to Bertie, that's going to be colossal. Brenda, did you know you were living with an organizational genius?"

"You're full of shit."

There was no more conversation until Brenda pointed and said, "That must be it."

There was no missing it. Two huge spotlights in metal superstructure were aimed at the doors of the Urban which led to the Franklin Theater. It was the only area of light on the darkened Fifth Avenue façade. We walked between the lights, through the doors, and into a small marble-floored anteroom. Others joined us and we were propelled through a second set of narrow red doors into the theater itself. Once inside, the people fanned out and dispersed. I heard the compressed babble of voices, felt a sudden rise in temperature. Brenda held my hand and pointed to a rear side aisle. I nodded in agreement, but O'Keefe said, "No, I have to be up front."

"See you later," replied Brenda, pulling me away.

We sat, I with my knees together and the mesh bag on top. The theater was three quarters full. The large audience undulated—shedding coats, folding them on laps, over the backs of chairs, rising to smooth them under thighs.

On the right wall was a sign which read SEATING CAPACITY 750 PERSONS. SMOKING PROHIBITED. Directly under the sign, leaning against the wall, were Rose Thomas, Peter Booth, and three other Art Workers. I nudged Brenda and directed my eyes toward them. "No idea," she replied. In front of the stage stood a cluster of photographers, each with an array of equipment dangling from neck straps. I counted fifteen cameras. Four were on one photographer, a big-assed female in bright-green slacks squatting in front of the others.

The stage itself contained the same two building models I had seen, a wooden lectern, and a microphone. At seven-forty-five Hayes marched on stage; the audience settled and quieted. Hayes briskly approached the lectern. He wore a dark-blue suit, a white shirt, a blue and white striped tie; his breast pocket revealed a bare quarter inch of white handkerchief. He tapped the microphone with one finger, causing a low wail. Placing one hand on each side of the lectern, he leaned forward and began: "Welcome to the Urban Museum of Art. I am Bartholomew Hayes, director of this institution, and tonight my job is both simple and delightful. It is to acquaint you with a magnificent gift, the Bertram Royceman Collection."

Hayes peered into the audience. (Look directly at the

audience, B.S., it shows sincerity. Aim your eyes at a spot in row 7, even if it's impossible to see over the footlights.) "I want to stress that it is you, the people of New York, who are the fortunate recipients of this unique legacy. We here at the Urban are the custodians of your property. We are proud to fulfill that function, and tonight we want to share with you our plans."

Hayes raised his left hand, the theater went dark, the models began to glow as before, the same pointer appeared in his hand. Here we go again, I thought. I reached over and touched Brenda's knee. Then I pulled off my cap and balled it up between my hands. Hayes began speaking, only this time the focus was completely changed. His speech reminded me of what happens to a microscope when you turn the wheel a fraction—an entirely different aspect of the specimen comes into view. Hayes kept referring to the collection as "yours." There was no mention of my father, of the building site (Central Park was never mentioned), and, of course, no mention of that "top-secret, hush-hush," twenty-seven-page contract.

Zags of light vibrated from Hayes's pointer, I could feel the restlessness, hear the rustling of clothing, the coughing. That moment when an audience becomes the captive of the speaker did not occur. I knew what it was like. I had seen it happen. My father spoke in a voice so low that people leaned forward in order to grasp his words. His interest was not in them but in expressing his own knowledge and passion: this was the contagion to which there was little immunity. Standing in the living room of the apartment, surrounded by a group of art-history students, my father struck his head and then his heart. "If it touches you in these places—trust yourself."

Hayes was an academician, discussing numbers, dates, statistics. He was saying, "For those of you who may not know, this collection encompasses over four thousand items. There are over six hundred Old Masters, two hundred thirteenth- to fifteenth-century Italian Primitives, a thousand fifteenth- to eighteenth-century drawings and watercolors, a thousand nineteenth- to twentieth-century paintings . . ."

An electric buzz reverberated and a screen began descending from the ceiling in front of the models as Hayes continued. "It seems presumptuous to single out favorite works." (Long pause.) "I shall anyway." Click . . . A slide projection of a painting appeared on the screen. "Giovanni Bellini's long career, stretching from the middle 1450's to his death in 1516, encompassed few works of the stature of this 'Virgin with Joseph and Infant.' This painting overcomes the restrictions of color and form to present a touching human portrait." . . . Click . . . "Botticelli's 'Virgin with Child,' measuring only 10 by 15 inches, glows with inner fire . . ." *My father's voice rang with pleasure: "I couldn't believe my eyes. It was Missy. The hair is the same exactly and the way it falls, don't you agree? I told Bernard, 'It's very small . . .'"*

Click . . . Click . . . "In Van Gogh's 'Portrait of Theo in White,' painted after a photograph, we observe how the artist transcended the mere recording of physical data to bring his own intense feelings about his brother to the canvas . . ." *"You're right, Jack, it was a ridiculous price. I can't afford it, but I thought, if I don't buy it, someone else will."*

Click . . . "El Greco's 'St. John' possesses demoniac fury." . . . Click . . . Click . . . "Gauguin's 'Tahitian Women,' executed in 1892, represents the mightiest powers of the artist and reveals . . ." Click . . . Click . . . Click . . .

Hayes's words drifted over my head: "One of the most superb examples of Mannerist painting in existence, the 'Countess Di Cavour,' by Ingres, is . . ." I grabbed Brenda's arm. The rigid-backed woman on the screen wore a voluminous oyster-gray dress, lace at the neck. Her tapered fingers clasped an ivory fan. Pearls glowed in her tightly rolled brown hair. My Ingres. Not his. But then it was gone.

Some minutes later the houselights came on and Hayes announced, "I would be glad to answer any questions you might have concerning the Royceman Collection. My one request is that you state your full name and organizational affiliation, if you have one, when asking a question. I enjoy knowing who you are." He gestured to a woman. She stood. "Lucy Stroller, no affiliation." (Some laughter.) "I would like to know if you plan to charge a special admission fee for viewing the collection."

"No," Hayes replied. "We do not contemplate . . ." I saw O'Keefe climbing the four wooden steps leading to the stage. Rose Thomas followed, then others. Each person held a glass jar. From where I sat the jars seemed to contain raisins or small brown nuts. Rose Thomas moved to the lectern, leaned in front of Hayes, and spoke into the microphone: "My good people, stop the Urban's monument to money. Art for the people. Look at the naked facts." With that, she tugged vigorously at the front of her blouse. It gave way and her breasts, which resembled pink plastic balloons, bounced into view.

People stood. There was laughter, hissing, clapping. The female photographer in green slacks rushed on stage. Hayes, standing directly behind Rose Thomas, grabbed her shoulders and tried to pull her from the lectern. He could not budge her. She leaned forward again, when two guards appeared and jerked her abruptly backward. A blond young man dashed across the stage carrying a brown suit jacket. He draped it over Rose Thomas's torso but she shrugged it off, her big breasts bobbing wildly.

By this time O'Keefe and the other Workers had formed a semicircle, holding their jars aloft. O'Keefe opened his jar and tapped the bottom vigorously. The contents fell, then came to life, and began scuttling across the stage.

I looked at Brenda. "Roaches," she said. "It's an old standby."

Peter Booth zigzagged across the stage like a broken-field runner, smashing his jar on the lectern. Fragments of glass and insects spewed out. Hayes jumped back, stumbled, then straightened up. The other Workers emptied their jars and proceeded in an orderly fashion down the steps and out a side exit.

In a burst of flashbulbs, Rose Thomas and O'Keefe both disappeared into the wings, squirming in the grasp of half a dozen guards.

Once again Hayes stood behind the lectern. He pulled the handkerchief from his breast pocket and swept the glass and remaining roaches to the floor. "I wish to thank those anonymous donors for the contribution they have just made. Perhaps they mistook us for the Museum of Natural History." Hayes laughed. "Now that the audience has been cleared of objectionable insects, I am once again open for business."

The questioning began. This was only the third meeting I had ever attended, but I observed certain patterns. Many people did not ask questions but made speeches. Some did not listen. (The same questions were asked two and three times.) A few asked question after question and expressed annoyance when Hayes called upon others.

I knew some of the questions had been planted by Hayes. Questions like, "In dollars and cents, Mr. Hayes, how much would you say this gift is worth?" To which he replied, "I am told the value of this gift is estimated at a hundred million dollars, but its value aesthetically is beyond price."

Slipped in with all the meaningless questions and the foolish questions were the questions I had been waiting for: the tough questions, the objections. I checked my tape to make sure it was recording and wrote the names carefully on my pad. I wrote quite a few names. I'd been right. The Art Workers weren't the only ones who would protest the Royceman Wing. Hayes had tipped me off to that with the arrogance of the complacent.

Later that night Brenda sat on the bed, munching potato chips from the top dresser drawer. "What did you think of Rose's tits?"

"Not much. You?"

"Exotic. Sort of free-floating. I liked that lecture to-

night though. I surprised myself. I've always thought
that art began with Jackson Pollock. I was so sorry he
died in that automobile accident. It would have been
something to have him fuck me. Anyway, it's nice to
know there's a collection like your father's, one that
goes back to the thirteenth century. I'm glad I went. I
mean, if I were you, I'd feel proud."

"If you were me, you wouldn't feel anything."

"You lie to yourself, Bertie."

"I don't know what I feel. Or if."

18

... *Johnson: I estimate that you intend to encroach on
approximately 31,500 square feet of park land beyond
the present museum line . . . Mr. Hayes, do you intend
to answer my question?*

Hayes: Did you ask me a question?

*Johnson: Do you intend to encroach on a vast area of
park land?*

*Hayes: No. We are utilizing a portion of our land
beyond our present building line but well within our
area of legal jurisdiction. We control all the land up to
and including the Central Park Drive. We plan to use
only a fraction of that land for expansion.*

*Johnson: Your model calls for the demolition of 500
linear feet, 21,000 square feet of the Central Park
Mall . . . Mr. Hayes, will you answer my question?*

*Hayes: If you expect me to answer a question, you
must ask me a question.*

*Johnson: Really, Mr. Hayes, you understand my
intent. Do you plan to destroy the mall?*

Hayes: No. We plan to relocate it.

*Johnson: You plan to relocate it without destroying
it?*

*Hayes: Mr. Johnson, what is the point of arguing
semantics?*

*Johnson: The point is that green space is our most
precious commodity and we must fight to protect it. If
we don't, New Yorkers will find themselves surrounded
with nothing but dirt, dust, mud, and buildings. . . .*

*Doyle: The model of the proposed Royceman
Pavilion which you have shown us tonight clearly*

demonstrates that over one third of the western façade of the Urban Museum is to be replaced with a glass wall. Is this indeed the case?

Hayes: ... Yes, Mr. Doyle, your interpretation is correct.

Doyle: You're demolishing one third of the western façade?

Hayes: To replace it with a glass wall which is, in fact, an integral part of our architectural plan. This will provide an unobstructed view of the lower galleries of the Royceman Pavilion.

Doyle: Mr. Hayes, surely you are aware that the western façade was designated a landmark in June 1957?

Hayes: ... Our charter enables us absolutely to reconstruct our buildings and to add such new structures as we deem fit.

Doyle: Your charter is over a hundred years old. It has no relevance whatsoever today.

Hayes: The Declaration of Independence, Mr. Doyle, is two hundred years old and yet we live by it. Age is no criterion to relevance.

Doyle: Am I to understand that you will not consider altering this plan in order to save a precious landmark?

Hayes: It would be impossible to do so.

Doyle: Why? Is this a conditional gift?

Hayes: The Urban Museum is solely responsible for selecting this architectural plan. We feel it is the best possible plan.

Excerpts from a tape recording of a public hearing at the Urban Museum of Art, December 11, 1972

———

"Who was that?" asked Ned.

"That's Walter Johnson speaking. He's chairman of the Parks Protection Association. I was very careful to write down all the names."

"What are all those pauses?"

"Hayes taking his bloody time. There was a water

carafe and a glass on the lectern, so every time he was asked a good question, he'd fill the glass and sip away until he thought up an answer.

"There's another part I want you to hear." I pressed Fast Forward. Then Stop. Then Start. A woman's voice asked, "Will children be admitted?" I'd gone too far. "I'll find it in a minute. I should have used spool tape instead of a cassette." I pressed Rewind. Then Stop. Then Start. A man's voice said, "You're demolishing one third of the western façade?" I pressed Stop. Then Reverse. Then almost immediately, Stop.

"I have it. This is Herbert Doyle of the Historic Landmarks Committee."

"I know him," said Ned. "He's the one who put up such a fight to save the old Metropolitan Opera. Didn't do too well."

I pressed Start. We listened. I pressed Stop.

"I wish I'd been there," said Ned.

"It was interesting. I sat on the side under one of the speakers; that's why the recording quality's so good."

"It's nice of you to bring it. Would you like some espresso?"

"No, Ned. I didn't come here to amuse you with my recordings or to drink your coffee." I tapped the tape recorder. "Did you hear Doyle ask if the gift was conditional?"

"What gift? I keep telling you, until our suit is settled, there's no gift."

"What I mean is, there's a secret contract between the Urban and Weisman. Twenty-seven pages. Of course the gift is conditional."

"How do you know that?"

"Hayes let me in on it when I visited the Urban. Ned, I want you to call Johnson and Doyle and tell them about that contract. The building must be constructed exactly like the model. Hayes can't make concessions. We can use these organizations to delay construction. We'll help them and they'll help us. My father had a theorem: 'If you want a good deal, make it good for the other guy.' "

"And you're sounding like a block off the old chip," Ned said, smiling.

Time racing, prismatic, my days began at six-thirty. I dressed, bought the newspapers, read them carefully, clipped everything I might use, and piled the clippings neatly on the near right-hand corner of the kitchen table.

At seven-thirty I began phoning. Ned was first on my list, then O'Keefe. I was learning the advantage of early-morning calls. People are pliable when all they want is to empty their bladder.

My father had a theorem: "You can wear out or you can rust out." He used to quote that one at me a lot. The implication being, of course, that I would rust out. That whatever I was doing, I didn't do.

Now I was performing, developing a routine and a plan. All I had to do was fix a thing clearly in my head and I could force it to become a reality. O'Keefe and Held seemed amazed by this. I was too. Me, Bertie the piss-ant, running the show.

No matter what time I arrived at the eye doctor's I had at least a two-hour wait. I hated going. This time Brenda went with me, which made it better. We sat in the crowded waiting room and filled in the *New York Times* crossword puzzle. Brenda knew all those little words like "zoa" that fit in the odd places. That took about an hour.

After that we just sat. Brenda tapped her foot on the floor and brushed her hair and read a magazine. That took a while too. Then Brenda got up and walked to the nurse's circular desk, which stood in the center of the room. "Can I help you?" the nurse inquired imperiously.

"I'm not sure," replied Brenda, giving the nurse her shy look. "You see, Mr. Royceman, Mr. Bertram Royceman, is due at his lawyer's office in half an hour to sign the final papers for the donation of the Royceman Ophthalmological Clinic. Of course we don't want to rush you, but I guess if it's going to be too terribly long I'll have to use your phone, since there are so many people involved. I won't have to call all twenty people personally, I could just call one of Mr. Royceman's secretaries and he could contact all the other people." Necks twisted; everyone within earshot turned to stare at me. The doctor took me next and pronounced me much better. Less than ten minutes later we were on the street. Brenda hugged me. I didn't get the joke. "Jesus, that was a god damn embarrassing thing to pull—stupid, tasteless, dumb-assed."

"It got us out of there, didn't it? Anyway, why are you yelling at me? I got the idea from you, from the way you got Booth inside the refuse room."

"That was different." I started to walk very fast. Brenda had to jog to keep up with me.

"It was exactly the same," she protested.

"Oh yeah? I didn't stand up in front of a roomful of people and throw my weight around and make an ass of myself."

"I see. It would have been all right with you if I'd strolled down the street to a booth and phoned it in."

"Jesus, Brenda, you have the sensitivity of a rhinoceros."

"Maybe. And maybe you can only be brave if you hide. That's what you do. You escape behind those shades and don't let anybody or anything in. Lately, you just sit at that table phoning and clipping and getting your kicks from some lunatic Monopoly game you've invented. You're one big shot of novocaine. You're turned off. I may not be anything great but at least I'm in touch with the world."

"Yeah, what's the world doing these days?"

"Don't be sarcastic with me."

"Then fuck off."

"I will. I really will." She turned and walked away from me.

I watched her until she disappeared around the corner. The afternoon turned rotten.

I walked, I thought without direction, until I found myself in front of Ellen's apartment building.

Ellen opened the door amid the clamorous cacophony of dog yelps. She led me into that disorganized morass she called a library. The desk was almost obscured beneath sheets of white paper, ledger books, random masses of checks, and an adding machine. "I've been working," she explained. "When Ben was alive I used to think I was an idiot about business. Actually, I've quite a knack. I was the best student in my bookkeeping course. I do my own taxes and everything."

"You can do mine."

"And incur the wrath of Royceman Brothers, the entire Wall Street community, and Jacob Weisman? Not me, I'm a coward."

"Don't worry. Saint Bertie will slay the dragon."

"Who's that, Weisman?"

"That's who!"

"Actually, he's not such a dragon. He was Daddy Bert's guardian angel."

"Who cares. It's all the same to us saints, as long as we get the job done."

"Well, in that case my fee is reasonable and I'll make you a sandwich for the same price."

"I'm not hungry." I moved to the desk and began stacking the checks in a pile. Crosshatched, flung every which way, they needed attention. I had to straighten them out.

Ellen watched me. "Bertie, what's wrong? You look so down."

I continued stacking those pale-green checks. "Insensitive people are a bore. Doesn't it bother you when people blunder into things they know nothing about?"

"What people?"

"People."

"Maybe."

"You're a big help."

Ellen regarded me with a slight smile. "What am I supposed to say? You're standing there with your coat on, sorting checks and not telling me anything, and I know if I say one wrong word you'll bolt out my door and I may not see you again for weeks."

"You can say any god damn thing you please."

"Good. I want to help."

"I don't need help."

Ellen laughed full out, her brown hair falling forward across her face. "Have it your way. No unseemly displays of emotion. So be it. Just take off your coat and sit down."

I dropped my parka on the couch and sat next to it, Ellen on the other side. "How's our illustrious brother-in-law?" she asked. "Still shining his shoes and getting us a zillion each?"

"He's under control."

"He called me this Monday and asked me to testify that Daddy Bert was senile. Did he get you to do that?"

"It's in the complaint somewhere. It's one of the 'few permissible legal objections.' "

"Is that so. Well, I told Ned, 'You may be crazy but Daddy Bert sure wasn't.' "

"Ellen?"

"What?"

"Why? Why do you care about it?"

"You mean about *him?*"

"Yeah."

"Sometimes, there was something. He could be very . . ." Her voice trailed off. "One afternoon when I was about six he came home and gave me a beautiful dark-blue box. Inside was a watch. I don't know what the occasion was, it wasn't my birthday or anything. He let me sit on his lap and helped me strap the watch on my wrist. Then he said, 'All right, Ellen, now tell Daddy Bert what time it is.'

"I just sat there, not knowing what to do or how to tell him that no one had ever bothered to teach me how to read time. I began to cry. I couldn't speak a word. I felt Daddy Bert squeeze me and he said, 'O.K., Ellen, turn off the faucet, because Daddy Bert's going to give you a lesson.' He closed the door and for the next hour

or so he taught me to tell time. He had that side to
him too."

"You shouldn't have to testify. I'll tell Ned to stop
bothering you."

"I don't need help either." Ellen reached out and
touched my cheek. "Hey, Bertie, last chance—going,
going, gone. Can I?"

"No."

When I left Ellen's, I started walking in the direction
of the Chelsea. At a small narrow-windowed store I
stopped to buy a bottle of Elmer's glue. That made me
think of Brenda and I found myself wanting her to be
there, waiting for me. She wasn't. I walked into the
bedroom and stood very still in the center of the room.
It took a long time before I could open the top dresser
drawer. When I did, I jerked it with a pull so strong
the drawer sprang forward, stopped abruptly, and began
vibrating on its metal casters. It was full. Peanut butter,
tea, immersion heater, saltine crackers—they were all
there. I felt a rush of warmth.

Brenda enjoyed sitting in bed eating those top-drawer
goodies, analyzing the world in general and me in particular. One morning she observed, "You were deserted,
so you either drive people away or pick ones who'll be
sure to split."

"Thank you, Fräulein Doktor. Ones like you?"

"Oh boy, I didn't think of that. Exactly. I'm a perfect
choice."

Everything has a time limit. I knew she wouldn't stay.
She was right about me: people desert me. I even knew
that fell into the category of self-fulfilling prophecy. It
didn't help. I knew all this, but three weeks after Brenda
moved in, early one morning after we'd made love, I
found myself moving my things from the top drawer to
the half-empty one below. In the mirror above the chest
I could see Brenda standing behind me, two dark-
haired child faces, a cameo from another century. Brenda kissed my neck. "Thanks," she said.

"For moving a few fucking things?"

"For beginning to make room."

I don't kid myself—the reason Brenda's with me is probably the oldest one in the world: she wants to change me. We screw well and she says we have "compatible skin and compatible heads," but what she really wants is to open me up. She says things like, "Bertie, life is active, not passive. Life is doing, not watching. Life is *feeling*."

Myths for modern living. They do not exist. I'm me. That's it. What Brenda doesn't realize is this: what you see is what you get. Brenda and Bertie are not a love story.

In a sociology class I once attended, the professor (a fantastic-looking woman who'd been a Ford model) lectured incessantly on the Map and the Execution. The Map was how things were supposed to be, the ideal plan. The Execution was what happened. They were always different, the Execution being the general mess we make of life.

Take my father and Missy. Map: brilliant investment banker, art collector, adds the most superb acquisition to his collection, a beautiful Wasp socialite who is to become chatelaine to his mansions and mother of the heir to the dynasty. That's true. Jack Weisman once (while a bit tight) asked my father if he remembered the advice he had given him about marrying Missy.

"What was that, Jack?"

"Grab her. If you insist on having a calf, it's better to buy a cow who's had one."

Execution: hatred. Missy hiding in a bottle. My object-obsessed father's favorite object (*his* son—*his* heir) discovered to be worthless.

We all have our maps, testaments to relationships that do not exist. Brenda and Bertie. Map: salvation through love. Execution: impossible. She—"no longevity." He—"turned off." Was I ever turned on?

It's as if there were a series of airtight compartments, separate, sealed. There is no flow between. I stand above, dropping each quantity into the appropriate compartment: here fucking, here eating, here my plan to win. I think if there were a flow, *if* there were, and these things could run together, the result might be a whole person. If such a thing exists.

I heard the door open and felt her hands on my shoulders. "Aren't you going to ask me where I was?"

"O.K., where were you?"

"How nice of you to ask. I was very angry, so I walked a lot, and then I went on a go-see and stayed to audition for a commercial. They called me back three times. I didn't get it though. They said I had old hands."

I reached up, pulled both her hands forward, and kissed each fingertip. "You have nice hands, very nice."

We lay on the bed smoking. Brenda's voice sounded dreamy and faraway. "I wanted to tell you about the time when I was a kid and my dad and mom took me out to a steak house. I still remember the name, The Char Pit. That was a big treat for me because then my father was just a used-car salesman who went to night school. When we were ready to leave my father said to the waiter, 'I'd like a doggie bag for Rex.' And I piped up, 'We don't have a dog, Daddy.'

"When we got home he beat me. First with a hanger and then with his belt. Then he cried. Later my mother told me to wear a long-sleeved blouse until the bruises on my arms faded."

"I don't understand. He did *that* over a doggie bag?"

"You see, that's my point. Maybe I don't understand the rich, but you don't understand the rest of us."

19

. . . EPTL 5–3.3 (subd. [a], par [1]) states that "an issue or parent may not contest a disposition as invalid unless he will receive a pecuniary benefit from a successful contest."

It is my decision that a clause providing for an alternative disposition of an excessive charitable disposition may deprive a parent or issue (the incompetent in this case) of any status to contest under EPTL 5–3.3. [Durkee v. Smith, 90 Misc. 92, affd 171 App. Div. 72, mot. to dismiss app. den. 218 N.Y. 619, affd 219 N.Y. (604)]

Excerpt from Opinion by Judge Samuel DiFalco, *Matter of Fitzgerald,* December 21, 1972

"Put your things anywhere as long as you don't disturb the disorder," said Brenda. Yards of unfurled tinsel covered the chair and a florist's box bursting with greenery lay open on the bed. Brenda stood on top of the oak dresser, a length of tinsel in one hand and a roll of Scotch tape in the other. She pressed the tinsel against the ceiling, pulled a length of tape, and bit it off. "How's it look? Is the swag even? I can't tell from here."

"It'll do. It sure makes a mess."

"Such enthusiasm. What's the matter, you anti-Christmas or something?"

I didn't answer.

"O.K., love, hand up a holly."

I removed a sprig of fresh holly from the green wax paper and handed it up to her. She deftly taped it in the middle of a swag. "When I was a kid, every Christmas my father would put up a plastic electric statue of the Blessed Virgin at the head of the stairs. There stood Mary in all her polystyrene glory, at least ten feet tall, with red and blue bulbs behind her. That's what I call a real Christmas."

Brenda gestured to me and I walked to the chest. She placed her hands on my shoulders and slowly slid down my body. When her feet touched the ground she didn't move away. She stood there pressed against me. Then she reached up and kissed me. There was a knock on the door. "Merde," said Brenda, "perfect timing." She moved away.

Ned Held stood at the door in a dark cashmere coat with a mink collar. His hands were encased in soft light-brown leather gloves. When I introduced him to Brenda, he shook her hand without removing his gloves. "Delighted to meet you."

He turned to me. "Bertie, you have good taste, she's a beauty. And this place—immaculate."

"Thanks. I do the cleaning."

Held pulled off his gloves and put them in his pocket. He carefully unbuttoned his coat, removed it, and handed it to Brenda. She looked astounded, as if presented with an unwanted animal or infant, dropped the coat on a chair, and headed for the kitchen. Held, swaddled in unawareness, said, "It was a rough drive down here, so much traffic we practically crawled." He looked around the room.

I read the signal. "Would you like something to drink?"

"Would I. Anything. On the rocks."

As I poured his drink Ned's words came out in a rush, striking my back. "The DiFalco decision came down yesterday, Bertie, and it's lousy for us. DiFalco decided for the archdiocese. He ruled against the incompetent son. DiFalco said he didn't need to reach the Cairo case. He went back to some case that happened over half a century ago where some guy wanted to build a park or a library or something, so he left his money for that purpose with the provision that if he'd left too much money to charity, the money would be given over to his trustees as individuals. He had, and the money went to the trustees, and they built the park or library themselves. In that case the money actually changed hands and it didn't here, but DiFalco used it anyway. It's anyone's guess, but I think he couldn't let the Catholic Church down. Those mackerel snappers always seem to stick together."

"So that's my Christmas present." I handed Held his drink. "No Ingres, no Degas, no money. Weisman must be happy."

"Not very. The court's appointed him preliminary executor of the estate, so he can pay debts, sell stock, and pay for the funeral. But he can't distribute the estate. Think of it this way, we've lost one round in a fifteen-round fight. We'll still win. We've got time, they don't. I plan to make this the slowest suit on record. Watch me. I'm going to object to every ruling, every everything. I intend to call so many witnesses it would take months to see them all. And guess what, I'm so busy I'm only able to work on this case one day a week. I'll creep along while they get more and more frantic. One question, Bertie: do you remember Ambassador Robert Royceman visiting your father in the hospital?"

"No."

"Unfortunately, Tammy says that too, and Ellen won't talk to me. It seems that in the last year of your father's life Ambassador Royceman spent most of his time in Washington, Virginia, and Europe. He maintains that being named Straw Man was a complete surprise to him, so that kills that accusation of collusion. But I'm getting affidavits showing the old man was senile when the will was signed, and I'm still working on collusion and undue pressure by Hayes. I'm leaning hard on him. He came down yesterday for a pre-trial examination and did I make him sweat. He came on very aggressive, lots of 'This is a ridiculous inconvenience' and 'How dare you impugn my motives.' Trying to pull that stuff. I answered, 'In April 1972 you announced publicly that you had secured the Royceman Collection for the Urban when, in fact, Bertram Royceman's will was not signed until May of that year and he did not die until September. I'd say you jumped the gun a bit on that one.'

"Hayes shot out of his seat and yelled, 'This man is trying to crucify me.' It was quite something." Held looked around the room. "May I use your bathroom?"

"Right through the bedroom."

"Thanks. Could you freshen my drink while I'm gone? A splash of water this time."

Brenda was standing at the kitchen sink, carrot scrapings mingling with the silver and turquoise of her rings. "Could you get some water for Ned's drink?"

"You mean, *would* I?"

"Would, could. What's the difference?"

"I could, but I won't, that's the difference."

"What are you talking about?"

"Damned anti-Catholic. I heard what he said. Him with his polished shoes, and his matching tie and shirt. He's so dumb he doesn't even know mackerel snappers are Irish, not Italian. DiFalco isn't a mackerel snapper, but *I* am. DiFalco happens to be a respected judge who wouldn't decide an issue on religious grounds. Someone should tell that stupid bastard Held that this is the United States, 1972, not sixteenth-century Spain."

"I'll get the water."

When I returned to the living room Held was perched on the faded arm of the couch, trying to blend in with the Chelsea decor. I handed him the drink. He took three rapid swallows. "Don't be discouraged, dear boy —I'm not. We've got a lot going for us, and I must admit most of it is your doing. When I told the people at the Parks Protection Association and the Historic Landmarks Committee about that secret contract, they decided to bring a public interest suit against the administrator of parks, since he's technically the landlord of the Urban. That secret contract won't be secret long. Right off, they'll start discovery proceedings—that's where they gather the pertinent information. If someone asks Hayes if there's a contract between the Urban and the Royceman estate, he will be under oath, so he's got to say yes. When he does, he'll be legally obligated to reveal its contents. Someone will ask."

"You've arranged that?"

"There are only five hundred lawyers in the entire world. Fortunately, I know most of them. The attorney for the public interest suit happens to be a close associate of mine, and so is the lawyer at Weisman's who slipped me a Xerox of the contract. Incidentally, Bertie, that contract has some pretty interesting provisions. The Urban can never sell the paintings, or even lend them to another institution, without the express permission of the executors of your father's estate. Someone certainly took care of Hayes's reputation for slick trickery with that one. I'm sure your father decided his collection would never go the way of the Tarkington and LaSalle collections, put on the block to give Hayes the cash to buy whatever happened to be his latest whim.

"Another provision says that at least seven rooms from your grandfather's townhouse must be duplicated exactly. I'll bet your father insisted on that. He was in love with the place." Held finished his drink and continued: "Some of the money goes to removing part of the western wall of the Urban and replacing it with a glass wall. It seems Weisman insists on an unobstructed view of your father's Taj Mahal. When all that comes out, it'll stir up a hornet's nest of criticism."

Something seemed out of whack to me. "What happens if those groups win their suit? Or if they delay construction so long that the building can't be built in time?"

Held rattled the ice cubes in his empty glass. "They won't. Actually, they don't have a case, but it's good for us, and I think . . ." Brenda walked into the room carrying a glass dish of carrot sticks. She placed them on the table and said, "I thought you might like something to nibble on. Am I interrupting?"

"Of course not," replied Held.

Brenda sat on the couch next to Held's perch and

tucked her legs under her. "Bertie tells me you're a brilliant lawyer"—she looked up at him with the toothpaste-ad smile—"and I'm desperately in need of some legal advice for my friend."

"Anything to be of service."

"Oh, how nice. My friend's really beautiful, half Dutch, half Cherokee Indian. That makes for spectacular bones and all. We used to model together."

Held concentrated on Brenda for the first time. "She sounds striking."

"She is. You should see her."

"I'd like to."

"I'm sure you would. What I was about to say was that my friend wanted to learn to give great blow jobs. She's a perfectionist. Some people just *are,* you know. She went to this queen who said he'd give her a course of ten lessons at fifty bucks a lesson. She paid in advance, the whole five hundred. After two lessons that old queen said she had no talent for sucking cocks. He just despaired of her. But he wouldn't give her any money back. I think he should give her the money back, or at least four hundred dollars. That would be prorated, wouldn't it?"

Held nodded frantically. He resembled a puppet with a coiled-spring neck who'd just been banged on the head.

"That's wonderful. Then you'll take the case. I'll tell her. She'll be so grateful."

"Wait a minute. Just wait a minute. I can't take a case like that."

"Don't you think justice should be done?" Brenda inquired sweetly.

Held's finger disappeared into his nose. "If it were *you,* dear girl, it would be different. But I don't know your friend and I make it a rule not to deal with strangers."

"That must limit your practice quite a bit."

"No, not really."

"Come to think of it, right before I came to New York there was this priest who was a very good friend of my father's, only I should have known something was up because, instead of masturbating like all the other priests, he picked his nose."

Held's posture stiffened. He quickly stopped probing and clasped his hands together.

Brenda plunged on. "Then one day he raped me. Right in the confessional. You know how strange and excessive we mackerel snappers are. I've been looking for someone to handle the case and since you know me, if you would . . ."

Held stood up, finally getting it. "I've got a long drive ahead of me. I must go. I think I've overstayed my welcome." He picked up his coat. "I'll call you right after Christmas, Bertie. Maybe we can have another meeting. Somewhere else," he added pointedly.

As soon as the door closed behind Held, Brenda asked, "Do you think we should throw out his glass and the hors d'ouevres plate, or will it be all right to just boil them?"

"It's no joke, he's my lawyer and he's helping me get what I want."

"Oh, that's great. Great. You know what's the matter with you—you're really narrow. There's a war out there and people are being killed and there's My Lai, but you don't know about that, or the rape of Bangladesh women by Pakistani soldiers or about political beatings or riots or anything because you only read *The New York Times* to find the blessed name of Royceman. You're not interested in anything except getting back at those people who put you down."

Brenda bit her lip. "Everyone wants to make a mark. I do understand that. That's why people go out and carve their initials in trees or spray their names in Day-Glo all over the subways. This is about the same, it's silly."

"It's something I have to do for myself."

"That's wrong. What's in it for you? To rub Weisman's nose in it, and Hayes's, that's all. If you lost your suit, if they didn't settle, you'd still be Mr. Rich,

Rich, Rich. You've got nothing at stake. You're committed to nothing. You don't really want anything."

"I want their respect."

"Don't expect me to believe that. You're substituting this crazy, obsessive activity for what you really wanted but could never get—*his* respect, *his* love."

"I guess you've convinced yourself that frankness is your most endearing trait. Sock 'em with the facts and leave 'em bleeding. Well, I don't buy your theories and I don't buy your act."

"It's no act. I just call things by their real names. You're the one who uses dirty language for effect."

"That's the way I talk."

"And telling your fat-headed, bigoted brother-in-law about how my friend likes to suck cocks is how I talk."

"No, it's not."

Brenda sat on the couch and bit into a carrot stick. "Cut it out, Bertie. Just cut it out. Don't think you're going to make my head all mushy. The next thing you know you'll ask me to wear lace and Chanel No. 5 and when we fuck you'll want me to call it *love.*"

"And what do you call it?"

"A lollipop. That's what. Just a lollipop."

20

PUBLIC INTEREST—WHERE?

. . . Since the gift of the Royceman Collection and Pavilion was announced at the Benefactors' Dinner last October, it has aroused a growing concern on the part of park lovers and community groups. Last week two civic organizations, the Parks Protection Association and the Historic Landmarks Committee, formalized their objections by filing a public interest suit against the administrator of Parks, Recreation and Cultural Affairs.

The suit seeks to compel review of the proposed Royceman Wing by the Board of Estimate and the City Council, and questions the right of the Urban to destroy a landmark façade, to relocate the historic Central Park Mall, and to encroach on 31,500 square feet of park land.

The Urban Museum has announced its intention to bypass the Board of Estimate, maintaining that its approval is not required since no city funds are involved. The museum will also ignore the Historic Landmarks Committee's recommendation not to destroy a portion of the western façade. Bartholomew Hayes said, "Such a recommendation is legally enforceable only on private buildings—ours is a public structure."

. . . Concerning the demolition of the Central Park Mall, Hayes stated: "The lease and charter granted us by the New York State legislature are clear—we can do whatever we want with that land."

It would seem that in order to claim an advantage, the Urban Museum of Art has wrapped itself in the cloak of public protection, but in no way does it serve the public interest. The proposed pavilion is essentially

a glittering monument to wealth and privilege. One
must agree with city councilman Donald Rose's obser-
vation that "the Royceman Wing is an affront to a
democratic people. It is unwise to build a glass house
on park property. Under these circumstances, any kid
with a rock could become New York's most valued
architectural critic."

Excerpts from an essay by Clarence Carton,
Op Ed page, *The New York Times,* January 9, 1973

Brenda sat opposite me, wearing my brown terry-cloth
bathrobe, her left hand spread flat on a paper towel.
She moved a stubby brush down each of her long fingernails, coating them with rust-colored polish. I flipped
through the clippings for a third time, occasionally
rereading a section and making notes on my pad.

"What did you think of Donald Rose's statement?"
I asked.

"Is he a friend or something?"

"No. I kept reading about him, he's come out for
everything from free public-school lunches to pooper-
scoopers for dog crap, so I put him in touch with
Carton."

"I've never heard of him."

"Sure you have. His picture's in the papers all the
time, looks about ten, patent-leather hair, no tie, white
shirt open at the neck. Ned says his family is rich and
politically ambitious. Sort of penny-ante Kennedys. Everyone's beginning to jump on our bandwagon."

Brenda looked over at me. "You know those toys
with the steel balls hanging in a row—you let the first
one go and it clangs against the second, which hits
the third; it sets up a chain reaction, each ball striking
the next, back and forth. That's what this is like. I think
it's scary."

"I hardly had to do anything at all. It just needed a
push to get things going. A few well-placed phone calls,
a little money, that's all."

"You're not listening."

"Sure I am. It's no chain reaction. I started it and I can stop it any time they're ready to settle. There must be hundreds of city agencies; I'm just scratching the surface."

"Does it feel good?"

"It's good to be busy."

"That's not what I meant and you know it. You're high on it. That phone hasn't stopped ringing all morning. People calling about schedules, meetings, interviews."

"I don't give interviews. Once you start, you've no privacy left."

"You know, Bertie, the only time I really like you a lot is when we're eating or when we're fucking." Brenda leaned way across the table and drew her brush down the length of the top clipping. It left a broad rust-colored streak.

"I'm going out."

"Sure." She looked down at her fingernails with intense concentration.

I knew exactly where I was going. I called from a booth on Thirty-second Street but they said she was "indisposed." Then I went to the apartment. An unfamiliar maid in a shrimp-colored uniform opened the door. Across the gallery I could see Gina framed by the open living-room doors. She was sitting at an octagonal burled-walnut table, holding a hand of cards. Opposite Gina sat a young gray-suited guard. He too held cards. Between them lay a pile of change, some bills, and the remainder of the deck in two piles—one face up, one face down.

The maid asked my name, but I ignored her and walked into the living room. Gina looked up and said, "Oh hi, Bertie. Want to sit in? I warn you though, I'm down twenty already."

The guard placed his index finger under one eye and pulled downward. His skin was the color of old newspaper. "Today. Yesterday she won four times that."

"I don't want to sit in," I said. "I want to see you."

"You see me."

"In private."

Gina glanced across the table. "I've got no secrets."

I put my hand on her arm. "Come with me. It'll only take a minute."

Gina stared at my hand. "All right." She pushed the stack of coins and bills across the table to the young man. It was then that I noticed scratches and gouges in the highly polished surface of the table and round black scars where cigarettes had been ground out.

"You sure?" the man asked.

"It's fine."

I steered Gina down the hall to the Impressionist Room. I seated myself on the far side of the desk, next to the telephone. Directly opposite me, turned so that it faced the wall, was a high-backed Régence chair. A series of crude concentric circles had been drawn on the beige damask with a black Magic Marker. One dart impaled the smallest circle—bull's-eye. White stuffing oozed from several wounds. Gina followed my eyes. "That one's mine. O.K., Bertie, what is this?"

"Get me the phone book." Gina opened a drawer on her side of the desk, lifted out a thick red book, and pushed it across to me.

"Not the classified. Regular."

Gina pointed at the drawer. "Get it yourself."

I walked around the desk, pulled out the correct book, looked up the number, dialed, and asked, "May I speak to the person in charge? This is Bertram Ogden Royceman speaking."

Gina wrinkled her forehead. I smiled at her across the desk. "You're home free." I spoke into the mouthpiece: "I'm calling to inform you that I'm sitting here with Mrs. Bertram Royceman. Perhaps you are unaware that Mrs. Royceman is the sole owner of the premises which she now occupies. I want you to know that if your men are not out of here in the next hour, we will be forced to call the police and have them removed. I have checked and this is well within our legal rights. Your men are here unlawfully, without consent. Mrs. Royceman will confirm what I have just said. You've got exactly sixty minutes."

I put my hand over the phone. "Just say *out*." I handed the instrument to Gina.

"This is Mrs. Royceman," she said in a clear, level voice. "I didn't realize what my stepson had in mind. Please ignore this call. He's right, I do own this place, and I'm quite satisfied with the arrangement. Thank you."

Gina hung up. She glared at me across the desk. "Why didn't you tell me what you were going to do?"

"What are you talking about? You asked me."

"You think you can come in here, pushing me around and telling me what to say." Gina gestured, a sharp upward jerk of her thumb. "And get out of that chair. It's not yours."

"You asked me!"

"That was a long time ago. If you were going to do it, you should have done it then. They're my friends now—my only friends. You know how long it took me to drop all those stiff, uptight phonies your father called friends? About two minutes. I don't have to be with those Tinkertoys any more. I can be with real people. I'm on my own and I've got my own and I'm going to be with people who have a little blood in them."

"I did what you begged me to do. I thought about you and this was the perfect solution. God damn it, I don't know what you think you're doing."

"What I want to do, not what you want me to do. Boy, big boss, do you ever remind me of someone. You want to do me a favor? O.K., do me one." Gina walked to the door and opened it. "Just get the hell out of here."

Brenda's wild hair was pulled back in a tight knot. Something else was different too. "How do I look?" she asked.

"Like a white rabbit."

"That's my eye shadow. It's called Lotus Pink."

"You don't look like you."

"I'm a restless, exotic creature with pink eyes." Brenda moved toward me with an exaggerated undulating motion of her hips. "I was bored so I played Make-up. Now that you're back we can play Doctor. Come here like a good little patient. Let's see what we can do for your poor dick. Caught in the zipper, eh? Just let this old doctor examine it." She extended her hand.

"Not now. I'm not in the mood."

"Me neither," snapped Brenda and withdrew her hand. "You certainly were gone long enough. All of Saturday shot."

I flopped down on the bed. "I went to see my step-mother. In true fairy-tale tradition she threw me out."

"What'd you do?"

"Not much. Fucked up. Hey, I'm sorry about this morning."

"Me too."

"Try to understand, I can't just let things happen any more, I want to work them out."

"You put a penny in the gum machine and you get a stick of gum?"

"That's right."

"Sure. Things are simple. People aren't. You can't tell with people."

Brenda lay on the bed next to me—near, but not touching. "You know what? I wish we lived in a tiny town in Spain where the sun baked the streets until they shattered. You'd tell them to keep all that money, that you didn't want it."

"How'd we live?"

"I'd be a hooker, solamente un poco. We'd have a whitewashed adobe house and at night we'd sit in front of a blazing fire."

"Your plans are hot, I'll say that."

"Stop interrupting. This is my fantasy. We'd sit there and read e. e. cummings aloud to each other, 'the sweet small clumsy feet of April came into the ragged meadow of my soul.' "

" 'And death i think is no parenthesis.' I'd like that."

"No, you wouldn't. Neither would I." Brenda looked up at the ceiling. "I'd better take down those Christmas decorations. There's nothing as bedraggled as tarnished tinsel. Did you ever wonder what happened to all those people who seemed so sure of where they were going? I had a teacher in a course in Shakespeare who told me, 'Brenda, you have a mind like a bright little goldfish. You flash around the bowl settling on nothing.' She was right, but what's left to settle on? I heard about this groovy plastic surgeon, Tom Rees. A lot of the time he sits around listening to some of his patients complain that he didn't take enough slack out of their chins or make their eyes wide open enough or remove enough flesh from their breasts. But one month a year —one month—he flies off to the African bush and operates there. It's part of a volunteer organization called the Flying Doctor Service. He saved a man who'd been gored by a rhinoceros. The man had waited a week for Rees to arrive, his intestines hanging out of his abdomen, tied with a piece of rope. Rees saved a baby who'd been bitten by a snake and developed gangrene of the skull. He cut off the whole top of his head. And others, a lot of others. I guess that's what keeps him straight: that one month of something worth doing.

"I've always loved St. Theresa, she's my favorite saint. I saw her finger in a glass case on a student tour in Spain. She's the one who was sleeping when an angel appeared and thrust a golden arrow into her heart. From that moment on she found a purpose in life. Bernini did that famous statue of her. In Rome. I'm sure you've seen it. She looks exactly like she's experiencing an orgasm. Theresa was meant to do big things and she did them. Reformed the whole religion, saved the children. If that angel came today, I wonder what poor Theresa could do. Nineteen seventy-three is definitely not a vintage year for saints."

21

SECRET ROYCEMAN AGREEMENT REVEALED

. . . The secret agreement revealed yesterday between the Urban Museum of Art and the executors of the Royceman estate came as a result of discovery proceedings in connection with the public interest lawsuit filed January 2 by two civic organizations. The agreement, a twenty-seven-page contract, stipulates that the gift of the Royceman Collection is contingent upon the fulfillment of stringent demands concerning both the design and location of the proposed Royceman Wing.

Clearly, this is a conditional gift, the first conditional gift the Urban has accepted in over half a century. (One might ask if it is a gift at all.) It would seem unwise on several counts. Why take priceless and fast-vanishing park land for this project? The Central Park Mall has never been violated by any structure. If it is now the victim of museum expansion, it will certainly set a precedent for further such acts.

Although the agreement specifies that construction costs, as well as substantial items of maintenance, will be paid for by the Royceman estate, the City is not a party to this agreement, and it could be changed at any time for any reason. . . .

Another contractual demand is that the collection be kept in solido *in perpetuity. Therefore, although the collection duplicates periods and artists already owned by the Urban Museum, these works can never be integrated into their proper departments. One cannot help but remember with pleasure that when the famous Havemeyer Collection was donated to the Metropolitan Museum of Art, it enriched virtually every department of that institution. If the Royceman estate wants this collection to remain together, why not locate it somewhere else? Royceman House, on East Fifty-second Street, has served as a museum—why not house the collection there? . . .*

It is indeed inappropriate at a time when museums should be increasingly interested in defining the relevance between the world of art and the problems of our age that millions are still being squandered on crystal palaces. At present, however, only this pending lawsuit, and one concerning the claims of Bertram Ogden Royceman, hold the bulldozers at bay.

Excerpts from an essay by Clarence Carton,
Op Ed page, *The New York Times,* February 15, 1973

A Bertram Royceman theorem: "When a man calls and says he must see you about something *important,* it's your job to figure out who it's important to." Hayes called. I figured it was important to me.

Sunday at nine-thirty: Hayes sitting in the pale morning sunlight on the main steps of the Urban. He saw me and shouted, "Over here." Together we walked through the Great Entrance Gallery, our footsteps echoing in the vaulted spaces. "Let's look at some Impressionists while we chat," said Hayes and bounded up the white-marble steps. We entered a gallery and he switched on the lights. Genre scenes in gilt frames glowed from the walls. "Your father helped us acquire many of these paintings. The ones he picked are the best we have. Can you guess which they are?"

"No."

"Try to pick your favorites. The ones that just say, 'I'm superb, great, stupendous.' Rely on your gut reaction."

"They're just so much wallpaper to me."

Hayes continued as if he had not heard me, "Your father selected the Cézanne, 'The Man with the Bowler

Hat,' Monet's 'The White Wave,' and my own favorite, the Degas, 'Woman with Roses.' That's something else again. Really terrific." He walked to a spot in front of the painting. "Just look at it, keep looking at it, absorb its nature, forget the label, forget it's a Degas, and try to see what that woman is thinking as she places the red roses in the vase. Concentrate."

"What's the point of all this?"

Hayes turned his eyes from the painting to me. They looked opaque, muddy brown. "I want to tell you something of what I know. I want to involve you in the workings of this museum. I feel you have been somewhat neglected by your father's estate, but I realize that you are the *future* and I want us to have a close and friendly relationship."

"And that's why you're giving me an art lesson." I spoke very slowly.

"In a way. This is a collecting institution. I want the objects we acquire to be the best in the world. Not the most, but the best. Did you know that last year we acquired a Rembrandt for two million three hundred thousand dollars? We did, and not because it was expensive but because it was great. It put our six other Rembrandts to shame and it formed the nucleus around which all the others could gather.

"You see, price is no object. There's not a trustee of this institution who couldn't write a check for three million dollars if the object were right. Your father helped me understand the importance of quality. He had an unfailing eye. I'd like to pass that education on to you.

"I took the liberty of calling Jacob Weisman to ask him if you knew the full repercussions of what you are doing. I will be frank and tell you that he said you had no love or appreciation for art and did not care about your father's higher purpose. I choose not to accept that. I choose to inform you of what we are doing, to set things right. I hate to see you being manipulated by charlatans."

Now we're getting to it, I thought.

"I think it was very unwise of Harold Linsky to introduce you to Michael O'Keefe. I know Linsky was responsible for that." Hayes sniffed the air as if smelling something rank. "O'Keefe and his Art Workers! Those people protest because they lack the talent to belong. They are talentless ingrates who express themselves by mocking the work of their betters. Not one person in that group has produced a work of art worthy of display in the most modest institution."

"Which this certainly is not."

"Are you being funny?"

"Obviously not very."

"If this is a joke—then the joke's on us. In the past, our method of dealing with these people was simply to go ahead and do what we knew was right for them—in this case, to begin construction. There is nothing like a fait accompli to drive away petty gripers. You can't sit in front of a bulldozer very long. And later, say five years later, does anyone remember the controversy? No, they only remember that we gave them something absolutely marvelous. Only we can't do that; your suit prevents us from going ahead, and it gives all the malcontents in this city time to mass their forces against us. This silly public interest suit is a perfect example. Those organizations haven't got a leg to stand on; our charter and rights are clear. And to attack us for secrecy—that's simply a political tactic. *Secrecy* is a public-relations term they've invented. We've always had private arrangements. We'll dispose of this suit soon, in time. All right, the simple truth is that it's your suit I'm worried about. We must begin construction, we're working under a deadline. Whatever your point was, you've proved it. Stop now, unless you wish the complete destruction of your father's wing."

"That's not what I want."

"Maybe not, but that's what's happening. You've opened a Pandora's box by encouraging protest against us. You've unleashed a monstrous force. We can have all the legal rights in the world, settle every lawsuit including yours, but if we don't move like quicksilver there may never be a Royceman Wing. We could be denied a building permit. Oh yes, that's the way public pressure works in this city. Concerned citizens going down to hearings and making all sorts of points, and the City Council simply says, 'The people don't want that and we're not going to do it.' That's happened time and time again: Forest Hills housing, the police stables in the park, the excellent first plan for the Ruppert Brewery, thousands of things. All the legal rights in the world, but if there are enough people against us, they can raise so much fuss that we'll be refused a building permit. No permit—no Royceman Wing. That's the bottom line."

"What do you want me to do?"

"Drop your suit, I implore you. Call off the Art Workers. We must start construction immediately or your father's collection will go to the National Gallery. He wouldn't have wanted that. It cannot be allowed."

Hayes was getting to me. "He did want it here," I said.

"We both know that."

What Hayes said next turned me off, fast. "I told Jacob Weisman that I could explain the whole thing to you. After you drop your suit and call off the protest, I'm sure he'll give you what you want. In fact, I can personally guarantee it."

"After?"

"You can't expect him to settle while you're still pressing suit."

"He can always get in touch with me. I'm in no hurry."

"No hurry? There's no time! I simply cannot lose that collection. It would be the greatest disgrace of my career. I have made my life here at the Urban. I want history to say that Bartholomew Hayes built the Urban into the greatest museum in the history of the world. I have dedicated myself to that ideal."

"Sorry, that's your ego trip, not mine."

"What does that mean?"

"I have to do what I have to do, that's all."

"Weisman tells me that by suing your father's estate you have lost everything. You must settle right away. If you continue to pursue this reckless course you'll be defeated, and what's more, you'll have no place as a patron of art in the future."

Me—a five-foot six-inch dropout—*patron of art*. I started to smile and then I could feel the laughter foaming out of me. Hayes regarded me icily, abruptly raised his hand, then, very deliberately, patted his hair. "That's it," he said in a choked voice, turned, and walked out of the gallery. I found my own way out.

"I thought he was going to hit me, but then he just patted his hair," I said.

"Marvelous," said O'Keefe. "Quite a victory, don't you agree, Harold?"

Linsky was slumped in a commodious armchair. His pallid face appeared pinched and distressed. "Great for you, but Hayes has *me* by the balls and he's squeezing hard. Yesterday he announced that he intends to trade a brilliant Jackson Pollock, a Franz Kline, and the best Willem de Kooning from my department for a Monet. These three paintings were part of the Crystal LaSalle bequest. Hayes did some job on her, Bertie. She was an ex-stripper—widow of a shipping tycoon. Hayes squired her around town and had lunch with the girl every Sunday. God, how he used to complain about those big turkey lunches in the middle of the day. Three years ago she left her entire collection to the Urban as an unconditional bequest. This year alone Hayes has sold seventy-three of her paintings. Luckily, your father was smart enough to protect himself from that fate. 'This Monet is absolutely seminal,' Hayes informed me. We have twenty Monets already and your father left us twelve more, but that doesn't matter to Hayes. He doesn't care about the Monet, he just wants to get at me by selling the best art in my department. And I can't stop him, he doesn't need my approval to sell or trade." Linsky's voice sounded thin. "What's even more humiliating is that we're being cheated blind by the gallery owner, who can probably sell the Pollock alone for what the Monet is worth. Hayes is trying to make it so impossible for me that I'll resign."

"Maybe he'll fire you and I'll have to support you," said Michael blandly.

"You don't give a damn about me. You don't care if I'm fired, as long as you're taken care of."

"Now, now, Harold, courage in the face of disaster and all that. If he was going to fire you, he would have done it by now."

"I think he's afraid of my friends and of what I know."

"Like what?" I asked.

"Like Max Dubrov. That could blow the lid off the Urban. Dubrov's our unofficial tax expert. Unofficial, because his suggestions are crooked. Last month we got rid of a painting worth three quarters of a million dollars. Dubrov arranged to sell it for three hundred thousand. The person who bought the painting also contributed seven hundred thousand from his charitable foundation to the Urban. That way we got a million dollars, the donor got a great bargain, and no one suffered."

"Except the people. Except us poor taxpayers," interrupted O'Keefe.

"True enough, Michael. It was ever thus. Dubrov's got a bag full of tricks. Let's say someone gives us a painting. In order to qualify for tax deduction, the painting must come immediately to the museum. But it's also quite all right if we write a letter begging the collector to keep the painting on his premises until we have room for it, which could conveniently be years later, or even upon his death. Then there's the time our trustee Rodley Clarke gave us a tiny Rembrandt, which we valued at a million four. Some whopping tax deduction there all right. Of course, the curator who insisted that it was a Nicolaes Maes, worth about a hundred and fifty thousand, was promptly fired."

"It's disgusting," said O'Keefe. "No one cares about art."

"My father did," I said without thinking.

"What?" asked O'Keefe.

"Care."

"Maybe," said O'Keefe, "but your father had a big fat contract with the Urban about the care and feeding of his collection. That's business, not art."

"My father's lawyer did that. My father really thought he was carrying on a tradition started by my grandfather. He didn't just buy art. He was a scholar, and after he made my grandfather's house into a museum, he'd go down there at night and just sit and examine his collection. Sometimes I'd go with him and I'd watch him sitting there looking at his objects with an expression of fierce intensity. Once I asked him, 'How can you just sit there like that?' And he answered, 'It's the best way to feel. I wish you could feel it.' "

"Bullshit," O'Keefe cut in, "you're romanticizing and sentimentalizing because he was your pater familias— pater unfamilias, I'd say, by the way you describe him."

"Bertie's right," interrupted Linsky. "That's the way I feel too. It sounds corny, but Bertie's father understood that art is beauty and agony expressing itself in an object. You don't understand that, Michael. You don't want to produce objects. You want to protest the bureaucracy that has grown up around objects, the parasites who deal and display and criticize. But if you manage to destroy the existing system, you'll also destroy the art. You'll throw the baby out with the bathwater, but you'll offer no replacement."

O'Keefe jumped to his feet. "You shit! If that's the way you feel, why are you with me?"

Linsky's answer was barely audible. "I'm fond of you." His voice grew firmer. "That doesn't mean I agree with you. I hate these protests, they're meaningless. This time it's my job if it gets out of hand."

"Don't worry."

"That's what you said before you destroyed the book shop at the Modern and before that terrible bloodbath."

"Terrible? It was funny. Get this, Bertie. Booth and I sauntered into the Modern one Sunday afternoon and he pretended to stab me in the chest. I had these plastic bags of pigs' blood under my coat and I broke them and writhed around on the floor. This big crowd gathered and one lady actually fainted, right then and there. Harold, you've no sense of humor."

"And New Haven?"

"What about it?"

"You just happened to be there at seven that particular evening and you just happened to have your camera with you and you just happened to take photographs of that art school at the exact second it was blown up."

"That's right. It was a coincidence. I keep telling you."

"Michael, promise me that this will be peaceful. I want you to promise. This time it's my museum and it's important to me."

"You've got that job for life."

"I'm not just worried about my job. Promise."

"Why not."

Clearly Harold was on the losing side. "I'm sure it will be all right," I said, trying to be conciliatory. "We do have a precise plan, you know."

Linsky looked at me questioningly. "I find it ironic, Bertie, that you, whose family has always stood for the elitist view, are sponsoring the Royceman Transfer."

"It is not ironic," said O'Keefe, looking menacingly at Linsky. "It's the right place for him to be."

"I disagree. With everything that's wrong, the Urban is still the place to be. It's an important place, and Hayes won't last forever. He thinks he can get away with giving people bread and circuses. He can't. They're beginning to care, to ask questions. I want to be there for the answers."

O'Keefe glanced from Linsky to me. "Don't let Harold smother you with his sob story, he's feeling sorry for himself today."

"You are not generous," said Linsky.

"You bore me."

"And you abuse me."

"Come on, let's drop the subject. What we need is a change of pace—exercise, fresh air, a free ride. Tonight we're going down to Royceman Brothers to pick up a load of stuff. It's piling up; in another month we'll have plenty—enough. Only we shouldn't set an exact day and time till the last minute. That way no one can interfere. Come tonight, Bertie. It'll be fun."

22

THE ROYCEMAN COLLECTION
MUST BE SEEN TO BE APPRECIATED

*The recent controversy over the donation of the
Royceman Collection to the Urban Museum of Art is
noteworthy in that the media has reported at length on
issues concerning this gift, including park encroach-
ment, decentralization, landmark destruction, mall
relocation—issues which, unless quickly resolved, will
cause the collection to be whisked away to the National Gallery in Washington. Only one issue has been
ignored, the fact that this is perhaps the greatest
private art collection ever donated to a public
institution. . . .*

*In the debate about the Royceman Collection we
forget that the collecting of art works in this country
has depended largely upon the initiative and enter-
prise of private individuals. Great tycoon collectors—
Morgan, Freer, Mellon, Kress—virtually overnight acquired an art heritage for our country. When their
collections became accessible to the public, the people
were vastly enriched educationally and aesthetically. . . .*

*Once the public sees the Royceman Collection it
cannot help but be grateful for the munificence of this
gift. It is my opinion that the controversy concerning
the collection will cease as soon as the public has
access to it.*

Excerpts from an article by Sophie Kleeger,
Art Affairs Journal, February 1973

I've read about people returning to places years later to find that they seem smaller (that's the most frequent observation) or altered in any number of ways. That sure isn't true for me. I was standing in front of Royceman Brothers, after almost a twelve-year absence, and it wasn't any different. Not in how it looked. Not in how it felt.

Surrounded by the faceless anonymity of glass skyscrapers, Royceman Brothers is an anachronism, a mole-gray granite structure, eighty feet wide, that resembles a sand castle, complete with rough-hewn turrets that seem to be stuck, slightly askew, to the sides of the sixth floor. My grandfather's luxurious office occupied this floor. When he died, my father turned Grandpa Paul's office into a conference room, electing to stay put in the office he was assigned on his first day at Royceman Brothers, an extremely small rectangle located on the third floor. I could tell you the color of the rug and how many bookcases he had, but I've recently come to understand that I rely on my ample store of this kind of gratuitous memorabilia because it's easy to deal with and it keeps me from remembering what it was really like inside that fortress.

My first day: In the cramped elevator I stood behind two men, dressed alike in gray pants, striped cord jackets, and gray-felt hats. They were quite young and those hats with grosgrain ribbon bands seemed an odd tribalistic touch . . .

"The old man's son is coming down this summer. Royceman called a meeting to request no special privileges."

"Clean that spittoon, young man, we have to break you in right."

"I told you, I want my coffee black, this has cream in it. You're fired, Royceman!"

"Collect your twenty million from the cashier and leave by the back door."

The doors opened and they stepped out, laughing.

I didn't just hate it, and I wasn't just inept. There was something more that I can't articulate. Tonight, even after all these years, when the dump truck stopped for a light in front of Reis University I felt again exactly what I had felt then. It had been a scorching 93 degrees that summer day. I walked up Broad, bought a book, and sat on a bench in a grassy square opposite Park Place, intending to read. It was too hot, the sun too bright. Across the square I spotted a building: Reis University, it said over the door. It appeared brand-new, its poured-concrete façade flawless. Kids my age were sitting on the front steps and around a reflecting pool which held a Henry Moore sculpture. It looked like a good place to be. I walked across the street, strolled around, climbed the steps, and opened the heavy glass door. A blast of cold air welcomed me. I found myself alone in a vast, vacant, rectangular area where both walls and floor were composed of slabs of travertine marble. On the wall to my left was a shining brushed-steel bank of elevators, to my right a billboard-size bronze medallion on which was emblazoned the two-dimensional face of a man. It took me a few seconds and then it hit me—it was my father's face. Above the medallion were the words BERTRAM ROYCEMAN SCHOOL OF FINANCE. I stood staring at that wall. How many places had my father endowed, occupied, owned, into which I would blunder inadvertently?

Royceman Brothers and, in fact, this whole section of New York had been imbued with the enormity of my father's presence. Now, looking up at the dark windows of Royceman Brothers, it was imbued with the enormity of his absence.

The evening had not started well. Brenda hadn't wanted to go, but I'd insisted. When we arrived at the Thirty-ninth Street Garage, O'Keefe was waiting in the driver's seat of a rented dump truck, Linsky by his side. Brenda and I crowded into the cab with them. In the open back of the truck, Amos Barth sat on a slatted wood bench. He was a small saturnine man with wiry gray hair. I remembered him from the Workers meetings. O'Keefe turned onto the East River Drive at Thirty-fourth Street. "No trucks allowed on the drive," Linsky informed him.

"You're right," agreed O'Keefe.

"Get off at the next exit."

"Can you smell the sea? Get a whiff of that air, isn't it something?"

"Michael, I said turn off."

"When I'm ready. At the Brooklyn Bridge exit. Just take it easy." O'Keefe reached into his pocket, removed a joint, lit it, and extended it to Harold. "Here, calm down."

I felt sympathy for Harold, and wondered how long he and O'Keefe would remain together. Brenda and I stood close to him on the pavement in front of Royceman Brothers as if our physical proximity might somehow demonstrate our friendship.

"Is anybody there?" Brenda asked, severing the thread of my thoughts.

"I'm here."

"In body only. Look, there's Booth." She waved.

Peter Booth stood below us at the bottom of a small flight of black metal stairs. "Come and get it," he chanted.

Amos Barth began moving down the steps. O'Keefe waited above, leaning against the iron railing, dragging openly on a joint. He was clearly illuminated by the streetlight. Linsky shook his hand rapidly back and forth, signaling to O'Keefe to move out of the circle of light. Michael O'Keefe bowed extravagantly from the waist but did not move.

Brenda placed her hand softly on Harold's shoulder. "You know that saying, 'I don't know why he hates me —I never tried to do him a favor.' That's your friend, Michael." In reply, Linsky managed a weak smile.

O'Keefe finished smoking, flipped the tiny butt over the railing, and joined Booth and Barth at the bottom of the stairs. The three began a circular route—inside, up the stairs, carrying gray plastic containers, dumping the contents into the open back of the truck, then back down the stairs for another load. "Can I help?" inquired Linsky.

O'Keefe stopped in front of him. "Not dressed in that jacket, it's brand-new. I told you to wear old clothes."

"You never mentioned it."

"You don't listen."

"You didn't tell me, either," I said.

"For Christ's fucking sake, we don't want help anyway."

"Let them do it," interjected Brenda with annoyance.

The round-robin procession resumed. We watched for about fifteen minutes as the truck gradually filled with refuse. "Up here, up here." O'Keefe climbed into the truck and stood with his legs wide apart, implanted in the debris. Barth handed up a gray-ribbed container; O'Keefe grabbed it and swung it in a pendulum motion, spilling out garbage. "More, more." Booth gave O'Keefe a container which he inverted. "I'm Colossus of Rhodes," he yelled exuberantly, as refuse poured from the container.

Barth carried up a final container, followed by Booth, who was empty-handed. The truck was now about half full, most of the trash piled near the open rear gate. Both men climbed over this obstacle and with their hands began moving the debris backward to distribute the load more evenly. O'Keefe helped them; then, slapping his palms together, dived to the floor of the truck and began rotating his arms, imitating a swimmer. "Come on in, the weather's fine," he called as ticker tape, newspaper, and coffee containers spurted around his windmilling arms. O'Keefe began rolling on the floor of the truck, laughing in short full bursts. Finally he stood, yelling to us, "Come on up, Harold. Come on, Bertie, Brenda. It's a trip and a half."

Linsky carefully removed his jacket, hung it over the railing, and walked to the back of the truck. O'Keefe reached down and pulled him up. Linsky gingerly began to redistribute the trash. Bending from the waist, he picked up small handfuls of material and tossed them toward the cab of the truck. Barth reached down and tossed trash at Michael O'Keefe. Peter Booth also began throwing paper and debris at him. Giant confetti swirled around the four figures in the truck. O'Keefe was yelping joyously as he began to pitch paper indiscriminately. Before long everyone was shouting with a high-pitched joy I remember from winter snow fights. O'Keefe scooped up a large armload of trash and dumped it over Linsky, who laughed and brushed at his shirt. O'Keefe watched him, then stooped and discharged a second salvo at him. The others pivoted and began following O'Keefe's example. As the shower of paper fell on Linsky, he kept making small brushing gestures with his hand. Then he shook himself like a wet dog and started to retreat toward the open end of the truck. O'Keefe blocked his way. Linsky tried to duck past, but O'Keefe put both palms on Linsky's chest and shoved hard. Linsky spun around, tripped, and sprawled facedown in the trash.

It turned ugly. Linsky tried to rise, but Amos Barth knocked him down once more. Then he pushed him deeper into the debris with his foot. Booth dropped a load of paper on Linsky. O'Keefe kneeled and began heaping loose material over him. There were wild bursts of laughter as the other two men fell to their knees and began helping O'Keefe bury Linsky in refuse the way you bury a body in sand at the beach. Linsky was struggling and kicking in panic. Whenever he tried to get up, O'Keefe would push his head down sharply. Linsky was still kicking. Barth stood up and stamped savagely on his back. That's when Brenda and I started moving. We scrambled up into the truck. Harold's body was covered with garbage, and O'Keefe held his head, so that only the smallest patch of black hair was visible. I dived for O'Keefe's hands and pulled one free. Next to me, Brenda kicked his other arm, dislodging it. Abruptly Linsky sat up. He began making sharp inhaling noises—halfway between gasps and sobs. Everything stopped. I saw a look of guilt and consternation on Booth's face, but O'Keefe and Barth were both grinning. Brenda kneeled next to Linsky and started brushing at his shoulders and shirt. His gasps subsided. I helped him to his feet and out of the truck. As we began to walk away, I felt Linsky shaking uncontrollably. I supported him on one side and Brenda held his elbow on the other. O'Keefe yelled after us, "Hey, don't go. Hey, Bertie, it was a game. Bertie, don't you get it? It was only a game. Hey!"

Brenda and I moved in our separate atmospheres. That sudden flare of violence seemed unreal to me. I tried to screen it out. Brenda, on the other hand, seemed furious, banging things around, impatiently whacking at her hair, punishing it with her hairbrush. Now she was stretched out on the bed, ignoring me completely, which was disconcerting. She held a small mirror in front of her face, in her right hand an eyebrow tweezer. I saw the tweezer flash as she began plucking viciously at her eyebrows. I sat on the end of the bed and spoke gently, "I'm sorry it was such a mess."

"I'm glad—it's what you deserve. Maybe now you'll see. Get out fast, Bertie."

"Soon as they settle."

"Oh God, that again. Don't you see how terrible it was?"

"O.K., it was vicious, but it was a lover's quarrel. Something between O'Keefe and Linsky. Don't make more of it."

Brenda sat up, abruptly slamming the tweezer down on the table. "You think that was a one shot? No chance. The protest is going to be O'Keefe's way of getting exactly what he wants—Publicity with a capital P. See me. See me."

"Actually, it's getting me what I want, not O'Keefe."

"Don't you believe it."

"I'm forcing Hayes and Weisman to settle. I'm in control."

"Like hell you are. Don't you understand, even now? Everyone out there is doing his own thing—your plastic brother-in-law and O'Keefe and the Art Workers—all of them."

"But it's what I want."

"I know the Art Workers. What we saw was a warm-up for next month. It's going to be awful, believe me."

"It's my plan."

"It's a roller coaster. Hang on for the thrills and spills."

"I'm driving."

"How can you think that?"

"I know. I've got them where I want them. Ned says they can't hold out much longer."

"And he hasn't been right about anything."

"I can tell, they're ready to settle."

"And if they don't?"

"They will. Hayes is panicked that there won't be a Royceman Wing."

"And you? Why aren't you worried? Maybe Hayes is right. Maybe you've done your job too well. Maybe even if they settle with you, people will keep on protesting. The arrogance of you: you're so self-important you think people are puppets you can manipulate at will. Who the hell taught you that? And, Bertie, did you ever stop to ask yourself if this is what your father wanted? Or do you want to get back at him too?"

"He wanted his collection at the Urban. It'll be there."

"And the rest—grabbing off people's land, excluding them?"

"I don't think that occurred to him."

"Well, it can't occur to him now, can it? But you're alive and you should think about it. All you're thinking about is showing how powerful you are with this stupid protest."

"I have to show them, Brenda. My father had a theorem: 'Own 51 percent. Then let them scream.'"

"Your father was a cripple. There's a whole world out there, Bertie, who never heard of him or his stupid theorems. A whole world who couldn't care less about that cripple." Brenda stood up and began walking rapidly in the direction of the bathroom. "You're a fool, Bertie, a first-class freak. Try anything. I'm not going to hang around for the Götterdämmerung." The bathroom door slammed behind her. I heard the bolt slide into place.

I sat in a chair reading. (Well, looking at the newspaper and trying or pretending to concentrate.) Exactly ten minutes later Brenda came out of the bathroom. Her face was powdery white, as if she'd dusted it with flour. She picked up her purse from the floor, walked to the oak dresser, opened the top drawer, and began dropping the contents into her bag. That finished, she carefully selected three strings of beads from the ones that hung on the corner post. She put them on, studying herself in the mirror. (I saw all this while appearing to be totally absorbed in the newspaper.) Next Brenda selected a cassette from the stack on the top of the dresser, inserted it, and pressed a button. Dylan's voice began to flow out into the room as she walked to the door, opened it, and left. We had not exchanged a word.

I sat immobile, but when the tape got to "Blue moon, I saw you standing alone, without a . . ." I got up and turned off the machine. It's not that I dislike Bob Dylan—for God's sake, he's a major talent and may emerge as the greatest poet of our century. He captures the mood of our times in a way that . . . What the fuck! The truth is that when Bob Dylan sings a corny old song like "Blue Moon" it can make you feel rotten. Correction: make *me* feel rotten.

23

. . . At the annual meeting of the Parks Protection Association, Chairman Walter Johnson stated his position in regard to the proposed Royceman Wing. He said, "It seems ironic that the Urban should pursue a course of action that will destroy precious open space at precisely the time when an unprecedented interest in natural environment is sweeping the country, at precisely the time when there is an increasing awareness that an institution on public land which receives public funds can no longer remain the private preserve of the super rich. . . .

"In 1972 the Urban Museum of Art received 4.2 million dollars in city, state, and federal government support for maintenance, guards, and insurance. This is taxpayers' money—the people's money—yet the people are not being consulted in the acceptance of this secret 'gift.' Only our lawsuit compelled disclosure of a secret contract with the Royceman estate which contains deleterious ramifications for the public at large.

"There is a similarity between the high-handed actions of the Urban and those of the United States government, where decisions affecting the lives and welfare of the people are being made in secret. Citizens feel their voice cannot be heard or is being ignored by the powerful men at the top. Their voice, however, is growing in volume. Many responsible organizations are joining with us in our protest of the proposed Royceman Wing."

Excerpts from the *New York Post,* March 12, 1973

Dark-blue velvet banquettes around the perimeter of the square room, dark paneling enveloping the ceiling and walls, the magnified babble of voices and clatter of silverware all contributed to my intense discomfort. It was like dining inside a jewelry box.

Held sat alone, sipping a drink. "I was afraid you'd bring that girl."

"She couldn't make it."

"Odd girl. Drink?"

"Not now."

"Tammy should be here any minute. She's at some sort of a charity-do."

"And Ellen?"

"Ellen?" Held shrugged. "Ellen's always late."

"In a way I'm glad they're not here yet," I said. "I want to ask some questions."

"Shoot."

"I can't understand why they haven't called to settle. Hayes was ready, I could tell. It's March and that leaves only thirteen months to get that building up."

"That's right. We're sitting in the catbird seat."

"So why haven't they called?"

"They will."

"I'm going to call Weisman."

"No you're not. I mean, I wouldn't do that. If you do, it'll show weakness." Held signaled the waiter and pointed to his empty glass. The waiter arrived with miraculous speed, carrying a fresh drink. "Calling, dear boy, would be just the thing they're waiting for."

"I want to settle it now, to call off the Art Workers."

"It's too late for that. After—they'll give in."

"I'm not going to wait."

"Look, Bertie, this is a social occasion. I didn't invite you here to discuss business. I can't talk about it now."

"Why not?"

"I'm not concentrating."

"Concentrate."

"My advice is to wait. Good things will happen."

"I'm not just sitting around. You call or I will. I mean it."

"I'm well aware you mean it. Tell me, exactly when is the Art Workers protest?"

"Wednesday—day after tomorrow—at three-thirty, but they're not telling anyone. It's supposed to be a surprise."

"I'll keep it secret, but I do want to see it. Tell you what—come to my office about an hour before it starts. Even though it's against my better judgment, I'll call Weisman. We'll talk about it and walk up together."

"You could contact Weisman tomorrow. Then I'd have time to call it off."

"You can't; it's our final gesture. If you don't do it, it will appear that we're throwing in the sponge just when we're about to win the fight."

"I wish it were over."

"It will be soon." Held waved his hand. Ellen was standing in the doorway. She acknowledged the gesture with a nod and began moving toward our table. She sat next to me on the banquette. "Sorry I'm late."

"No matter. Would you like a drink?" inquired Held.

"What are you drinking?" she asked.

"A Bombay martini."

"Is that vodka or gin?"

"It is gin, dear girl," said Held. "Dry gin." There was forbearance in every syllable.

"What's in it? Why is it a Bombay martini and not just a martini?"

"Bombay is the *name* of the gin. My martini contains Bombay gin with a breath of vermouth."

"Oh, that's nice. I'll have a rye and soda," Ellen declared.

Held grimaced.

"Me too," I said.

Ellen kicked me softly under the table.

"How's my bookkeeper?" I asked.

"Fine."

"It's odd about your being a bookkeeper," interrupted Held. "I've never thought of bookkeeping as a profession."

"You mean a proper profession for a lady of substance?"

"Something like that."

"I believe one should do what they can do."

"I agree," I said. "I'm an expert in nothing, so that's what I do."

"That's not true," Ellen protested. "You do a lot of things."

"Like build model ships and clean the apartment?"

"You have to find something that interests you. You're smart and talented; you could do anything, Birdie." Ellen's voice sounded forceful.

"I just have to find myself, right?"

"Sure," chimed in Held. "That's right."

"Let's see, I'm almost thirty. When do you think I'll find myself, Ned? I'd better start looking right away." I picked up Ellen's purse, opened it, and peered inside. "Hey, are you there?" I asked. "I'm way down here, trapped under the keys," I answered in a tiny falsetto. "I think I've found myself," I announced solemnly to Ned.

"Kidding aside, Bertie, you should begin to think about the future. I agree with Ellen—you could do anything. All you need is a little self-discipline." He said this with lugubrious sincerity.

"I could even be a lawyer like you, right?"

"I believe you could."

I let him have it. "The trouble with you lawyers is that you spend your life masturbating while persuading yourselves that you really do have a function. Take me. I came to you with a relatively simple request and you said you'd help me. It seems you lawyers drafted a law that says you can't leave more than half your estate to charity. You lawyers also arranged that this law doesn't apply unless someone challenges it. Then you stipulated that in order to challenge it you must stand to benefit directly from such a challenge.

"Next, members of your esteemed profession devised a Straw Man to prevent just such a challenge. This is the way that jerk-off device works. If there's an excess gift to charity it goes to the Straw Man. The direct beneficiary can't challenge because he can't benefit. The Straw Man can't benefit either, because now no one is left who can challenge the will. So that's the end of it. Right?

"Wrong. It's the beginning. We, that is you and I, Ned, decide to knock over the Straw Man device. At least to fake it, so they'll settle fast. But my case is special because you legal fellows have invented an *in terrorem* provision that says if I object I lose everything. So I can't object. Right?

"Wrong. Ned Held, eminent lawyer, fixes that. If I object, my share of the estate goes to Tammy and Ellen. So you draw up an agreement where they'll give me back my share. No risk now. Right?

"Wrong. Because in spite of your assurance, they won't settle. So we wait to see how Judge DiFalco rules in a pending case. DiFalco rules the wrong way for us. The Straw Man stands. Why should they give me anything now? We're in trouble. Right?

"Wrong. Actually things begin to look pretty good. Guess what, it's not because of the legal measures you've taken but because O'Keefe and I have a loony idea. We decide to dump some garbage behind the Urban Museum and say I sponsored it. That gets people angry about my father's collection. I make them even madder by revealing a secret contract between the Urban and my father's estate. People hate secrets and criticism mounts. Suddenly we're doing fine, only I don't know what your legal crap has to do with it. We're doing fine for other reasons, and you and your fucking profession have built a structure so phony, complex, and incomprehensible that it astounds me. You've buried me under the pile of shit you so-called men of importance heap up to justify your existence, to lend a purpose to your nothingness."

"Christ, Bertie, you're shouting," said Held. He looked ashen.

Ellen began gently stroking my hand. "I don't understand what Birdie is saying, but I agree with him," she declared gravely.

I had to smile.

"What's funny?" It was Tammy standing beside the table.

"Not much," I replied.

"Ellen dear," said Tammy, "why don't you scoot over next to Ned so I can sit next to Bertie."

"I'm comfortable here."

"But it's not proper."

"I arranged it this way," I said.

"Oh, all right." Tammy sighed and slid in place next to Ned. She put the tips of her fingers to her lips and blew me a kiss. "Hello, all."

"How'd it go?" inquired Held.

"Beautiful. You should have seen those adorable children. It was for the B.C.F., that's the Battered Children's Foundation. It's the hottest ticket in town. Everybody wants to work for it, but we prefer to keep it small. Order me a vodka on the rocks, will you," she instructed, without so much as a glance at Ned. "We wanted to have a benefit, but all of us had already sold so many tickets this year, we decided that by spring no one would give us another penny. I got the idea that if each of the thirty members would contribute five hundred dollars, we could present a check for fifteen thousand to the organization."

"What kind of an organization is it?" asked Ellen.

"A wonderful one," replied Tammy. "We wanted to find a small charity that no one had heard of, not a big thing like Cystic Fibrosis where our contribution wouldn't have any impact at all. Our center provides medical care, recommends legal measures—that was Ned's idea—and specializes in counseling. The children come with their parents to our center and we have trained psychologists who see them free of charge."

"And it works?" asked Ellen.

"We don't have statistics on that," replied Tammy sharply. "Anyway, that's not my field of interest. The check presentation was my project. That's why I had to be there to the end. We did it at Rhinoceros, that new discotheque. I arranged to have ten of the children attend. Not the parents though, because I thought they might be, well, I don't know, rather unattractive? Helen Atwater presented the check to the most beautiful little girl. She was delicious."

"You ate her?" I inquired.

Tammy did not answer, but her fingers began to drum the table. Tonight they were bare except for one small ring composed of three plain gold bands. She saw me staring, slipped the ring off, and began rolling it between the thumb and index finger of her left hand. Then she said, "I don't think it's appropriate to wear a lot of jewelry to a charity benefit. You can't be too careful with the press around. Eugenia Sheppard was there, Suzy too. It was a great success. It provided good will for the B.C.F., maximum publicity for Rhinoceros, and maximum exposure for us."

"Let's order," I cut in. "I have to be home by ten-thirty." Once again I felt Ellen's tiny conspiratorial kick.

"I want an order of oysters to start," said Tammy.

"You want to live dangerously," said Held. "With the pollution this year I wouldn't order oysters anywhere."

"March has an R in it," Tammy replied.

We ended up eating a mediocre dinner, but it must have been expensive because Ned complained to Tammy about the check.

They offered us a lift but I said I wanted to walk Ellen home. The crisp night air conveyed relief and release. Ellen took my arm. "Every time I see them I feel as if I had a harelip or a club foot."

"Then why did you come?"

"You know."

"I do?"

"I'd walk a million miles for one of your smiles, my Bir-ir-die."

24

. . . At a meeting in the Board of Estimate chambers last night, hisses greeted the statement by the Urban's director, Bartholomew Hayes, that they must remove a part of the present western façade, replacing it with a glass wall, in order to fulfill a stipulation in the contract between the museum and the executors of the Royceman estate.

There was a wave of cheering and clapping, however, after Donald Stewart said, "Community Planning Board 8 represents 500,000 people. Our jurisdiction is the Central Park area from Fifty-ninth Street to Ninety-sixth Street. We are dismayed by your institution's determined efforts to create a monstrous environment over park land." . . .

When, in the final moments of the meeting, Hayes appealed to the audience, saying, "If we do not clear up these lawsuits immediately, we must forfeit this glorious collection to Washington," another wave of cheering and clapping engulfed the audience. . . .

Excerpts from the *New York Post*, March 13, 1973

———

Wednesday: Held was in his usual place behind the desk. "Did you see yesterday's *Post* and Carton's editorial about the abuse of park property in today's *Times*? Who would have thought a mere art collection could generate such controversy?"

"Did you call Weisman?"

"Sit down. It's time we had a frank little chat, but the way you enter a room makes me feel that any second you might be sucked backward out the door."

I continued to stand, looking down at Held.

"The trouble with you, Bertie, is that you don't understand the nature of the lawyer-client relationship. I'm the kind of person who has to have the complete trust of my client because I'm out there fighting for him. You, however, are constantly looking over my shoulder."

"Did you call?"

"As a matter of fact, I spoke to Weisman. He offered us nine million, your paintings, and an apology. He gave me a lot of bull about how even that amount would endanger the building of the wing, about how they might have to sell off some paintings to do it because they couldn't touch the maintenance money. I said, 'Sorry, Jack, no deal.' He went off like a Roman candle. I must say, it was more satisfying than an orgasm."

"What the hell do you think you're doing? I'm picking up the phone this minute and telling Weisman that I'll settle."

Held smiled. "You can if you'd like, it really doesn't matter any more. You see, Bertie, we've already got eighteen million in the bag."

"Christ, what are you talking about?"

"When the twenty-month time limit runs out, the collection goes to the National Gallery. They're committed to build a wing and maintain it on their own. Eighteen million was designated to build and maintain the collection at the Urban, but *only* at the Urban. So next April, eighteen million will automatically revert to the residuary estate—that's you, Ellen, and my dear wife. We'll have six million smackers apiece, dear boy, less estate tax, because it's no longer a charitable contribution."

"You never told me that if the National gets the collection we get all the Urban construction and maintenance money."

"I forgot to mention it, but now I'm absolutely sure that the National Gallery will get the collection. There is no way to settle in time. Even if you drop your suit, there's still the public interest suit and all that brouhaha out there. It could take years to resolve. Am I clear?"

"Jesus, that's why you've been dragging it out, encouraging me to organize protest against my father's wing. 'I forgot to mention.' Shit." I looked at my watch. Forty-five minutes till Transfer time.

Held pulled at his nose. "To mention it early on would have just complicated things. At first I was completely willing to make a fast settlement. They brought this on themselves. Early on, I didn't think we had much chance of stalling that long, but public pressure is miraculous. It's done our job for us and more effectively than we could do it."

"There must be a way to stop this."

"No way. I am convinced of that or we wouldn't be having this nice truthful talk. Next April we get eighteen million. Then there's nowhere to go but up, which is exactly where I want us to go. It's just one tiny step further to break that will. Think of it, Bertie, an estate worth at least one hundred and forty-two million dollars—that's real money. How powerful you'd be if that were yours. And don't play the innocent with me. You knew I always wanted to go all out. I said so."

"No. You said you couldn't do anything without me. You said we'd challenge the Straw Man and contest the charitable bequest and then they'd settle."

"And I was perfectly willing to settle, wasn't I? They messed it up. And I still can't do anything without you, Bertie. As for the Straw Man, I knew you'd be interested in anything as outrageous and tricky as that device. I knew it would encourage you to assert your rights. But, Bertie, if we were only going to question the Straw Man, we wouldn't have needed the agreement with the girls to avoid the *in terrorem* provision. That provision doesn't apply in the case of mortmain statutes."

"What?"

"The hand of the dead cannot hold you back. You're allowed to lodge a charitable challenge, no matter what provisions are directed against you."

"I could have challenged the Straw Man without risking my inheritance?"

"That's it."

"That agreement, you only set it up so you could ring Tammy in on any money we might get."

"I told you long ago that we needed the agreement because, if we ever decided to break the will, we couldn't come back later with new objections. We needed to do everything at once, if only to look like we meant business."

"You sucked me in with the Straw Man. Threw me a fucking red herring."

"Not so. If you let us go ahead and we knock over the Straw Man and win our charitable challenge, we'll be entitled to at least another twenty-nine million, over and above the eighteen we've just secured, because that's the difference between half your father's estate and what he's actually given to charity. You wouldn't have needed the agreement for that, I admit. But, as I said, if we only went after the charitable challenge they'd know we were bluffing. Look, I did two quite separate things: I went after the charitable disposition, but I also used the prescribed ways to break a will. I did both, which is the way you do it, the usual procedure in these cases. I know your reaction to this may be to contact Weisman, but before you do I want you to know that it's all up to you now. I've gone as far as I can. I need your cooperation to go any further. You're still in charge in spite of your vicious attack on me the other night."

" 'In charge.' Ned— Oh God!"

"What's so terrible? Think about it. Tomorrow you'll say I'm a hero." Held stood and moved toward me.

"Where are you going?"

"With you."

"No chance. You come one step closer and I'll fix that nose of yours. Forever."

I thought about it. I'd been had. Held needed *me* to sue the estate. I was the only one who could do it. He'd used the Straw Man to bait the hook. And I bit. But it was my idea, mine alone, to toss the fragments of dissent that caused the avalanche.

I had not known because I had not allowed myself to know. I had played a sterile cerebral game of self-delusion. I headed for a phone booth and dialed O'Keefe. No answer. Then I got the number of the Garden City warehouse and called there. With each unanswered ring I heard, *Sign by the X, sign on page 7, sign all four copies.* Don't ask, just sign. It was too late. As I hung up, I acknowledged, perhaps for the first time, exactly what I felt. I felt fear.

I walked rapidly, almost running, across the parking lot, and turned the south corner of the Urban. The large crescent-shaped field of brown stubble that lay between the back of the museum and the mall was empty. On the far side of the mall, the traffic on the park drive hummed with the steady vibration of a tuning fork. The western façade of the Urban resembled a wedding cake, layer upon layer of intricately carved white marble, city-smudged. There were three separate entrances, the one nearest me distinguished by carved-wood twin eagles over the doorway, their claws clutching a banner inscribed "U.M.O.A." This doorway was the designated rallying point. It had been selected because it was where my father's wing was to go. The trucks were scheduled to arrive from the north, traveling down Fifth Avenue. If I was there when they came, perhaps I could intercept them. I cut over to the mall and walked up until I cleared the north end of the museum and could see out to Fifth Avenue. I moved in about twenty feet (which I thought would be roughly the path of the first truck). Because there was nothing else to do, I waited. Small gusts of cold wind at my back caused dead leaves to swirl around my body.

Then they came. The first truck was bright red. I saw it speed down Fifth Avenue, jump the curb, and head across the open field. I ran toward it, waving my arms, but it didn't stop. Another truck, this one a mottled yellow, followed the first. I waved frantically. It too sped on. Another and another. They shot across the field and halted abruptly near the south end of the museum, over a block from where I was standing. Jesus, why had I moved out of position. I raced across the field as trucks zoomed past me on both sides, making great whooshing sounds. Everything was happening too fast. When I finally caught up to the trucks (there must have been at least twenty-five) they looked like a bunch of casually tossed pickup sticks, until I realized that roughly half of them were positioned with their backs almost touching the wall of the Urban. The rest of the trucks were strewn across the open field in a ragged line, waiting to move in. They were indeed following a plan—my plan.

People began jumping out of the trucks, slamming doors, shouting orders, sprinting past me. The back of one truck flipped open, lifted at a steep angle, and paper and debris tumbled out against the wall of the Urban. I saw Peter Booth wave the truck forward. It pulled out, turned left, and disappeared in the direction of Fifth Avenue. Another truck began dropping an enormous mass of gray paper at the foot of the Urban doorway. I spotted O'Keefe's bright-red hair. He stood beside a truck, a camera pressed to his eye, turning this way and that, photographing the chaos. I moved toward him; he waved and called out, "Your mountain is rising."

"Tell them to stop."

"Forget that!" O'Keefe began photographing the pile of material, which was rapidly expanding, as three trucks discharged their contents. I reached out and pulled the camera from his hand. "Stop them," I shouted.

"Get off my back." O'Keefe grabbed for the camera but I held fast. We were surrounded by frantic activity: Art Workers standing in front of the trucks signaling directions, paper cascading around us, trucks pulling in and out. Nearby, two trucks collided, the front bumper of one ramming squarely into the rear of the other.

The drivers leaned out of their cabs and began to scream at each other. Torval Einsig appeared, wearing his black and red flannel shirt. He stood in front of the first truck. "Drive out, you bastard," he ordered. The driver obeyed, and the other truck followed.

I kept yelling at O'Keefe to stop the protest, holding his camera in one hand while I tugged at his arm with the other. He, in turn, kept trying to push me away with small jabbing motions of his fist. I heard a footfall behind me; then an arm snapped into position across my chest and a hand closed painfully around my ribs. I was lifted off the ground, my feet thrashing the air. "You're in the way, rich boy," the voice of Torval Einsig announced. O'Keefe recognized my helplessness, retrieved his camera, and began to photograph my futile struggle.

I felt myself being carried away from the activity to a spot where the last of the trucks waited to move in. Einsig turned me as if I were a piece of sculpture and plunked me down facing the museum. The instant my feet regained the ground I strained forward with all my strength, but Einsig merely shifted position, sliding his arm down around my waist.

I watched the last three trucks roll toward the museum, dump their loads, and leave. It had taken only a few minutes to create the great mound of paper that leaned against the wall of the Urban. In front of this mass, Art Workers shuffled back and forth through a wide area littered with debris and paper. Four months' worth of paper, Royceman paper, the paper of my life. Ticker tape spun in tornado spirals, typing sheets were plastered against the wall of the Urban, newspaper blew past me and whipped onto the park drive. I heard honking and yelling and, turning my head, saw that traffic on the drive had halted. Dozens of people were climbing out of their cars and some were scrambling up onto hoods and roofs to get a better view of the demonstration. From nowhere a crowd materialized.

People kept moving in front of me, oblivious or indifferent to my efforts to break Einsig's grasp. After an

unusually violent wrenching on my part (which did absolutely no good at all), Einsig hissed in my ear, "You
watch this. Watch good," and squeezed me viciously,
causing my breath to burst from me in a short, painful
spurt.

Hayes appeared in the center doorway of the Urban.
He made his way down the steps and trudged through
the accumulated trash as if it were snow. He stopped
directly in front of O'Keefe, who stood with several
other Workers at the foot of the enormous heap. "This
is private property," he intoned in a singsong voice.
"What is the meaning of this outrage?"

O'Keefe called out his answer loudly: "This is a
work of Destructivist art, a demonstration against the
capitalistic enslavement to which you are trying to subject us. We protest the Royceman Mausoleum."

Hayes's voice was a weak treble reed piping, "I will
meet with your committee in my office but I cannot
allow this desecration."

O'Keefe's arm swept the air in a wide arc. A storm
of paper drifted down on Hayes. About a dozen Art
Workers were stationed on the roof of the Urban,
emptying burlap sacks in unison, aiming the contents
at him. "Stop this abomination," Hayes cried.

Einsig began to laugh, his body vibrating against
mine. I had not known that there would be Art Workers
on the roof. That was the beginning of what I did not
know. O'Keefe and the others walked away from Hayes
so that he stood alone. Two Art Workers on the museum roof took careful aim and urinated on Hayes's
head and shoulders. Hayes touched his shoulder with
his fingers, examined them, glanced up, and gasped.
He lunged at O'Keefe, slapping him with great force
across the cheek and jaw. O'Keefe retaliated by simultaneously pulling Hayes forward by his necktie and
jabbing his fist again and again into that startled face.
Blood spurted from Hayes's nose and flowed down the
front of his shirt. He turned, raced back up the Urban
steps, and disappeared into the museum.

A clump of people, glued together, moving as one,

advanced through the field of paper. Photographers skittered like water bugs on the periphery of this group. Floating above their heads, at the absolute center, anchored to a tubular black steel pole, was a figure—a man—life-size, frock-coated, top-hatted, a broad green streamer angling across his chest. The figure possessed a white bond-paper face, silver coins for eyes. The mouth orifice was stuffed obscenely with a mass of mock paper money. Straw innards oozed below the jacket cuffs and pant legs. The black pole twisted, spinning the figure in a constricted circle.

I felt Einsig move behind me and looked up to see him beckoning to the group. They adjusted direction slightly and headed right for me.

Then the flame— Suddenly the figure was imprisoned within a sheath of jagged yellow and blue. Face, body, legs were trapped in heat and light. The figure writhed and vibrated as if trying to escape the agony of the heat. The face was full of animation—grimacing, shriveling, becoming a gaping wound. The neck snapped. The head fell forward and came to rest antically on the chest. The top hat tumbled off and disappeared beneath the advancing feet. As they carried that maimed form toward me, the body began disintegrating, chunks of it dropping into the tight group, causing it to break apart and reunite.

They moved steadily forward. When they stood directly in front of me, I saw the bright flames biting viciously at the green ribbon, which seemed to bind together the remains of the torso. I saw the letters before they blackened. I could read them clearly. On that burning ribbon was the name. His. Mine.

A disheveled Rose Thomas popped out of the group. "Turn him around. Get the kid in the shot with it," she commanded. I was shoved forward, tripping over my feet. Other hands joined Einsig's in holding me, pushing me, dragging me, spinning me around. I felt a hand tearing my glasses from my face. Flashbulbs exploded.

There was screaming, a whirring motion, and through

the white spots in front of my eyes I saw policemen making quick forays into the group, swinging nightsticks, striking people, dragging them away. I felt the hands holding me loosen; then, like the snap of a rubber band, I shot free.

Instinctively I headed for the park drive and the safety of that clot of immobile cars and observers. I stood behind a cab in the midst of the crowd, gasping for breath and shaking. When I looked back, three Art Workers were running at top speed across the littered field, the police in close pursuit. One of the Workers held the smoldering form above his head as he ran. It was Einsig. The police caught up with him and began striking him with their nightsticks. Einsig and the effigy crashed to the ground together. Seconds later Einsig was on his feet again, lashing out at policemen, wildly punching as he tried to break away. They imprisoned him in a tight circle of flailing sticks. Einsig crossed his hands in front of his face to ward off the rain of blows, sank to his knees, and disappeared from sight. When the circle parted he lay unconscious at the center. The police dragged him off.

From the place where the effigy lay, a network of bright veins spread over the debris, flowing together until there was a field of fire. Then the enormous pile of material heaped against the wall of the Urban ignited, flames leaped past the roof, the wings of the twin eagles were adorned with shimmering golden coats. Two windows imploded, the entire south end of the museum was on fire. A kaleidoscope of images assaulted me—I heard sirens, saw blinking red lights; firemen appeared, dragging huge flaccid hoses; pieces of fiery debris flew into the crowd. More sirens, water began taming the blaze, billows of dark smoke, confusion.

I turned then and ran from the holocaust, from that place, and I understood. Understood, finally, the purpose of the Royceman Transfer: that symbolic Destructivist act was meant to destroy what I came from. It was meant to destroy me.

As I ran I could see the Royceman Wing in perfect

detail, the way Hayes had shown it to me; only now that giant ice cube was melting in a great conflagration, steel supports flowing in silver streams over the macadam. The building was consumed in flame, and at the heart of that flame, trapped in that terrible inferno, I saw my grandfather, my father, and me. I was what I had always wanted to be, irrevocably fused with them. While I sought to refute, to deny, to desecrate—all that time—I had been a part of them and they of me.

I ran. I walked. I do not know how long, but later, much later, I returned to that place. In back of the Urban a sodden mass remained. Police barriers cordoned off the area. The south end of the museum had been brushed with an immense black paintbrush, several windows were broken, a moist dark mound still blighted the doorway. I knew what must take its place. I knew there must be a Royceman Wing. Call it mausoleum, monument, gift to the people, munificence or selfishness: it was his wish, my heritage, and inescapable.

25

. . . Furthermore, a spokesman for the museum's restoration department gave every assurance that the twenty-five smoke-damaged paintings can be restored with relative ease. In this we are indeed fortunate.

The question remains: Was the fire a deliberate act of violence? Perhaps we shall never know. Although this act was reprehensible and cannot be condoned, one must acknowledge that, on a purely philosophical level, it provided a devastating commentary on the way the media are beginning to control us all. Along with severe censure, the Art Workers deserve a nod of recognition for an elaborate criticism on a subject of deadly seriousness—man's loss of trust. The Royceman Transfer reflected an aspect of our time, as any work of art must do willy-nilly, and did so by plan.

We must give thought to the persistence of destruction as a factor in the ideology of the artist in the twentieth century. This preoccupation with destruction has a positive facet of sorts in the effort of the artist to clear his decks of a past that has piled up for so long that he feels stifled under an excruciating load. . . .

Excerpt from an article by Clarence Carton,
The New York Times, March 16, 1973

———

The New York Times ran a photograph of Hayes pressing a bloody handkerchief to his nose. The *Daily News* had a photograph of me. My arms were held behind me by Einsig and three other men. In the background was the flaming effigy. Anyone with half a brain could see that I was crying.

The newspaper accounts reported that, miraculously, the museum had suffered little damage and no paintings had been destroyed. The fire seemed to turn the tide of public opinion; suddenly almost everybody was *for* the Royceman Wing. The Art Workers got plenty of publicity—not the kind they wanted. They were depicted variously as "demented children," "dangerous pyromaniacs," and a "radical fringe group." Only Clarence Carton of *The New York Times* saw beyond the violence and found some value in the protest. But his reasoning was so convoluted and obscure that I don't think he got his point across. At least not to me. I didn't understand what he was trying to say.

A Bertram Royceman theorem: "If you want to discover a solution—explore the problem."

This time Jack Weisman stood as I entered the room. I walked up to the photograph of my father and read the inscription: "To my dear friend Jack. With deep affection, Bert." Not much.

As I read, Weisman said, "I've asked myself fifty times this morning why I bother to see you."

I turned. We faced each other, both standing, the desk between us. Then I told him my terms—the paintings my father had promised me, his cuff links, his watch.

"Are you aware that we have already made a much more generous offer?" Weisman asked in a carefully measured voice.

"Yes, I know about that."

"To be precise, the figure of nine million dollars was offered as part of the settlement."

"You'll need that to maintain the collection. I've heard the public's not supporting private manias these days."

Weisman's lips compressed, causing quivers in his jowly chin. "I had a rather unpleasant call from your counsel, Edward Held. He instructed me to ignore any terms you might offer. He says he alone is empowered to act on your behalf."

THE STRAW MAN 235

"He's stopped being my lawyer."

"And you're willing to withdraw your suit with no cash settlement, if we give you two paintings and the personal effects you mentioned?"

"That's right. There is one other thing. I want the stuff that's going to the Urban out of that apartment. Send it now, put it in storage, but I want it out of there—away from Gina."

"I see." Weisman walked around the desk and stood beside me, a quizzical expression on his beefy face. "I don't understand it. If what you really wanted were just those two paintings and a bauble or two, we could have worked it out. All you had to do was ask."

"I asked."

"I guess you did," replied Weisman, shaking his head, "but when you sued we knew, at least we thought we knew, you wanted to upset the whole apple cart. We figured the *in terrorem* provision couldn't stop you from questioning the charitable bequest, but we counted on its preventing you from further suit by making you lose your entire legacy. When it didn't stop you, it was our natural conclusion that you were out to play a desperate game. I for one never imagined you'd settle for what you'd originally requested. I was sure I was right when Held started out by trying blackmail."

"Blackmail?"

"What else would you call Mary Constanziakias?"

"Me? I'd call her my father's assistant curator."

Weisman studied my face as if to gauge whether I was telling the truth. Apparently satisfied that I was, he shrugged and said, "I should have realized Held was capable of that kind of deception. Mary Constanziakias was your father's, I believe the euphemism is, 'great and good friend.' Last fall Held threatened to expose the relationship and the fact that I was going to give her the ninety thousand left to me in the will, if we didn't immediately settle your suit."

"Why would you give her your money?"

"Your father requested I do so. It wasn't meant to be mine. He didn't feel he could mention her name in his will. He knew such a legacy would be a clear declaration of their relationship. Somehow Held got on to that and demanded an immediate settlement of nine million, your paintings, and some sort of letter of apology from me. He also threatened that if we didn't settle, he'd hold up construction long enough for the twenty months to run out. The way I figured it out was this: knowing Held, if he had a chance of getting eighteen million, he wouldn't be willing to settle for nine. Also, only Mary and I really knew about the arrangement, and in any case, I couldn't actually give her the money until everything was settled. I said no. I was sure we'd get your suit on the court calendar and thrown out—pronto. Then I tried to talk sense to you. I figured Held had set you up. He'd use you to sue. If he could blackmail us, great, but if not, and you lost your legacy, his wife would get half the money."

"No, he didn't do that. We had an agreement: if I lost my share of the estate, Tammy and Ellen would give it back to me."

Weisman struck his head with his hand. "So that's why you could ignore the *in terrorem* provision. I guess there were some things I didn't begin to understand."

"That makes two of us."

"For one thing, I'll never fathom how all this got out of control. Once public opinion began to build against the wing, it became impossible to get your suit thrown out. They refused to speed it up on the docket. By February we had our backs to the wall, time was running out. I asked Hayes to persuade you to settle. When he couldn't, I just swallowed my pride and called Held. By that time he wouldn't settle. He refused every offer. Held kept saying he'd hold out until the twenty months were up and the eighteen million reverted to the residuary estate. He said that was when the real trouble would begin."

"There won't be any trouble."

"Not from you, and I'm terribly pleased you've decided to do this; but I'm afraid there is trouble. Too much trouble. I think it's too late. I tell you, Bertie, from my own point of view, I'd like nothing better than to donate that collection to the National Gallery, where it would be appreciated. Imagine having to fight to give away a treasure like this. If I had my way, I'd tell them all to go to hell, but I don't. He chose the Urban. It hurts me to feel I'll probably fail him in this."

"I think maybe there's still a way."

"Sit down, won't you? We've both been standing a long time." It was a request, not an order. I sat down. Weisman pulled up a chair and sat facing me. "Let's hear your idea."

"Build it over the south parking lot. You wouldn't have to take any park land for that. We could use some of the money to restore the western façade—only a little of it was damaged in the fire."

"How large is that area?"

"Twenty-one thousand square feet."

"Are you sure?"

"I'm sure. I got the idea the night of the fire. Since then I've studied that whole area. I know it quite well."

"I'm afraid it's not enough space. Legally, we can't build higher than the present Urban roofline, and it's quite low on the south side. Even if we could, in this unsympathetic climate, people will be out there screaming that we're taking away their parking lot and erecting a skyscraper in their park."

"We could put two stories above ground level. One floor could be below ground level. Parking could go under that."

"It won't be grand enough. That isn't at all what we planned. He wouldn't have wanted that."

"How do you know? My father said he wanted a 'suitable edifice.' All the rest was laid on afterward. What he really wanted was a replica of my grandfather's house, but he compromised. He had a theorem . . ."

"A what?"

"My father taught me something. He said, 'The

straightest line between two points is called a compromise.' "

A gargoyle smile enveloped Weisman's face. "That sounds like Bert. You've certainly thought about this." Weisman sat quietly, his head bobbing slightly. After a time he said, "That public interest suit is based on objections to our use of park land and to the removal of a landmark façade, which I must say is rather academic now that a portion of it is ruined. I think we'd be heroes if we restored that façade, and we'd certainly pull the rug out from under their objections. It could work. At least it gives us a chance." There was another extended silence. Then Weisman asked, "Do you remember the day you came here with your friend to ask me for money to invest in *Hair?*"

I nodded yes.

"I've often thought how wrong I was in denying you. I realize, looking back, that my judgment wasn't based on the offering circular, which was sound, but on appearances. Your friend, sitting on the floor like a frog, and you, talking about peace—it seemed so unprofessional, to say the least. But I was mistaken and I'd like you to know that. Sometimes you can go wrong judging people. Take your father—he was a brilliant man, intuitive about business and art, about most things really, but . . ." He stopped in mid-sentence, then began again. "When I told Mary Constanziakias about the money, you know what she said? She said, 'I never really knew him.' Your father was well fortified, but I was extremely fond of him."

Again we sat in silence. No motion. No gesture. At last Weisman stood and said in a bombastic tone, 'Bertie, regarding your trust fund. There are certain stocks that I'd like to sell as quickly as possible. I would like to buy safe but slightly more speculative stocks with a higher yield. I think that would generate more income without incurring undue risk. And we must discuss what you plan to do with your London house and with Birdwood."

"Yeah, that's right. Some other time. Let's go."

"Where?"

"To see Hayes."

"Is that your solution? An open admission that we have been overpowered by the lunatic fringe—the bird watchers, tree worshippers, self-aggrandizing politicians, architectural purists, and demented decentralizationists who want to put Renoirs in the latrines of the House of Detention?"

Hayes, standing between two of the familiar Renaissance chairs, curled his fingers into a fist, which came crashing down on the highly polished surface of an Irish hunt table. "We too have power." He struck the table another blow. "Every year we bring millions of people to New York. People who spend money going to restaurants and the theater and staying in hotels." He struck the table a third time.

"I hope you don't do that to the chairs," I said.

"What?"

"The chairs. They're from my grandfather's house, aren't they?"

Hayes flushed. "In point of fact, they came up from the Fifty-second Street house last week. Until completion, I thought they'd be safer here than in storage."

Weisman's face brightened. He quickly readjusted the climate. "What do you suggest we do?" he asked Hayes.

"That public interest suit is sheer rot, bunkum. It will be thrown out."

"In the interest of time," said Weisman, "we would prefer to see it withdrawn."

Then I said, "It was you who told me that even if the suits were settled you might be denied a building permit."

"All too true. It could happen, and whose fault is it? That building would be halfway up by now if not for you."

"Maybe it will be built better this way," I said.

"What, with your simplistic suggestion? You expect me to stand here and congratulate you for this stopgap solution—this last-minute effort to clean up your own mess? Well, I won't; I'm not a hypocrite. These are complex issues. Have you ever considered that certain works demand natural light? Statuary, temples, monuments that have stood for generations in fresh air cannot be consigned to a vault."

"Really," interrupted Weisman, "there is very little of that nature in this collection and there's plenty of room on the main floors."

"Consider the cost of going underground. It will be exorbitant."

"You have eighteen million, which, I must say, is nine million more than you had a week ago."

"To burrow like a mole in the earth. It will set a precedent for other institutions to follow."

"Our interest is solely in facilitating the construction of the Royceman Wing. Suggest another way and we will discuss it with pleasure," replied Weisman.

Hayes dropped his head dramatically onto his chest. His shoulders rose in a minute shrug.

"I take it then that we are ready to amend our contract. Also, I have a request from Bertie that Mr. Harold Linsky become curator of the collection."

"Unfortunately, Mr. Linsky is no longer with us."

"Hire him back," I snapped.

Hayes's neck pivoted, he glared at me, lemur-eyed. "You're not serious! You envision Linsky as the curator of a hundred-million-dollar collection? You are a perverse little fool, an irrational, meddlesome know-nothing. You are . . ."

Weisman's booming voice cut him off. "We suggest you honor the request of Mr. Bertram Ogden Royceman."

"Yes, yes, yes, and yes," Hayes hissed. "I capitulate. Breeding is gone, elegance is no more, and your people have broken the barriers and are running the show."

"I understand you all too clearly," replied Weisman.

Hayes threw his head back and gulped air. "I meant no such insult. None. Only what kind of future will it be when we are faced with people who would rather have a picnic on a filthy piece of earth with soot falling on their heads than see the most magnificent art in the world?"

"Maybe they'll do both," I said. "It's comforting for me to know that there are some people who wouldn't trade a blade of grass for a Rembrandt."

"Lunatic," muttered Hayes under his breath.

26

. . . With the withdrawal of this public interest suit, it would seem that the last legal obstacle to construction has been overcome. . . .

The Urban Museum is now accepting bids on the revised plans for the Royceman Pavilion. Allan Tanger, architectural director of the museum, stressed the fact that the construction bids will have a guaranteed ceiling price, to avoid the type of criticism that plagued the Hirshhorn Museum in Washington when the Piracci Construction Company of Baltimore underbid competing concerns by more than two million dollars and then demanded additional payments, claiming increased costs in connection with the project. This led to accusations that the firm was "buying in," a practice used by Defense Department contractors who submit an unusually low bid in order to win a contract and then ask for more funds because "modifications" have resulted in higher costs. . . .

Excerpts from *The New York Times*, April 5, 1973

Missy phoned. It didn't surprise me. "Darling, Birdie darling."

"Yeah, how's Jamaica?"

"I don't know what's happening down here. It's taken two hours to get through those surly operators. All the waiters smoke marijuana—it's too hot to play tennis—and Pappie says that this year Round Hill has been taken over by parvenus. We went there for a buffet yesterday. It was disgusting. The buffet table was sixty feet long, full of lobster moldering away in mayonnaise in the sun—ptomaine time. By the way, Tammy called last night; she was very upset. Birdie, are you listening?"

"Yeah."

"Well, say so, so I know my sweet boy is still there. Birdie, there are very few things you can count on in life. Tammy tells me you are turning down millions. I can't believe that, darling. Not in this uncertain world. And it's wrong. Morally wrong. You mustn't do it. Security is all we have."

"It's pretty complicated."

"I'm sure it is. But I'm going to tell you something: if you could get that money, take that collection and break it up, you'd be doing a good thing, a brave thing. What is that collection but misery and selfishness? It was such a big thing to him. Such a big thing. What did we get? Nothing. Don't have any misplaced loyalty, it's cursed us all. Whatever he felt went into that stupid canvas and bronze and porcelain. If you could smash it, I'd congratulate you. Take what you can get. You owe it to us and to yourself. Do it, please."

"No."

"I'll have Ned call you tonight. Let him do it. He's strong and he's there to help you."

"No."

"Don't go against me. You don't know what it is to be without. Don't do it. If you love me, don't."

"I've got to go," I said. She was pulling the wrong string.

"But, Birdie," she said, "you know how I . . ."

That was it. I broke the connection.

I'd arranged to meet Tammy at the zoo cafeteria in Central Park at four-thirty. The downtown side of the Urban was a field of mud. A gray wooden fence, half completed, ran around the perimeter of the parking lot. Already, it was covered with graffiti: bright red poppies, a yellow sunburst, FUCK YOUR FRIEND, a devil with a green tongue, MAN WITHOUT GOD IS LIKE A FISH WITHOUT A BICYCLE, THE ESTABLISHMENT SUCKS, a green and black snake, JESUS IS COMING. Under that, in small green letters: "Not if he's taking the A train."

A line of pickets moved single file up the mall, cut diagonally across the moist earth, and began circling the fence, walking now on asphalt, now on mud. Three of them carried signs that read: PRIVATE INTEREST, PUBLIC LOSS; WHY NOT QUEENS? and DECENTRALIZE. A girl in a green dress with red apples on it bumped into me, hooked her arm through mine, and pulled me into the group. I smiled, removed her arm, and walked away, the mud sucking at my shoes.

When I reached the cafeteria Tammy was already there, sitting outside. She wore giant blue sunglasses, which engulfed her face, and she sipped a Coke. "I dropped off a pin to be fixed at David Webb: then, since it was such a perfect day, I walked here. I was a bit early," she said brightly.

I sat down.

"Last night I was wearing the emerald crown pin David made me when I looked down and the biggest emerald was right there in front of my feet. It's a miracle I found it. If I hadn't just happened to glance down at that moment, I don't know what might have happened. I love that pin, you know. It's so beautiful, and whenever I wear it, I feel right somehow. David's man said this has never happened to them before. You want something to drink?"

"Later."

"Bertie, I want to talk to you about our settlement. I know Ellen goes along with you, but I don't."

"It's finished, Tammy."

"You and Ellen. The two of you were always a closed corporation. No way in. No matter how hard I worked to make a place for myself, to be excellent, you two didn't even notice."

"We were never that close."

"Yes, you were. I was always alone." She looked over toward the rectangular pool where sea lions rolled like overstuffed sausages on their concrete slabs and then dived into the murky water below. "I don't know why you picked this place. I hate zoos. Animals lose their color when they're caged up." Tammy reached for her glass and lifted it to her mouth. As she tilted her head back, I saw behind her glasses. Her right eye peered out from a swollen mass of red, gray, and green tissue.

She saw me staring. "Ned," she said.

I whistled.

"He asked me to see you today, Bertie, to tell you there's been some brand-new legislation that makes it look good for us. Ned says he could reopen our suit as a result. He says what's happening in the Mark Rothko case makes it a sure thing that you can knock over the Straw Man."

"Tammy, I never wanted to break his will."

Tammy leaned across the table so that her face was close to mine. "Ned was counting on that money, Bertie. We really need it. There are so many expenses, what with schools for the kids and the house and the club. I don't know what will happen to us. He acts as if it's all my fault. As if I did it. He won't leave me alone."

"It's finished," I said again. She knew I meant it. After a while she left.

27

ROYCEMAN PAVILION GALA OPENING

The long-awaited Royceman Pavilion officially opened at nine o'clock last night when over 2,500 New Yorkers sipped champagne and strolled freely through the various galleries, which house some 4,000 objects, including an outstanding collection of Italian Primitives, Old Masters, Impressionists, and Post-Impressionists.

The Royceman Wing, constructed in only eleven months, showed signs of speed and incompleteness. Exposed wiring hung from the ceilings, walls remained unpainted and roughly plastered, in marked contrast to the immaculate installation of paintings and objects. Both the men's and the women's lavatories were inoperative, a situation saved only by the fact that the party overflowed into the Great Entrance Gallery of the Urban Museum proper. . . .

New York celebrities rubbed elbows with members of Old Guard society as black-gowned dowagers, bedecked with ropes of pearls, sipped champagne next to nymphets in see-through blouses. What passes for society included politicians Jacob Javits, Andrew Stein, and Donald Rose; curator Harold Linsky; art critic Clarence Carton; Woody Allen and Tony Perkins; Ruth Ford, in a feathered headdress; Andy Warhol and his entourage, including Fred Hughes in a tuxedo with red satin lapels and Betsy Ross, Warhol's latest superstar. Miss Ross wore her floor-length Halston caftan soaking wet. Early in the evening she had taken a plunge in the Tarkington Patio fountain. . . .

At about ten-thirty Bartholomew S. Hayes entered the Royceman Wing accompanied by a select group of approximately one hundred trustees and benefactors who had dined in one of the period rooms on the second floor of the museum proper. Mrs. Gaston Bergé was overheard recounting how one of the braziers used to serve the zabaglione dessert had ignited a nearby tapestry. "It gave us quite a turn," she remarked. . . .

Bartholomew Hayes refused to comment on the Royceman Collection, saying only, "This is a party. The collection speaks for itself." His comment was apt, however, in that the Royceman Collection is magnificent. The two upper glass-enclosed floors contain twenty galleries in which the paintings, sculpture, and porcelain are ingeniously displayed in a variety of ways: in vitrines, cabinets, within glass pillars, on free-flowing walls. The subterranean floor is equally handsome. It contains seven rooms reproduced exactly as they appeared in the original Royceman mansion. . . .

In one room, paintings of the French Post-Impressionist and Fauvist periods, as well as a rare Giovanni Bellini and a Francesco Guardi, hang on brown velvet walls with matching draperies. The room contains a Renaissance table, chest, and chairs. One wall of glass shelves holds over three hundred examples of Venetian glass. Another room—the dining room in the original Royceman House—has a twelfth-century refectory table and chairs, and a priceless Aubusson tapestry depicting Judith and Holofernes. A vitrine on the left wall of this room contains many examples of superb majolica, including the famous plate "St. George," by Giorgio Andreoli.

A bedroom contains a canopied bed, once the property of Marie Antoinette at the Petit Trianon. On the wall are four paintings by Giovanni Battista Tiepolo, as well as his ceiling of an enthroned Madonna and Child with two monks; a Giovanni

*Domenico Tiepolo painting, "Punchinello," completes
the room. . . .*

*Never before has the Royceman Collection been
displayed in its entirety under one roof. Gathered in
one wing, as it is now, this dazzling collection is com-
prehensive enough to create a major museum in itself.*

*This morning at ten it was reported that the line to
see the Royceman Collection stretched for seven
blocks. The wait was estimated at six to eight hours.
Therefore, many visitors will not see the inside of the
Royceman Pavilion today, but those in line will be
given preferential tickets enabling them to move to
the head of the line tomorrow morning.*

Excerpts from an article by Suzanne Swan,
the *New York Post*, March 28, 1974

———

"A famous collector goes into a gallery and buys a
painting of one red dot. The next day he goes back and
buys a painting of two yellow dots. The next day he
goes back and the gallery owner shows him a painting
of one red and two yellow dots. He refuses it. He says,
'It lacks purity.' "

Laughing, I asked, "Where'd you get that?"

Brenda was sprawled diagonally across the bed wearing my shades, sections of the Sunday *Times* crazy-
quilting around her body. "Dial-a-joke, 999–3838.
Yesterday, I tried Dial-a-Prayer, 246–4200, but I got a
sermon. I asked for my dime back. The operator said,
'It's not our fault if they've changed the prayer to a
sermon.' "

One morning last April I looked out of my window
on the bleakest of scapes: improbable city-soiled snow
spotted the street and roofs of the buildings. I called
Linsky and asked him to locate Brenda. When I had
her address, I went out and bought the biggest lollipop
I could find, thirteen inches in diameter. It looked like a
target with circles of red, blue, yellow, green, and, finally, a tiny center of white. I bought some brown wrap-

ping paper, string, and stamps, and lugged everything back to the Chelsea. I found a piece of paper and wrote the following message:

I put it in with the lollipop, made a neat package, and addressed it. As I was gluing the stamps in place, I began to feel uneasy, as if I were doing something cowardly. Don't do it this way, I told myself. Do it straight. Try to be honest. And vulnerable? Sure, that's the chance you take. I took out a clean sheet of paper and wrote:

> Brenda,
> I want to see you.
> I love you.
> > Bertie

Then I threw the package away and mailed the note.

Two days later Brenda appeared at my door, dragging a green canvas duffel bag. "I'm scared," she said.

"See, we do have a lot in common."

Naturally, I've thought about all that happened (in regard to my father and to me) and on some levels I consider it a work of concept art, with appropriate documentation, of course. The memory exists in the documents. I've saved as many as I can. I've filed them, according to date, in a gray four-drawer filing cabinet I bought for that purpose. One can reread the hundred-page will, the twenty-seven-page contract with the

Urban, my trust agreement, newspaper articles, letters, press releases, tape transcriptions, legal tomes concerning the legislation about the Straw Man. You probably wouldn't want to. But you could.

The emotions—those painful pulses—were never written down and cannot be used as proof. But they too exist. It was Brenda who said: "Beginnings are beautiful, middles are O.K., and endings are endings." For her it was all very neat, but for me there were no clear divisions. I never knew when anything began, because it started before I was aware of it, and sometimes it ended that way also. It was preordained. I don't feel that any more. What I do can matter. A little. You can't fix thirty years' damage with a gesture. You begin.

We didn't go to the opening of the Royceman Pavilion, although I read it was grand. I've clipped the articles and put them with the rest. I've almost filled three drawers.

Next Tuesday Linsky is coming down here for my paintings. I don't mind about the "Girl Combing Her Hair," but I will miss my countess a great deal. Degas could freeze an instant in time, but Ingres is forever. My countess exists in a timeless vacuum, monumental against a white void, serene, lofty, luminous—perfect. My father must have loved her too: his first lady, his first acquisition.

The reason I'm lending my two paintings to the Urban is that Brenda and I have decided to travel. Brenda says New York is turning into a place where all you do is take a number and wait in line. We're taking off, heading for Iowa, South Dakota, Montana, Idaho, Wyoming, Colorado, Utah, Arizona, New Mexico, Mexico. Brenda says the only way is to drive. She's going to teach me.